Lord, Now What?

a novel

Judith L. Dammons

Lord, Now What?

Copyright 2012 by Judith L. Dammons

Published 2012
Printed in the United States of America

ISBN: 1480050059

Dedication

This book is dedicated to all the women and men who stand on faith, stand on commitments, and stand their ground!

Cousin James,
Thanks for being a blessing and supportive.

Judy

Acknowledgements

First and foremost I'd like to give honor to Jesus Christ, our Lord.

I'd like to thank my mother, Flaura Dammons, for all of her continued love and support.

To my editor Rev. Stephen Wilson, your help is making the second novel easier to write.

Professor Patricia Taliefero-Griffith and Stephanie Randolph-Norris, your early critique and reading was greatly appreciated.

Long-time friends Vanessa & Carl Duson, Kendra & Michael Branton, and Brenda & Rod Sawyer, your encouragement and inspiration has meant a lot more than I can express in a sentence.

To Katie Paulson and my pals at IKEA-Bolingbrook. You helped put a lot of fun in work, as we cheered on the White Sox and Bears.

Tina Toles and the Dayton Christian Writer's Guild, you helped me finally get over the hump.

To my aunt, M. Loretta Gray for helping me look great for the photo shoot. And my cousin and computer wizard, A. Renee Crutcher, for the great shots we took at the lake.

A sincere and heartfelt thanks to all!

All Bible verses are from the New Living Translation

Cover photo taken at Caesar Creek Lake in Ohio

Chapter 1

Sara hollered with a girlish giggle, "OUCH", after popping herself with the WWJD expression band on her left wrist. She had come home after a ten hour shift at work and plopped across the bed. It was only five o'clock but it already felt like bedtime. Twenty minutes had passed and instead of focusing on the highlighted calendar dates, indicating the busy Christmas season ahead, her attention had drifted to the pictures of the male model featured on each of the twelve months. His dark complexion, long braids and well chiseled body was commanding her attention at the moment. This guy is probably half my age anyway. Not that a forty-two old don't still enjoy looking! Hastily flipping through a few more pages with a constant smile, she applied one last hard pop on the wrist and drew her attention back to reality.

After an eighteen year career working in manufacturing she had been downsized from a large telecommunications company three years earlier. The company relocated its operations to an Asian country where the labor was cheaper, leaving thousands of Americans in the unemployment line. For the past thirteen months, Sara has been working as a quality auditor for a small company, that manufactured a variety of cylinders. After overcoming the significant pay reduction associated with being a department manager, she concluded this job had its rewards and that she'd perform it with due diligence. It was definitely less stressful, had shorter work days, and Sara felt blessed to receive a weekly paycheck again, something many people in recent years longed for. Besides, the mandatory two-week inventory shutdown was just three weeks away and she was ready for a break.

It was the week after Thanksgiving and December was going to be a busy, fun-filled month. Her day planner and calendar read something like this:

2nd- youth rehearsal 7pm
3rd- dinner preparation
4th- dinner at Hazel's House
8th- 3T's play and party
10th– CLEAR farewell party
13th– Toastmasters
16th- last day of work
17th– Chana's party
18th– youth ministry Christmas pageant;
24th-28th – home for holiday
31st- New Year's Service.

This layout gave the appearance of a well-organized life. But as she lay there, getting ahead of herself, she was overwhelmed, looking at all the activities, causing a little unnecessary lightheadedness. Slowly and repeatedly taking deep breaths in and out, eyes closed, she meditated on Rev. Steven's weekly benediction from Psalm 118:24, *This is the day the LORD has made. We will rejoice and be glad in it.* Reciting this to herself, had a calming effect, slowing her heart beat back to normal. If she was going to make good on these commitments, in addition to her daily routines, Sara knew she had better start by getting up from this prone position and complete the remainder of this day or else.

Friday, December 2nd
Rarely did Sara say no when it came to helping with the youth ministry. Some of these young people had already seen more bad times than she'd ever

experience in her lifetime. Children raising children, parents absent from the home, grandparents raising grandchildren, and the list went on. Sara knew she could not correct these problems, but she could help alleviate some of the pain and suffering by acting as a surrogate mother, a mentor, a big sister, or whatever role she needed to take on at any given time.

So here she was on Friday night, helping with the Christmas pageant rehearsal. Of course, the children were all over the place, laughing and talking about what took place at school, what was on their Christmas wish-list, who liked who and on and on...everything except practicing the lines they were required to learn.

"Okay young people," said Rev. J.C., "let's get serious for a few minutes before I start giving you a beat-down with my belt the way my momma and the women at my church used to do us!" Of course, the children got a big kick out of this coming from the youth minister, whose thirty-two years of age could easily be mistaken for nineteen. He was young, single, and energetic, gaining the respect and love of everyone who knew or came into contact with him. As some of the young people put it, *he's da man!* "Sisters Sara, Payne, and Hemings along with Brother Charles could be doing something else tonight other than babysitting."

"Who're they babysitting? Ain't no babies here!" cried the voice of Trent Miller, one of the more vivacious youth, as well as Sara's neighbor.

"Well, then let's act like the young men and ladies that we are and let's get busy," replied a very patient minister. And just like that, the rest of the rehearsal went as smoothly as possible for a bunch of adolescence on a weekend night.

Rev. J.C. had written a gospel rap version of the Christmas story, as found in the second chapter of Luke. As with his previous works, this production was sure to be a crowd pleaser.

Saturday, December 3rd

Food preparation and gift wrapping was the order of this chilly, Fall day. Rosebrook Community Church fellowshipped annually at Hazel's House, a non-profit shelter for women and children. A holiday feast of turkey, dressing, roast beef, candied yams and collard greens were a mere portion of the menu. Sara's contribution in the kitchen was to do as she was told by the real cooks, such as peel potatoes, snap green beans, or chop onions and peppers. She was the first to admit that homemade cooking wasn't her specialty or something she did on a regular basis. The truth was she had no desire to perfect her culinary skills. She got by on a few simple dishes, which usually came from a can or box. This was a known fact to her family and friends.

After a couple hours of kitchen detail, Sara went shopping with the First Lady of the church, Portia Stevens, and long-time member Adelaine Richardson, to pick up a few more items for the gift bags to be handed out to the shelter residents. Portia, all the adults were comfortable being on a first name basis, preferred to stay out of the kitchen also. She loved to shop, especially for others. It didn't matter if the occasion called for bargain buys or exclusive specialty items. She could find good deals on anything and says it's in the giving that she derives the most pleasure.

Adelaine is like a personal attaché for the First Lady, usually just a few steps from Portia. Maybe this is where she drew her pleasure. She and Sara had a cordial relationship at best. Sara was not exactly sure what caused their acquaintance to be shallow, although she has a pretty good idea. Whatever Adelaine may know about Sara predates Rosebrook. But during Sara's freshman year at the church she politely asked, no insisted, that Sara refer to her as Sister or Mrs. Richardson. Sara obliged. It wasn't until Portia made mention of the formality that Adelaine reneged her order. Two years later, Sara felt at ease enough to do so with discretion, such as when they were in the presence of a buffer, like Portia. Today she would be sure to exercise caution so as not to unleash any harbored ill feelings.

In the late afternoon, assisted by a few teenage girls, all of the gift bags were completed. The food from the kitchen smelled so inviting that Sara had to wrestle with herself to leave without doing any taste-testing. A local drive thru restaurant would have to satisfy her hunger this evening.

It felt good to lie back on the couch relaxing with a Rodney Posey CD in the player. Had the clock stopped or was it really only 7:15 p.m.? Her heavy eyes were in the closed position more than open. As she was unwinding and dozing off a little, the phone rang. She owed this time of solitude to herself so she let voicemail handle her business.

Suddenly, she sat straight up when the phone rang again. Checking out the time, she saw that it was now 8:05 p.m., although it seemed as if the calls were back-to- back. Too late, she missed the second one also. By now, she needed to relinquish her comfortable position and proceed with the Saturday night ritual of getting ready for Sunday morning. Rousing herself by making a hot cup of lemon-honey tea, she decided to check her voice mail first.

Hello Sara, I know it's been a long time. Found your name and number on the internet and thought I'd give you a call. I'd like to see you the next time I'm in Chicago. Not exactly sure when that'll be but I'll call first. By the way, you probably don't recognize the voice. It's someone from your past. Take care.

Replaying this recording twice, she still had no clue as to who this mystery man from her past was. "Unknown" name and number was displayed on caller ID. *Hmmmm, no help there.* She moved on to the next message.

Hi girlfriend, the twins and I won't be able to join you at Hazel's House tomorrow. They're not feeling very well so I'm going to keep them home. I hope they aren't trying to catch a cold. Anyway, give me a call when you get a minute Miss Busy Bee. Smooches!

Krista. Sara was praying for the day her good friend and mother of her twin goddaughters would join Rosebrook, or any church for that matter. Sara took comfort in knowing that the Lord would direct their path in His time. She sure hoped the time would be sooner rather than later.

click, dial tone

Once again she replayed the first message and still couldn't place a name or face with the voice. Never mind, she decided. She was not going to lose any sleep over it...hopefully.

Sunday, December 4th

Abused and abandoned women and children held a special place in Sara's heart. Everyone at Hazel's House had a story that could break a person down. But on this day, the Rosebrook church family was here sharing the good news about the Lord's blessings, even in the midst of what appeared to be the most desperate of situations. And indeed, they did just that. The young people got everyone on their feet as they performed a gospel stomp, joined by Rev. Stevens' hilarious dance moves. Rhoda Hemings, musical director and Sara's neighbor, brought her karaoke machine, lending itself to the entertainment. Her ever playful and lovable husband, Jed, took over the microphone with his version of *White Christmas*, in his own tune and tempo. Jed, was that person whose presence enlivens any occasion, no exceptions! Whether he wanted to be or not, he was always a crowd favorite.

As for the feast, judging from the empty plates and satisfied look on the faces of everyone, it was greatly appreciated with enough leftovers to feed the residents for another meal. Everyone received gift bags, candy, hugs, kisses and a day to remember.

Sara went home that night full of joy, thanksgiving and a deeper meaning of love as written in Matthew 22:37-39: *Love the Lord your God with all your heart and with all your soul and with all your mind. Love your neighbor as yourself.* As she thanked God for another beautiful day she drifted off to sleep knowing that she had a few days to recuperate before the next scheduled activity.

Thursday, December 8th

Taking an afternoon off work to be present at the Mae Jemison Academy's Christmas Explosion, the young thespians had Sara as excited about this event as they were. Among the children who had a role in the program were the Miller siblings, more commonly known as the three T's,-Trent, Tyree and Tamala. They lived with their grandmother, Miss Lizzie, directly across the street from Sara. In this closely knit neighborhood, everyone assisted Miss Lizzie however they could with raising those three adorable, but often, trying children. Ever since Halloween, the children had been telling Sara to be there to witness their performances. Promising that she would not disappoint them, as she had not with any other function, she arrived early for the talent showcase and party. Joining her were the Hemings as well.

Tamala, the youngest, had a non speaking role as a snowflake, dancing about the stage with eleven other beautiful little girls in their white and silver glittery attire. Tyree, the shy one, had a traditional role as one of the Three Wise Men. He had one line to recite which he said rather quickly and quietly, generating a little laughter from the audience. Trent, the oldest and most outgoing one, was a show stealer, playing a modern day version of Scrooge. He ad-libbed lines such as "Yo, dude, I said chill out" and "Quit hatin' on a playa!"

Trent could sometimes test everyone's patience, but, the neighbors loved all of them, which is exactly what the three T's had needed when they came to live with their Granny more than a year ago.

After the festivities, all of the neighbors took the children out for pizza in celebration of a job well done. Sara went back to Miss Lizzie's house for a while as the excitement of the day started winding down. Tamala was fast asleep before 8 o'clock, but it seemed Trent and Tyree were getting a second wind. While the boys amused each other, Sara sat and talked with Miss Lizzie in the living room for over three hours. This was normal for the two women. Just before midnight, Sara was definitely ready to join Tamala and declare this night over. By then both boys had fallen asleep on the family room floor in front of the television. After a final goodnight to Miss Lizzie, she languidly walked back across the street to her quiet haven.

Sara glanced at the telephone when she entered the house and noticed the message indicator light was blinking.

Click, dial tone.

Hi Sara, don't forget to bring your taco dip tomorrow. It's so good and fattening. I love it and you too!

Gloria. How could Sara forget about her sisters, especially since their circle of reading friends would soon change, dramatically. Gloria was really emphasizing the taco dip, one of Sara's favorite social snacks, embedded in her limited cooking capabilities.

Breathing, click, dial tone.

What's up with all of these recent hang ups. Sara was registered on the Do Not Call list so they shouldn't be telemarketers. A bill collector would leave a message, but she was on time with all her payments. "Unknown" name and number was displayed in the window again. Is this still the man from her past who's obviously not ready to reveal himself? Why not? What does he have to hide? Shrugging her shoulders and knowing another day was done she proceeded to bed.

Saturday, December 10th

The group decided to keep this final reading club gathering casual, simple and having nothing to do with a book. CLEAR (Christian Ladies Enthusiastic About Reading), deviated from the book discussion and had a farewell party for their long-time friend, Danielle. A recent widow, she was moving back to her hometown of Oakland, California. Her twenty-nine year marriage to Nylan Grant ended late last year when he lost his brief battle with cancer at the age of fifty-three. An empty-nester at age fifty, she wanted to be closer to her aging mother and siblings. This was Danielle's day.

"Danielle, do you think the men in the Bay area are different from these Chicago brothas?" inquired the single and free spirited thirty-one-year-old Nia.

"I'm not the least bit interested in what the men on the west coast are about," replied the attractive and unassuming Danielle.

She still grieved the only love of her life and was not concerned about another man any time soon. She'd heard enough about dating in the new millennium from CLEAR's single pundits, Sara; Taylor, thirty-three, saved and holding out for God's gift; Gloria, fifty-one, divorced for fourteen years and pledged to a life of a no more commitments; and Cecily, forty, who had an unhealthy relationship with long-time live-in boyfriend, Ramon. Admittedly unhappy, CLEAR continued to pray for her deliverance from a life that may have acceptance in the secular world, but not in the Christian realm. Cecily was often reminded that God won't bless a mess, and she knew she had a big one on her hands. Balancing out the group were Erin, forty-five, and Serena, forty-six, happily married and cherishing their lives as devoted mothers and wives.

That was the make-up of CLEAR. They were first and foremost Christian ladies who love to read. Taylor stayed up on all current events through media such as USA Today, The Chicago Sun Times and The New York Times. Gloria read mostly mystery and detective novels. Nia was the wiser in the lore of African American history. She should have been teaching with the wealth of knowledge she had attained as a hobby. Serena and Cecily traded off on love stories while Erin enjoyed nonfiction and biographies. As for Sara, she supported the works of many African American female authors, most of which were works of fiction. With these varied interests, CLEAR was exposed to a lot of different literature, making for some fun and lively conversations. At times, they got a little controversial, and even argumentative. But by the time the two hours were up, the ladies were always hugging and praising the Lord for another blessed experience.

"So Danielle, are you going to look up any old flames?" asked Gloria as the others laughed along. "I know your mother has told everybody that you're on your way home. I bet there's an old high school sweetheart who can't wait to show you how much Oakland has changed since you've been gone." Danielle, who was always calm and no nonsense, just smiled slightly and said, "Who knows and who cares?"

The ever romantic and teary-eyed Serena cried, "You know I'll be out there in a quick minute to help you plan your next wedding when you meet Mr. Right, again. God knows you were a good wife to Nylan and He's got another man waiting for you."

Erin said, "Let's continue to show these single divas what they're missing by not having a wonderful and loving husband in their lives. We've got to keep marriages alive and in demand."

Sara felt compelled to add her words of advice. "Danielle, enjoy each day of your life to the fullest, and don't waste one precious minute hoping, wondering or imagining if some man will be your next husband. Remember what is written in Proverbs 18:22: *The man who finds a wife finds a treasure, and he receives favor from the Lord.* You are going to be a blessing to everyone you encounter just as you have been to all of us."

"I'll drink to that," chimed in Nia. Then they all lifted their glasses of sparkling juice or soda and saluted Danielle. The tears flowed as the ladies' evening of good food, singing, dancing, and great conversation started coming to an end.

Tuesday, December 13th

Was this an unexpected snowfall or did Sara just not keep up with the weather report? It wasn't a heavy accumulation, but the big, wet, white flakes slowed traffic and extended the commute, in this case, to a Toastmaster's meeting. She'd been a member of this non-profit organization since high school where she began to hone her natural communication skills. As a youth, Sara was often told that she talked too much in school and church. High school helped put her talkativeness to good use. Currently though, her activity level with the South Suburbanite Toastmasters was minimal at best. Tonight's appearance was more to see some friends and pass on holiday greetings, not deliver a speech.

One of John Legend's CD's was in the player and she was getting in the groove when the car behind her failed to follow her lead and stop at the red light.

BAM! *(The sound of the fender bender was worse than the actual damage.)* The driver, a young woman, jumped out of her car, appearing to be a bit shaken. She came up to the door of Sara's four-year old Nissan Altima just as she was getting out.

"I'm so sorry", she cried. "I've got two little ones in the back seat crying and they distracted me for a few seconds. Please let me call my husband then I'll give you all of my insurance information?"

"It's alright, honey. Nobody's hurt. Go ahead and make your call," Sara said hoping to calm the young mother a bit.

An unmarked police car passed, heading in the opposite direction. The car made a U-turn and then pulled up behind the driver's dark green Ford Taurus. When the approaching officer got closer, Sara wanted to climb back in her car and just drive off. Lieutenant Marcus Richardson, of all people, had to be the one at this time and this place.

"Sara J, I hope you're all right?" he said as he shot her a wink.

"Yes, Mr. Richardson, I think we're all fine. Isn't this street patrol and minor accident investigation a little beneath you, Lieutenant?"

"I was just driving by when I saw one of my favorite ladies in distress. You know I'll stop for you any time, any place."

"Thank you, sir. We'll just exchange information and be on our way. As you can see there's not much damage to either car," she said even though her car would need to be repaired by a body shop.

"Come on, Sara J. Quit the formalities with all of this 'Sir' and 'Mr. Richardson.' I'll handle this in no time. Now, why don't both of you ladies get back in your cars so you won't get soaked. Sara J, I wouldn't want you to dissolve out here on the streets," he smiled as he took their license and insurance cards and gave her another wink.

Even though Marcus had been promoted to this lieutenant's position in Calumet City, just a few miles from where she lived, it had been more than three years since she last saw him. As she sat in the car, waiting for the return of her personal information, she had to pop herself on the wrist with her WWJD band. *The past is just that, she told herself as thoughts whirled around in her head.* The tinge of the rubber expression band bought her back to the present. It had probably been less than twenty minutes before he was tapping on her window although it seemed like hours.

"You'll need this accident report for your insurance company. Why don't you stop by the precinct tomorrow. I'm usually there between seven and five. Maybe we can have a cup of coffee like old times. It's good to see you again, looking good as always," he said along with wink number three.

"Thanks for your help Lieutenant Richardson. It's been a pleasure," she replied, knowing good and well that she was not about to stop by the station and share coffee or anything else with him.

That little incident left her in no mood to go to the meeting to which she would now be quite late arriving. Running into Marcus like this killed her merry mood more than the damaged car. Making the time to get the car repaired had to be squeezed into her busy agenda. Why she still allowed him to unnerve her is even more frustrating. Was this minor collision a test of faith, trust and forgiveness? If so, this was a personal examination that she must pass, with a perfect score.

Friday, December 16th

For the next two weeks, the first thing that came to mind was not having to set the alarm for the arduous task of getting out of bed, the hardest part of her day. Once dressed, the next sixteen hours were typically a breeze. So it seemed was the sentiment of the employees on this blithesome day, counting down the minutes to begin doing whatever was planned to occupy their time until the first week of January. Not much coaxing was needed as Sara had agreed to join several coworkers at a popular bar and grille for some holiday cheer. Afterwards she and Marilyn, another auditor, would go to a couple of stores to complete their gift-shopping and make it back home by mid-evening. It sounded like a good plan when they plotted their course of action on Thursday.

Hours of munching on nachos, chicken wings, potato skins and a variety of beverages, highlighted by some of the most horrendous and fun karaoke, the ladies didn't step into the first store until nine, later than they had planned. Determined not to return home until they could boast mission accomplished, those words were not spoken until four hours and six bags later. This was quite a feat for Sara since she avoided most shopping as if it were associated with a serious plague. Marilyn seemed to enjoy their meandering in and out of stores, even indicating that she would do more buying before and after Christmas. Sara knew this was it for her.

Tired feet, a full stomach, and the thrill of victory thrust her into the house, falling face down on the bed. The shopping bags would rest on the living room floor until later that afternoon when she wanted to think about getting out of bed.

However, the 'message waiting' indicator light piqued her curiosity even though no calls would be returned until much later.

Hi Sis! Just calling to see when you'll be arriving home for the holidays. Give me a call back when you get a chance. Love ya!

Big sister Eddie. Sara would return her call when she had plenty of time. Eddie was quite a talker. Sara had fallen asleep in the middle of one of her stories about her adult children, grandchild, or some other family member.

Hey baby cakes! Just a reminder that I expect to see you at the party tomorrow night. No excuses! Don't make me come over and drag your butt out of the house. You know I'll do it if necessary! Love ya!

Charles Nash, better known to her as Chana, the best friend anybody could ever ask for. Sara wouldn't miss this for anything, probably her last social outing with him as a single man.

Girlfriend where are you? I haven't talked to you in several days. What's going on? Of course if some man is holding you hostage then I'm not mad at you. Shout at me as soon as you can. Smooches!

Krista. That woman was always overly dramatic about everything going on in her and Sara's life. They just spoke on Wednesday afternoon, making plans to get together on Sunday for the pageant. The truth was, Krista thrived on getting attention, always had and probably always would. She and Chana were Sara's family away from home.

click, dial tone

Delete!

The final order of business for Sara that night was simply sleep, and that's what she did. It was one of those deep restful sleeps that you don't want to end. Unfortunately it seemed Sara had just closed her eyes when the phone rang.

Saturday, December 17th

Managing to open one eye wide enough to see that it wasn't even 8a.m. startled her for a moment. Focusing on her surroundings, she put a time and place to the situation. *My bed, my room, no work!* That thought gave her a reason to smile and grab for the phone on the fifth and final ring.

"Wake up sleepy head!" Chana hollered out. "Where were you hanging out last night?"

"A little holiday celebration after work and some last minute shopping."

"You must have really tied one on," he said facetiously.

"Yeah Chana, that Diet Pepsi on the rocks can do it to you all the time. What are you doing calling me this early, interrupting my much needed beauty sleep?"

"Come on, good looking. You get any more beautiful and all the ladies are going to be envious of you tonight." There was a reason she loved this man. He could always make her feel good even in the midst of not-so-good times. "You got my message about the party tonight? I mean it. I'll drag you out of your own house if you try to bail on me."

"Chana, you know I don't pass up an opportunity to step with you. Especially since I'll have to give you up in a few weeks," she answered, referring to his upcoming marriage.

"Baby girl, you know you will always have a place in my heart and a small part of me will always belong to you. Now does that mean I'll see you tonight?"

"Absolutely!"

"Good, you can go back to sleep now. Got a kiss for you later."

With that said, he hung up and Sara lay there smiling at how lucky she was to have had this man as her best friend for all these years. Suddenly, she began to ponder what she was going to wear? It had been a while since she put to use that one little black dress that most women have tucked away in the closet. Hopefully, she would be able to fit into it later today. With that thought, she settled back in bed in an attempt to return to sleep. Finding just the right comfortable position, Sara was starting to drift off when the phone rang again.

"Sara Joy Deyton, where have you been or should I say whom have you been with?" demanded Krista.

"I could make up a lie that I know you'd love to hear or just tell you the truth. Which shall it be?"

"Fine, Miss Waiting-for-Mister- Right, the truth." Which Sara recounted did in detail, especially the minor car accident. "Does Marcus still look as good as he did back in the day?"

"I really didn't notice since it was wet and cold that evening," Sara answered slightly downplaying the encounter, then quickly changed the subject.

"Are you and Bradley coming to Chana's company party tonight?"

"No, Brad has to work and I don't like going to Christmas parties by myself."

"Excuse me, since when have I been that bad of a date?" Sara teased.

"You know what I mean, silly girl! You go and have a good time. Tell me about it tomorrow and don't leave anything out. I've got to get the girls some breakfast. Smooches!" Her signature ending disconnected the call.

By now, Sara was wide awake and to lay in the bed any longer would be a waste of a wonderful day, doing much of nothing. But before her feet hit the floor she returned Eddie's call.

"Hi big Sis! How's it going?"

"Good morning, and where were you last night?" inquired her older sister.

"Out!" *How dare she question my whereabouts like I was some teenager with a curfew!* "Yes, I got your message. I'll be home on the twenty-fourth."

"Why wait until then? Come on home now?" Eddie replied.

"No, I have too much to do including getting the car repaired." She informed her of the minor accident. "Besides, I can use a couple days of total down-time."

"Well, if you change your mind, you know everyone will be glad to see you and your mother would love it if you stayed longer than your usual two days and out. All of the kids will be home this year. Girl, you won't believe how much all of them have grown, especially your great nieces and nephews. Everyone talks about how little we see of you. Are you sure you can't come home before then?"

"I know, but all of you seem to forget that I do have a life over here in Illinois."

Sara felt that her family thought that because she was still single she probably got lonely and should spend more time at their homes. What a spurious notion to entertain. Her plate was so full of activities and events that sometimes she could use a cloned twin or perhaps even triplets to get everything done. Not only that but when she was home, even at age of forty-two, she still heard some of the same old boring comments such as, Where is your man? When are you going to get married? Don't you have any kids yet? What are you waiting for? blah! blah! blah! Everyone seemed to want to interrupt her singleness. Since she was in no hurry to hear the same tired questions that everyone knew the answers to, driving home the day before Christmas is soon enough. Eddie was about to kick into full gear about the happenings of some family member, so Sara knew she had to get off the phone, quickly.

After breakfast, while wrapping the gifts she purchased last night, mostly for the children in her life, she reminisced about her childhood years. Sara's parents had instilled in the three of them the importance of being happy in the giving, and not just at holidays. The receiving would come in various ways throughout the year. As kids they didn't quite understand this concept. But as the years progressed and they matured in the true meaning of Christmas, their giving became a fun sibling competition. Their parents would always declared her brother, sister, and herself undeniable winners.

At last, the gift recipients were all accounted for, but she still felt a sense of incompleteness. Retrieving her debit card from her desk, Sara made an additional generous donation online to the World Food Program and said a prayer of thankfulness for her abundance. With that, her afternoon of gifting and fond memories of yesteryear was now complete.

As the minutes ticked away into hours, Sara danced around her house while getting ready for the party. Although the little black dress still fit, she arrived at the evening affair dressed in gold and winter white. Immediately spotting Chana, she headed straight to his table, greeted by a hug and kiss. Making her way around the table, she said hello to Olivia, his fiancée, who introduced her to two female friends. Then Sara literally came to a complete halt in the presence of the last guest.

"You must be Sara? You're more beautiful than Charles described," the handsome man said as he took her hand laying a flattering kiss on the back of it. "I'm Jonathan Tate and it's definitely my pleasure to finally meet you."

Chana never mentioned this man to her, but this meeting went a long way towards explaining the phone call he made last night and this morning. There must be something about this one because Chana was as particular about the men Sara met as she was. Her initial impression of this man was highly favorable, as it probably would be with most women. Jonathan was quite handsome, tall, of medium build, with a dark complexion, and a head full of small twist, with a sprinkle of gray. Before her, he stood aplomb, appearing to lack nothing, waiting for her to respond. Somewhat awe struck she simply replied, "Yes, I'm Sara. It's good to meet you too, Jonathan."

He pulled her chair out and asked what she wanted to drink. When she told him a Diet Pepsi he gave her a warm smile and said he'll make that two. Being a gentleman, he checked with the others at the table as well before going to the bar. Trying hard to keep her composure she was hoping this wasn't a dream.

"Chana, you never mentioned him to me," she said with an ebullient utterance.

"You know how you can be about meeting men, so I just thought it would be better this way."

"Come on, I'm not that bad, am I?" Even Olivia joined Chana in giving Sara a look that spoke much of her cautionary stance when it came to making a new acquaintance. Cold, picky, unrealistic, and stuck up are just a few of the terms used by others to explain why she wasn't in a dating relationship. Sara's reaction to them was just a shoulder shrug indicating her favorite response of, life is what it is. The two of them made Sara laugh out loud.

"So have you finished talking about me?" Jonathan asked as he made his way back to the table with the diet sodas and wine for the other two women.

"For right now," Sara managed to say as he positioned himself next to her.

They spent the rest of the evening dancing, laughing, and comfortably getting to know a little about each other, oblivious to the entertainment and the rest of the table.

"We're getting ready to call this a night," Chana said as he and Olivia rose from the table. "I trust I can leave Sara in your hands man?" he asked as he and Jonathan shook hands.

"Of course man, you know I wouldn't let anything at all happen to this precious woman," Jonathan said as he stroked Sara's cheek with the knuckle of his index finger.

The four people at the table departed, leaving Jonathan and Sara on the dance floor, joining a line-dance already in progress. Unaware of the time, over shadowed by all the fun, it was evident by the moaning of the remaining crowd, when the bright lights came on, that Sara wasn't the only one who didn't want the night to end.

They strolled to her car with Sara still idly chatting as if that would put more distance between them and the car. Reaching the departure point, she could not think of anything else to say without coming across as stalling the inevitable. The bright moon on this chilly night was the backdrop for what she felt was a living dream. Like a rehearsed script, Jonathan turned to Sara and looked straight into her eyes without saying a word. With his big masculine hands he cupped her face, softly kissed her on her right cheek, then the left, before planting a lingering one on her forehead. That was all that was needed to say goodnight. She tried to wipe the Cheshire cat grin off her flushed face when she climbed into the car, but to no avail. One final wave and she pulled away, without having said another word. No need. The many happy thoughts racing through her head was worth a zillion words.

Coming off a delightful night, before cuddling into bed, she was led to read the scripture of Matthew 6:33: *Seek the Kingdom of God above all else, and live righteously, and He will give you everything you need.* Sara knew if Jonathan would have any significance in her life, it would be the work of the Lord, since she had already experienced a big mess by doing things her way!

Sunday, December 18th

Two nights straight, she'd gone to bed much later than usual, and for the second morning, her peaceful sleep was invaded by a ringing noise. This time, it was the alarm. Tapping on the snooze button three times, she firmly clutched the blankets, not wanting to relinquish that which was shielding her from the early Winter cold that crept into her bedroom. Knowing that Rosebrook's service started exactly at 10:30, and she fashioned herself with being on time, Sara rolled out of bed with a good feeling. Noticing the festive clothes laying on the chair in the corner and remembering the part of last night that was not a dream, she had several new reasons to be thankful for this day. Scurrying to get dressed, she was clapping and swaying to the music of the praise team's first song with plenty of vim.

The youth ministry's Christmas pageant would take place this afternoon. Sara had just enough time to pick up Autumn and April, Krista's twin daughters, and grab a big bag of potato chips and a gallon of punch. This accompanied the light lunch at Miss Lizzie's house of chicken salad and a fruit medley. She didn't want the children to get too full and sluggish, causing them to forget their lines or, in the case of Tamala, not wanting to perform at all. Miss Lizzie, who was known for her exquisite cooking, said the real food would be served after the program.

Miss Lizzie had been busy in the kitchen the past couple of days preparing the turkey, dressing and all the fixings. She loved all holidays that gave her the chance to showcase her cooking talents. And without failure Sara was always glad to be entertained by her culinary creations. Miss Lizzie was a big fan of cooking shows, having garnered all kinds of recipes and cookbooks over many years. As with every other occasion, tonight's meal was sure to please!

Rev. J.C. and Chana had most of the props set up when they got there. Other young thespians were starting to arrive, eager to do their part for moms, dads, grandparents, and all the other relatives and friends that came out to support them. Seeing the sanctuary fill up was a testimony to how much people encouraged youth to stay away from the evils of the world, such as gangs, drugs and sexual activity and live according to the will of God.

Rev. J.C., (short for Jeremiah Cooper), was answering God's call to service. He had the know how to attract young people. Even some of the roughest and least disciplined respected and admired him. His gospel/rap/jazz version of the Christmas story had piqued the curiosity of many, a testament to the large turnout by the time the pageant began. One hour and twenty minutes later, after rapping wise men, line-dancing angels, and a joyous Joseph and Mary doing a choreographed praise dance after the birth of baby Jesus, it was all spiritually well received to a three-minute standing ovation. Sara smiled, assured Jesus was smiling upon his children as if to say, "Well done good and faithful servants."

Back at Miss Lizzie's house, they were joined by Chana, Olivia, Rev. J.C. and Taylor. Everyone was elated. Jed Hemings stopped in to congratulate the children, handing them presents to put under the Christmas tree. This gesture enhanced their hyper activity, but they deserved it. The adults let all the children just have a good time and be kids.

Sara joined Miss Lizzie in setting up the buffet-style meal, which was even more of a palate pleaser than she imagined. Rev. J.C. blessed the food and everyone helped themselves to what appeared to be a never ending feast including desserts. Miss Lizzie's cooking was the best gift you could ever receive from her, and all most people ever wanted.

Taylor volunteered to help them with the clean-up, but they encouraged her to keep Rev. J.C. company. Besides, it was Sara and Chana who, earlier in the year arranged a meeting between the two. Thus far, it appeared that was really a match Heaven sent, although Chana loved to take credit for their relationship. It seemed everyone, including her family, thought they were an ideal couple. No one dared to attempt to rush them into anything, although they secretly prayed for a marriage in the near future.

Finally, the events of the day were starting to show in the weariness of the children. As the evening fell upon them, Miss Lizzie's guests all said goodnight and departed with a heightened love and joy for this Christmas season. Chana offered to take his goddaughters home, but Sara knew Krista wanted the details about the party as much as she wanted to share them. The twins slept the short distance home, only waking when she turned off the ignition. Krista heard Sara pull up and greeted them at the door. The two friends helped the girls get inside, struggling to climb the steps to their bedroom.

"Why don't you stay for a while since I haven't seen you in a few days. How was the party last night? Meet anybody of interest? Come on, sit. Want something to drink? I want to hear all about everything, including your encounter with Marcus." Krista could talk nonstop if you let her! But Sara was in no mood for what could turn out to be one of their all-night girl talks.

"Krista, I'm really tired after today. By the way, you missed a wonderful program," she said, hoping to change subjects.

"Sara, I know I should have gone, but I'm just not in the holiday spirit."

"What's going on with you, may I ask?"

"Bradley really seems to be distant a lot lately. When he's here, he gives the girls a whole lot more time and attention than he does me. And, he gets more and more calls to fill in for someone who didn't show up for work. So after the girls get in bed he dashes off to that part-time job even though it's supposed to be his night off and he keeps promising to spend more time with me. But," she paused, then didn't finish the sentence.

Although Sara was not at all surprised at what Krista had just said, she was still sympathetic to her obvious pain.

"Kris, you know I'm in no position to offer any advice about your marriage. So I'm going to do the only thing I can do and lift it up to the Lord. You know Jesus can work it out." Then to bring a smile to Krista's face, Sara started singing and dancing a little, *"Jesus can work it out, Jesus can work it out!"* Her performance worked. Krista was laughing as she went upstairs to tuck in the girls.

She came back, finding Sara stretched out on the recliner with her shoes off and one of Krista's beautiful throw blankets covering her. So much for going home at a decent hour for the third night, if she'd make it home at all. Since Sara didn't have to be at work in the morning, there was no need to rush home to her empty house. Besides, Sara already felt at home with her long-time friend's family. So, as usual, they talked and talked and talked about everything that took place over the past few weeks. Krista wanted to know every detail, even if Sara had to make up a few. It was no surprise to Bradley when he came home from work in the very early hours and found the two ladies laughing and behaving like the college girls they once were.

"Carry on," he said after greeting them. "Sara you'd better not drive home at this hour." Then he marched on up to their bedroom.

As April and Autumn made their way downstairs the next morning, they giggled as they approached Auntie Sara in the recliner, their mother stretched out on the sofa, just like they were the night before. Only this time, they were sound asleep!

Saturday 24th

The week went by so fast, highlighted by lunch with Jonathan on Wednesday and a full body massage on Friday afternoon at Serenity Day Spa. Sara returned the rental car, got hers back from the repair shop, then headed home to Dayton, Ohio to spend time with her immediate family. Eddie, the family historian, had been unable to link their last name with that of one of the founders of the city, Jonathan Dayton. Although a different spelling but same pronunciation, the Deyton's, Sara's family, still couldn't claim fame or a piece of the city known as "the birthplace of aviation". However, that hasn't deterred Sara's brother or uncle from using the name as a pickup tool.

Sara's family consists of her mother, Rose, older brother, Kenneth Jr., and sister, Edwina Grace. Uncle Dillon, her mother's baby brother, nicknamed the siblings Kid, Eddie, and Lovejoy. Only Uncle Dillon could get away with calling them by those names, although her sister answered to Edwina only from her mother.

Saturday evening they were lying around her mother's living room, poking fun with one another as relatives do.

"Hey, Lovejoy, how come you came home by yourself? When are we gonna meet that man you got held up over there in Illinois?" Uncle Dillon started in on her for the millionth time, after several shots of Jack Daniels. This was coming from a man who was twice divorced, father of seven and living with his current girlfriend.

"I told you, I'm single, happy, and loving it," Sara replied, wishing her family would quit trying to interrupt her singleness.

"You don't know anything about happiness until after you get married. Then you'll really know what it is to love the single life," he quickly replied.

"She's smart in that respect. I say stay single lil' sis, and you'll always be happy," laughed Kid, father of four, divorced and barely tolerating his second marriage.

"Sara, don't let them get next to you. You know how they are," said Eddie, divorced with a grown son, daughter, and granddaughter.

"If I didn't hear this bantering when I come home, I'd think something was wrong," Sara said, although she was thinking enough was enough!

Her mother, a widow for almost ten years after a thirty-nine year marriage, came to her rescue. "Leave Sara Joy alone. She just hasn't met a good man yet. Anyway, the Lord will send her one when He's ready."

"Thank you Mom."

"Don't hold your breath waiting for that to happen. There are a whole lot of women asking the Lord to deliver a decent man and they've been waiting and praying for a long time," Eddie stated, who happened to be one of those women.

"Thanks to all of you, I'm in no rush," she reminded them for the millionth time.

"Amen to that!" shouted Kid after he finished the bottle he was sharing with their lovable uncle. This was the Deyton's family way of saying Merry Christmas.

In the early afternoon the day after Christmas, Sara, her mother, and sister were sitting around the kitchen table, eating and talking about everything but nothing particular. They were both telling Sara of their activities at the church her family has attended for more than ninety years. Then they jumped to other social events that kept them busy. Not short on words or things to talk about, the discussion shifted to Sara's nieces, nephews, cousins, and everybody else she knew, didn't want to know, or could barely recall. Hours passed as they continued to find more food to eat, hot and cold beverages to drink, and things to talk and laugh about.

When one of her nephews entered the house with a cell phone to his ear, Sara decided to check for any messages she may have received. Of the five messages only two caught her attention and interest. The others were immediately deleted.

Hello Sara! I hope you're having a wonderful time visiting with your family. I'm sure you helped make their holiday brighter. If I can be a little selfish, I wish you were here making mine a little happier. But, I guess I'll just have to wait. Take care and call me as soon as you get back in town.

Jonathan. She replayed the message twice, her smile increasing with each word.

Merry Christmas Sara and I wish you nothing but the best for the new year. I can't wait to see you in a few months when I come back to Chicago. We'll have a lot to catch up on. Happy New!

She still couldn't put a name or face to that man's voice. Since he still wasn't ready to reveal himself she just deleted the message.

Breathing, a cough, click, dial tone.

Delete.

Anyway, Sara replayed Jonathan's message one last time. Here she was, home for the holiday, but

Jonathan's message sounded so inviting. What should she do? She loved being with the family, but loved being at her own home as well, especially with her newfound friend so close by. So Sara said goodbye a day early and was back in Illinois before dark.

Saturday 31st

New Year's Eve, Sara had every intention of being at the church service that night. If she wasn't ringing in a new year in such glamorous places as Paris, Montreal, Times Square, or the Bahamas, she joined the hundreds of other saints at Rosebrook. Jonathan had already made plans for this night, which she did not expect or want him to change. So church was her midnight destination as she lay across the bed enjoying a lazy Saturday. Then the phone rang.

"Sara, I just had a wonderful idea. Since you're not spending the midnight hour with anyone, although I can't understand why not, and Bradley only wants to be with his drunken family, how would you like to join me and the girls downtown to watch the fireworks?" Krista knew Sara usually jumped at the chance to see one of the great Chicago fireworks displays. It didn't matter how often she saw them, Sara loved a good pyrotechnics show any time. However, there was also something in Krista's voice that told Sara she needed to talk or be in her company. Without an argument, Sara consented.

"You know a way to my heart don't you?" Sara laughed. "By the way, I was going to be spending the midnight hour with about three hundred people, not just one person."

"Yeah, I know, Rosebrook. Well, you need some excitement in your life and who better to help make it happen than your three favorite girls? I'll pick you up around eight for pizza then we can head downtown. Sound like a plan?"

"It's a date!" Sara exclaimed.

She was still relaxing on the bed when she heard the doorbell ring, several times, followed by a rhythmic knock with two hands, then the doorbell again. That was the signature announcement that either one or all of the three T's were paying her a visit. At the door stood the threesome.

"Good afternoon Trenton, Tyree and Tamala. Come in, what a pleasure to see you today."

"Why you gotta be so formal Miss Sara Smile? It's just us," said Trent the usual spokesperson. They started calling her Miss Sara Smile after a block party where Jed Hemings, playing some old school songs, serenaded her to the Hall and Oates classic, *Sara Smile.* She told the amused young audience the song was written for her and hence Miss Sara Smile was born.

"Okay, so what are you guys up to?"

"Nothing much. Are you gonna go to church tonight, too? Granny wants us to go, but we wanna stay home this time." Their little solemn faces suggested they were in need of a little diversion and she had just the remedy.

"How would you like to join the twins for pizza and fireworks tonight? Of course your grandmother would have to agree."

"Yeaaaa" they shouted jumping up and down. So across the street they scampered to get Miss Lizzie's approval.

"Now Sara, don't you have better things to do than bring in the New Year with a bunch of kids?" Miss Lizzie teased her.

"No, not tonight. Anyway, don't you want to take a break and spend some time by yourself? Or maybe even find yourself a date?"

"Please, child! My date is with the Lord. There hasn't been and won't be another man like my Grayson Payne." They had been married for forty-one years when he died three years earlier of a heart attack.

"Well, you go on to church and the seven of us will party tonight until we drop," Sara said looking at Tamala. She wasn't sure the little one would last but Tamala insisted she wanted to go and be with the other kids. Miss Lizzie would make the three T's take a nap so they would be awake for the midnight pandemonium.

Krista was right on time arriving at 8 o'clock. The seven of them piled in her Minivan, stopping first at Beggins Pizza Restaurant, one of the kid's favorite spots.

Although it was crowded, they only had a short wait for a table. Party hats and horns were distributed to patrons by the staff, not that they needed any party favors to add to the children's excitement. Krista and Sara just looked at each other and knew they had to talk louder. Two hours later, the minivan headed east on Interstate-94 into Chicago, joining hundreds of thousands of other revelers.

Krista managed to find a spot on Randolph Street just north of Michigan Avenue to watch the fireworks near Navy Pier from the car. As suspected, Tamala fell asleep, but the other four kids stood outside the car so they could get an unobstructed view.

"Sara, please pray for me and my marriage," Krista said. "It seems to be slipping away and I really don't want it to. You know I believe in my vows and I'm in this one for the long haul. We're almost at ten years and my dream is that we see at least fifty."

"Krista, you know your family is always in my prayers. God will bless you. It would help if you do more than just visit Rosebrook occasionally," Sara replied then became quiet as the sky lit up. Sara looked towards the heavens and whispered thanks for whatever the next twelve months would bring.

Happy New Year!

Chapter 2

January was somewhat of a sleeping month, with cold, long, dark days being spent sheltered indoors. The highlights for Sara this month were her birthday and preparing for Chana and Olivia's upcoming wedding.

She shared the same birthday as Dr. Martin L. King Jr., on the fifteenth. Her preferred celebration for his holiday was to go to work as an appreciation for his dedicated years fighting for the civil rights of African Americans. This year's recognition, albeit the second Sunday, would be a low-key jubilation of life.

Sunday January 15th

The day was filled with phone calls from family and friends beginning as early as midnight. After church Sara was treated to brunch at a popular country club by Chana, Olivia, Taylor and Rev. J.C. They left the restaurant three hours later, full of good food and spirited dialogue. Later that evening, Krista's household was the place for her favorite cake, yellow with milk chocolate icing, baked by the women of the house. Even Bradley was home all night for the occasion, playfully taunting Sara about one thing or another, especially the new man in her life.

Krista Katherine White Barrett Cunningham and Sara had been friends since their freshman year as Boilermakers of Purdue University. During an orientation, everyone turned to the person next to them and stated their intended major. After Sara said, Industrial Management, Krista replied an MRS. degree. And she was just as successful in her pursuit as anyone else. In her first year, she met Winston Barrett III, a serious minded, good looking, dean's list, third year student. Holding her own academically, she pledged a sorority in the Spring of her second year while maintaining a relationship with Winston. Returning for her third year, she completed the first semester, then left to marry Winston, who was now working in Chicago. By the end of that year, she gave birth to a beautiful baby girl, Whitney. Two years later, they welcomed a son, Kendall. Unfortunately, two years later Winston and Krista were divorced.

Tumultuous was a mild word to describe the next four years for Krista. She fought constantly with Winston over child support and alimony although he was very generous when it came to his kids. She kept trying to get back in the dating scene but realized that not many eligible men in their twenties wanted a ready- made family. She was miserable being single again. But with the love and support from her family and friends, she was persuaded to finish her degree and get on with her life. Eventually, she completed her business management degree, met and married the inveigling Bradley Cunningham and became the proud mother of twins, Autumn and April, born on the first day of Summer. Whitney and Kendall had never accepted Bradley as a stepfather so they went to live with Winston, who was still unmarried. Krista had yet to have a career outside of being a stay-at-home wife and mom, loving every minute of it!

Sara and Krista were like sisters, being with each other through the good times and those which could be much better. Today was a good day as everyone laughed, danced, and ate plenty of cake and ice cream in celebration of forty-three blessed years. The festive occasion would be repeated in May for Krista.

At the end of the evening, having made her way back home, Sara felt exuberant and about five pounds heavier. Checking the voice mail one last time there were six more well-wishers that she was pleased to hear from. However, the notable exception was Jonathan. Maybe he had an extremely busy weekend, she deduced, to soothe her emotionally wounded soul.

Monday's workday couldn't end soon enough as Sara dashed into the house and headed straight to the telephone. *Yes, messages!* Two were from friends with a belated birthday greeting, but not Jonathan. Tuesday she followed the same routine except with different results.

Hello, Sara. If I'm not mistaken, you're celebrating your birthday today. I remember it's around Dr. King's holiday. Sorry I missed you again, but I hope this is a very special day for a very special lady. See you soon.

This phone message made her a little uncomfortable. Who was this man from her past that knew where she lived, her home phone number, compliments of the internet, and remembered her birthday? News reports were full of stories about women being stalked by men, often with a tragic ending. Trying not to entertain such negative thoughts, she decided to approach this a little more seriously. Instead of replaying or deleting this message as she did the others, it was saved in the archives, in the event that further action was needed. Seconds later, as she walked towards the bedroom, the doorbell rang, rattling her nerves just a little.

"Who is it?" Sara shouted defensively.

"It's me, darling, Jed. I have something for you," he said, calming her. By the time she opened the front door, she was all smiles. It grew broader when she saw what was in Jed's hands.

"Is that for me?" she loudly shrilled at the sight of the beautiful birthday bouquet of balloons and flowers.

"Yes, honey. You didn't think I'd forgotten your birthday, did you?" he replied, although Sara knew better than that.

"Come on in, delivery man, so I can see who these are really from. But thank you for bringing them to me. They must have come while I was at work." She rested the vase on the coffee table and grabbed the typewritten card.

Happy Birthday
This is only the Beginning
Jonathan

"When you wipe that grin off of your face, are you going to tell me who my competition is, or do you want me to leave you and the flowers alone in your thoughts?" Jed said, snapping Sara out of utopia. For a fleeing moment, while opening the envelope, it crossed her mind that these could be from the mystery man. Thank goodness they were from the man she was anxiously waiting to hear from the past three days. He had not forgotten and he did want to be a part of her birthday celebration. She was now ecstatic! Could this be an answer to her prayers, a blessing from above? She had to take a few deep breaths and relax.

"They're from a friend of Chana's that I met a little while ago. This is awfully considerate of him and very unexpected," Sara tried to say without showing her true emotions, but Jed wasn't buying it.

"Seems to me like he's more than Charles' friend and wants to be more than a friend to you. By that glow on your face, I think you want that too. I'll get out of here so you can keep blushing over your present. But I want you to know that I will have to check him out to see if he'll pass the test before you are allowed to get too involved with this Casanova," Jed said before leaving.

Sara's face was probably still flushed red as she danced around the house to the music of popular artists from the 80's, keeping her eye on the bouquet and perusing the small card over and over. *What did he mean by This is only the Beginning? The beginning of what? Us? A life with him? More surprises?* Sara was beginning to act like a love sick school girl, but she didn't care. She was so happy she wanted to share this joy, maybe not with the world but at least with Krista. So she picked up the phone and jabbered fervidly for over an hour. The beep during their conversation informed her that another call was waiting. Looking at the caller ID display, she politely dismissed her girlfriend, as Krista had done with her numerous times, and received the one Sara had been waiting on.

"Hello precious lady and happy belated birthday. I hope you had a good time all day Sunday eating and partying with your friends. Now it's my turn to help you celebrate. You didn't think I forgot did you?"

Gaining her composure and being somewhat honest, Sara replied, "It's good to hear your voice, Jonathan. Thank you for the beautiful birthday bouquet. I'll admit, since I didn't hear from you, I briefly thought you may have been too busy to remember."

"Now, Sara, give a brother some credit! I'll never be too busy to celebrate such a wonderful occasion as your birthday. We wouldn't be talking now if you hadn't come into this world then and blessed my life now."

"Okay, Jonathan you can quit laying it on so thick," Sara said, blushing while taking it all in.

"Charles told me about the plans for brunch and dessert with Krista so I decided I'd let your friends have you on Sunday, and this weekend will be mine. How does that sound?"

"What exactly do you have in mind?" Sara asked, a little more subdued.

"I happen to know an excellent chef in Chicago who has a fantastic view of the city. We have reservations on Friday night. And Saturday, one of my buddies is hosting a stepper's set in the south suburbs to which I have secured a couple of tickets. Now it would really break my heart if you say something like you've already got plans for those nights."

"As a matter of fact, my date book is completely empty this weekend" Sara Said, hoping he wouldn't sense her excitement.

"Good, I'll pick you up at six o'clock Friday. And by the way, this is casual."

"I'm looking forward to it already. A comfortable, casual, excellent dinner with great company, what a birthday present!" Sara exclaimed! When they hung up, the anticipation of the upcoming weekend helped her get through the rest of the week, quicker than most.

Friday, January 20th

Friday at last! Sara tried on four outfits before choosing a pair of yellow leggings with a matching V-neck angora tunic sweater, gold ankle boots and her favorite pair of gold and multi-color dangling Monet earrings. Jonathan rang the doorbell at six o'clock sharp with a single pink rose in his hand, handsomely dressed in a black turtleneck and slacks.

They wasted no time departing for their dinner destination while Sara pleaded to know where they were going. She was a bit surprised to hear him finally give in and say his sister's house. It didn't matter that they were not going to a restaurant, she just wasn't quite ready to start meeting the family. Barely acquainted with him for not even a month, she felt they were still at the getting-to- know-you stage. But, these were his plans and she would just have to trust his judgment. Besides, to date he had shown nothing but good taste in everything he had said or had done.

On the drive to his sister's house, Jonathan shared some background on his childhood. He was the youngest of six children born and raised on Chicago's south side. His parents were deceased. The oldest was a boy who began serving a life sentence for armed robbery before he was twenty. That left Jonathan with four older sisters who escaped the life that could have made all of them a statistic of their environment as well. The eldest girl lived in Mississippi with her husband of thirty-four years. The next sister was killed many years ago in a car accident on the Dan Ryan Expressway. His youngest sister was an Emergency Room nurse at Cook County Hospital. And lastly, Rebecca, whom Sara was about to meet, was a single, forty-nine-year-young partner at a prestigious law firm in the Loop, or downtown. Jonathan thought Sara reminded him of Rebecca in many ways, which is why he wanted them to meet.

"How did you get her to cook for us tonight?" Sara asked him upon arrival.

"Not only is she an excellent cook, but she has a new man she's trying to impress. We decided a double date would be comfortable for everyone," he said with a wink. A very good idea Sara thought. No doubt in her mind the suggestion came from Rebecca.

Rebecca met them at the door, accepting a bottle of white wine from her brother. "Thanks, Nate, but you didn't have to bring anything except your date. Sara, welcome and please make yourself at home," said the petite woman, who easily looked ten years younger than her actual age. Sara's presumption that Nate was Jonathan's nickname was correct.

"Thank you for your generous hospitality," Sara replied as she scanned the immaculate condo in the high-rise, offering spectacular views of the lakefront and Chicago skyline. Later, Rebecca revealed that her leather and wood contemporary living room came straight out of a window display in Paris. The Fall colors ensemble had caught her eye while she was casually walking down a street off the famous Des Champs Elysees, in the City of Lights. She went into the store and had the entire showcase shipped to her home. Sara admired her bold, classy, good taste.

About fifteen minutes later, the doorbell rang and Rebecca buzzed in her date to the twenty-ninth floor condo. Her brother was quite surprised to see this much younger man make his entrance holding a bottle of wine and dressed in a black sweater and slacks, too. Sara teased her date about this being the Friday night dress code. Once again, Rebecca gained more points with Sara as she applauded her taste and capability to attract a man almost twenty years her junior.

"What playground did you pick him up on?" whispered Jonathan to the two ladies.

"Behave yourself, little brother," Rebecca mildly scolded him as Sara gave him a slight nudge, agreeing with Rebecca.

Jonathan was also right about her culinary talents. Rebecca's seafood dinner was superb. It consisted of crab cakes with Remoulade sauce, broiled lobster tails, pan seared asparagus with hollandaise sauce, wild rice, Waldorf salad, and homemade sour dough bread. Cooking was a hobby she thoroughly enjoyed and it showed! Sara admitted to her that if she ever returned a dinner invitation it would have to be at one of her favorite dining spots. Even with her best prepared meals, she couldn't come close to this culinary delight.

Jonathan spent a good portion of the dinner conversation quizzing Vincent, a sign of his protective nature. "So Vincent, my sister tells me you're with the public defender's office. How long have you been volunteering there? We know it doesn't pay much." His inquiry caused his sister and Sara to raise an eyebrow.

"Eight years. You're right about that though. It doesn't pay much. If it was about the money, I would have joined one of the big firms that made me an offer before I graduated. I'm one of the brothers who's attempting to make a difference in the lives of some of these young knuckleheads. You see, I grew up in Detroit with my two sisters, raised by our mom. My alcoholic father walked out on us when I was so young I don't remember anything about him. We had it rough financially but my mother was determined that her kids were going to have a better life. She fought hard to keep us away from gang violence and drugs. It's because of her that my oldest sister is an attorney also and my baby sister is working on her doctorate in psychology, specializing in adolescent therapy. When I was in law school I met Johnnie Cochran and was impressed with his road to prominence. I chose this route to get my feet wet and gain valuable experience about the law and how it really works."

"Bravo my brother, I'm impressed," Jonathan said, speaking for Sara as well. "But why did you leave the Motor City?"

"I have too many family members and guys I grew up with in the system. I wanted to go someplace where I didn't know names and faces but the problems are still the same. Chicago is close enough to home so that I can get back there often and check on my women," Vincent said fondly.

"Yeah, I keep tabs on all my women too," Jonathan responded as he squeezed Sara's hand and winked at Rebecca. "You've got it going on. You just don't look old enough to have accomplished so much."

"When my dad disappeared, I became the man of the house. Been making money since I was ten, graduated high school and college in six years and finished law school and the bar in another three. I felt I owed it to my mom so she wouldn't have to spend all her life working hard for us kids."

"That makes you what, somewhere around thirty?" inquired Jonathan.

"Nate!" shouted Rebecca. Even Sara gave him an eye of disbelief that he would be so bold for no reason.

"It's alright, ladies. We men understand. I have no secrets. I'll be thirty-one on April fourteenth. Is that a problem for you, man?"

"No, and I apologize if I came across like a jerk for even bringing it up.I can identify with you in a lot of ways and protecting our women is one, if you know what I mean. For what it's worth, I'm forty-five."

Rebecca and Sara said nothing for a minute until she realized this was Jonathan's way of bringing peace back into the room and the comfort level they all shared before his dialogue with Vincent. Being a bit bodacious, she casually stated, "I turned forty-three on January fifteenth." Rebecca finally broke her silence. "Alright, I'm thirty-nine." By now, they were all laughing again and lifted their glasses in a toast to birthdays.

For the next three hours, they relaxed in the showcase living room over dessert, after-dinner drinks, and all kinds of conversation during the fun card game Phase 10. Finally, Sara convinced Jonathan that they should give Rebecca and Vincent a chance to spend some time alone. So they made their exit, ending yet another heavenly night. An elated Sara thought how much this man had rocked her single world in less than thirty days.

Sunday, January 22nd

Yes, they did go out dancing for a little while Saturday, but Sara wanted to make it an early night since she attended church just about every Sunday. And they did without any hesitation from Jonathan. Hearing the phone ring early that morning while she was dressing for Rosebrook, was a pleasant surprise.

"Good morning, beautiful. Are you about ready to go to church?" asked Jonathan.

"Good morning, yourself. I'll be walking out of the door in about ten minutes," she said proudly since she wasn't rushing to make it to Bible class on time.

"I just wanted to make sure you hadn't overslept from being up too late," he commented.

"Not a chance. Rosebrook is like a second home to me and my extended family will come looking for me if I'm not there, especially Chana."

"Very well, then, I'll talk to you later," he said and hung up before she had a chance to say another word.

Fifteen minutes later, as her garage door opened, she got another surprise. There he was, parked in the driveway, waiting to join her for Bible class and church service. Sara was too delighted to introduce him to the Rosebrook family. She took this as another sign from heaven that Jonathan was in her life for a reason. But what?

Rev. Wallace and Portia Stevens invited the new twosome to have dinner with them, but Sara graciously declined and accepted their open invitation. All the usual suspects, Miss Lizzie, Jed and Rhoda Hemings, and Rev. J.C. gave him a plausible nod. Even Adelaine Richardson shook his hand, cordially greeting both of them. But, that's the Rosebrook way, making all visitors, feel welcomed and like family.

Mother Bertha James, Rosebrook's proud matriarch, came their way. "Young man you know you're with one of the best women a man can find, don't you?" Sara blushed from embarrassment.

"Yes, ma'am, and I totally agree with you," Jonathan said as he applied one of his signature light kisses on her cheek.

"You take care of her and I want to see you here more often. The Lord is going to continue to bless Miss Sara and he'll bless you too if you're doing the right things." Mother Bertha didn't hold back on speaking her mind. Sara was hoping she didn't have anything else to say, but just in case, she jumped in.

"Mother Bertha, Jonathan is visiting with us today. I'm sure his pastor doesn't want him missing too many Sundays to attend Rosebrook," she said while adding a kiss to her cheek as well. Suddenly, a question popped into her head after she made that remark. Just where was his home church? "But you know you'll see me next week as usual." Then they started making their way towards the door where Chana was standing.

"Man, the Lord does work in mysterious ways, and that's a good thing," Chana chided as he and Jonathan greeted one another. "I've been trying to get you to visit for months."

"Well, now I have an even better reason, wouldn't you say?"

"One of the best that I can think of," Chana replied giving Sara a hug. "What are you two doing this afternoon?"

"We're having lunch and a quiet afternoon at my house," she spoke up. They had spent much of the weekend in the presence of others and she desired some uninterrupted time to hear more about this man who was warming her heart with every beat.

"That's good to hear. Enjoy yourselves." Then Chana whispered something in Jonathan's ear, he replied, and they shared a laugh. That kind of male bonding was allowed. Sara figured women don't need to know everything that a man is thinking or doing. Women are God's wonderful creatures who relish unexpected surprises at unexpected times, like Tuesday. Whatever was said she'd more than likely be privy to at the right moment in the future.

Back at her quiet haven, Jonathan lit the fireplace while she ordered a pizza for delivery. The cozy fire slowly started adding a little more warmth to the room, raising the level of comfort up a notch. The crackling sound of the dry oak and maple wood drew them to sit on the floor and be themselves, pretense left outside the front door.

"I'm glad I got a chance to meet some of your family, even if they aren't your blood relatives. I just hope I passed the initial test," Jonathan smiled as his finger stroked her face.

"You don't have to worry about that. Everybody appeared to like you. Besides, any friend of Chana's will be accepted by the entire Rosebrook congregation. Everybody loves him."

"Can I ask why you call him that?"

Sara laughed and shared with him their platonic twenty-year relationship and explained how that nickname came about. Actually Krista and the twins were the only other people who called him Chana.

"If you don't mind, I'll stick with calling him Charles."

"Of course not, Nate," she said playfully.

He stroked her face with his finger as they just sat there silently gazing into the fire and each other's eyes. He slowly leaned in to kiss her and she acquiesced, when suddenly the doorbell rang. Saved by the pizza man!

Half way through lunch, she began visualizing spending more time with him. In one month she had met a man who was occupying more space in her mind and heart than she would have imagined. Krista said she fantasized, but Sara referred to them as moments of visualizing the way she wanted her life to be. An array of visualizations included the perfect career choice, her physical appearance, the ideal family and home life. To date, some of her visions had eluded her. The visions dancing inside her head disappeared when she was reminded of Rev. Stevens' message today, *"Wait On The Lord"*. A condition of the waiting process was to get to know more about this figure of her visualization.

"You're not eating much. Is anything wrong, baby?"

"No, nothing is wrong. Actually everything seems right. Too right."

"What do you mean by that? What's on your mind? Talk to me, Sara?"

"I'd like for you to open up like Vincent did the other night and tell me things about Jonathan Tate that I don't know yet. All that I ask is for you to please be honest and release only the information you want me to know."

"Okay, fair enough," he said as he finished the piece of pizza that was in his hand. Slowly, he began to be selective in what he was about to reveal. "My name is Jonathan Paris Tate, born on September 29th. I told you about my siblings, so now I'll tell you about my personal life. After I graduated high school, I took a job as a janitor at the Ford plant in Ford Heights. The job wasn't anything I wanted to do all my life, but for a kid who had nothing growing up, the money was good. My sisters kept encouraging me to go to school. At first, I just shook my head yes to keep them off my back, but, eventually I listened. A year later I started going to Kennedy-King College during the day while I was still working full time on second shift. In the Fall of that year, I met a fine student who wanted to be a nurse, Rosalyn Silverman. She turned my head and world around. That following May she told me we were going to have a baby. Yes, I panicked at first but I knew I had to do what I had to do. In October, we welcomed a beautiful baby girl, Jasmine Athena. Rosalyn's parents were not very pleased that we had not gotten married and put pressure on me. So, I succumbed and we were married at their home in March. Here I was at twenty-one, a husband, father, part time student and full time janitor. But I kept pushing forward and so did she. Rosalyn became an LPN the next year and by the time I was twenty-three, I had received my associates degree in business administration. As a graduation gift, my son Johnny Roman was born in June. For the next two years, I struggled with this whole family thing, trying to figure out what else life had to offer me. The only difference was that I now was working as a machine operator at Ford. Finally, at age twenty-seven, I thought I was missing something in my life and I was determined to find it. However, I thought having a wife and two kids in tow would hinder me, so I bailed out of the marriage. I'm not proud now, but for a few years I only provided financial support to Rosalyn and the kids, being an absent father. Those years were spent being all about me. I did drugs, slept with more women than I care to remember, and worked the party scene nonstop."

Jonathan paused, taking a few sips of his soft drink and collecting his thoughts. Sara knew these words were coming from his heart. She rubbed his hand, showing her appreciation for his openness and honesty. He smiled and continued.

"Finally at thirty-three, I met a woman who settled me down......a little. Candace was a very attractive mover and shaker in the real estate business. I moved in with her, quit my job at Ford, got my license, and started selling real estate. She taught me everything I needed to know and we were doing quite well, financially. Both of us drove nice cars, dressed to the hilt, dined out like we didn't have a kitchen, and continued to smoke weed daily. One of the best things she did for me was insist I own up to my daddy duties. I began spending more time with the kids. She also encouraged me to get my bachelor's degree, which I did from Chicago State. For me, life was going great and I was pretty happy, but it was obvious that Candace did not share my happy feelings. She wanted us to get married and have our own family. The thought of marriage didn't rest well with me at this time either. Once again, the pressure was on and I still wasn't ready to make that commitment. So, on my fortieth birthday, Candace asked me to leave and I can't say I blame her. I was a financial mess after I left because she handled all of the money. I had to start all over again. The good thing is I learned to be a lot smarter now with my finances."

Jonathan's mood was now melancholy as he recalled this time in his life. Sara listened with intent, but did not want him to feel pressured to continue.

"Remember, you only have to release whatever you want me to know," she empathically whispered.

"I know, sweetie," he said as he kissed the back of her hand. "I have nothing to hide." Shifting his body into a more comfortable position and adding a little smile to his face he starting recalling happier moments.

"Jasmine is a real gem, like her mother. She has never given us a minute of trouble. She breezed through school always on the honor roll and dean's list. After graduating from the University of Illinois with a degree in Finance & Accounting, she followed her dreams and moved to New York City. At twenty-five she's working on Wall Street and appears to be having the time of her young life, in addition to making the big bucks. We are so proud of her."

"I can tell from the glow on your face," Sara eased in.

"Now Johnny, he's a different story. He's lazy, graduated high school with only average grades, not that he couldn't have done better. He spent one year at Southern Illinois in Carbondale and didn't go back. He came home and his uncle got him a job at the M & M Mars company. While he was there, he took the police exam and passed, but decided that's not what he wanted to do and neither was working at the candy company. Right now, he works at UPS delivering packages. Of course, we keep hearing the story about going back to school. Yeah, right, I'll believe it when he graduates. I've asked him to work with me in the real estate industry, but he says that's not his thing either. Baby, I know you're a praying woman, so please keep him in your prayers."

"I'll add him to the prayer list at church. You and your family have been in my prayers since I met you. I always pray for my friends and their loved ones. Now I know who I have been praying for and I can be more specific."

"As for Rosalyn, she is still a beautiful woman and because of the kids we remain friends today. She remarried after Johnny finished high school and seems to be very happy."

Jonathan stopped talking and just stared into the fire as Sara let him have those quiet reflective moments. He stretched out on the floor laying on his back, looked up at her and said, "Now that I've spilled my heart ,I think it's your turn."

As if right on cue, the clock chimed indicating the seven o'clock hour. They had been sitting on floor eating and talking for several hours. To quote an old cliché, Sara had been saved by the bell.

"You're absolutely right and I will, the next time we get together. There are some things I need to do in preparation for next week. Let's call it a night and at our next gathering, I'll introduce you to Sara Joy Deyton." The complete truth was that she wanted to process the information he had shared with her. Sara's first reaction to his story was that Jonathan was a commitment phobic. If that was the case, she might be wasting her time and emotions. Sara whispered to herself ,"God, we need to talk!"

"Is that a promise, sweetheart? I hope I didn't say anything to scare you off."

"No, quite the contrary. You've added more sparks to the flame," she correctly stated. Her heart and mind was now burning with curiosity.

They engaged in a tight embrace at the door, followed by a short, guarded kiss. After Jonathan left, she threw her body on the couch and laid there for more than an hour, *visualizing*.

Saturday, January 28th

Chana's wedding was only two weeks away and Sara was pushing it to find a dress for the lovely affair. Gloria assured Sara they would find a dress on a trip to one of her favorite malls, the Lighthouse Place Premium Outlets in Michigan City, Indiana. In fact Gloria would dress her from head to toe. Taylor joined in as the three of them made a day of shopping the last Saturday in January.

Two hours and five stores later, she saw the perfect dress in the Anne Klein shop. There it was, a pretty purple and cream sleeveless dress with gold accents. The dress flared at the waistline with a matching purple long-sleeve jacket, highlighted by a single flower-shaped cloth button. Although it wasn't an exact fit, Gloria's tailor could make the needed alterations. Now that the biggest problem was solved, they continued to shop as they accessorized the ensemble with earrings, shoes and handbag. Sara was sure to look extra special for her best friend's big day.

Gloria had driven them in her burgundy Lexus SUV that she had bought a year ago. Although they were a little tired after the full day's excursion that included several snacks and a full late lunch, the ladies gained a second wind engaging in all kinds of conversation on the ride home.

"Sara, can I ask you something personal and I hope you don't take offense to it? How do you really feel about your best male friend getting married? I know you and Chana are really close and have shared a lot of good times together. I'm bringing this up because my mother taught me big changes are about to take place," said the serious Taylor.

"Well, Taylor, they have been dating for almost three years and I've already taken a back seat to his relationship with Olivia. That's the way it's supposed to be and the way it is. No offense taken, by the way."

"Has she ever commented on the nickname you gave him?"

"No, not to me. Should she? Chana has not mentioned anything either. Why would she? I've been calling him that for twenty years. There's nothing secretive about how Krista and I derived at his nickname."

"I know and it may seem innocent and fine with you, maybe even to Charles, but, he's a man and may not be sensitive to his soon-to-be wife's true feelings. My mom told us when she married Daddy that she became so protective of him, almost to the point of smothering. She wanted to know everyone he knew, how he knew them, how long, how they met, and so on, you get the picture. She says a marriage is a partnership and his role as husband and potential father was different than that as a single man. So she wanted people to see him in the same light as she saw him. Therefore, Daddy had to change some of his habits as well as Mommy. It got easier with time and she loosened her grip on him. She said the single man eventually died out and her husband emerged in full. He had a couple of female friends that slowly but surely faded away. This could happen to you, my dear. I just don't want to see you get hurt."

"I love you and appreciate your input from a potential married woman's perspective. My relationship with Chana is more like that of a big brother than anything else. And believe me, since he met Olivia, we have slacked off a lot with things we use to do together. I'm very happy for both of them.

They deserve each other. So, yes, I'm prepared to keep my distance," Sara sincerely replied.

"Girls, when I first married that ex of mine, I thought I was the luckiest woman on this earth. That feeling lasted for maybe the first six months. After the tenth year, we were just together for the sake of our three kids. When the children were in high school he had women calling and coming by the house looking for him. At first, it hurt but after it went on long enough, I didn't care. Let me tell you, before I kicked that no good man out, I was trying to get anybody, man or woman to take him off my hands." Gloria said all of this as she kept her eyes on the road and hands on the wheel. Sara and Taylor burst out laughing. Gloria always had stories to tell that would make any woman want to remain or become single.

After five minutes of side-hurting, eye-tearing laughter, mostly from Sara, Taylor tried to make marriages look attractive. "Ladies, all marriages aren't that bad. My parents have been happy for thirty-six years. Before them my grandparents celebrated sixty-three years together."

Then Gloria opened up the envelope that Sara hadn't been quite ready to reveal its contents. "So Sara, who's this man you've been seen with around town? I know you didn't think you could keep him from me, did you?"

"I'm not trying to hide the fact that I met a wonderful man at Chana's Christmas party. There's not much to tell. Yes, we've been out since then but we're just letting nature take its course. I don't know where it will lead but for now I'm just enjoying the journey. Not only that, I don't want to scare him off by introducing him to CLEAR too soon. You know how you ladies can be!"

"Now, you know we wouldn't do anything to disrupt any relationship for you. I'm happy that you finally met someone who's caught your interest. But, I'm curious, when are we going to meet him? From what I hear, he's not only something to look at, but a man who seems to have it together," Gloria commented.

"And who have you been talking to?" Sara blushed.

"I've got my way of finding things out. But just remember what your elders always say; the devil is a liar," stated Gloria.

"I know, so you can understand my not wanting to rush into anything with him. Fools rush in and I've been there before. Don't want to repeat that mess again."

"So, at least tell us his name? My sources didn't have all the details."

"Jonathan Tate."

"Why does that name sound familiar?" Gloria asked with a look like she was trying to take a trip down memory lane.

"I don't know," was all Sara could say, hunching her shoulders.

Chapter 3

Sara met Charles Nash the first week on the job after she had graduated college. He was an electronics engineer with two years under his belt. They hit it off from day one as friends and to this day has maintained a true platonic relationship. He was named after his grandfather and uncle. His cousin named his first son Charles after his father. His mother had remarried and her second husband's name was Charles Franklin, who had a son Charles Jr. There were just too many Charles' and it's variation of Charlie, Chuck, and Chucky. At first, Sara started calling him Charles Nash and he said that was too formal. So she shortened his name to Chana, taking the first three letters of his first name and first two of his last. He didn't have a problem with it then and still responded to it twenty years later.

Chana was a quiet warrior. He was a God fearing man who served tirelessly, especially with Rev. J.C. and the young people. His handsome caramel complexion, medium build, five feet-nine inches, didn't draw attention or stand out in a crowd, just the way he liked it. Chana tended to be a little on the conservative side. Once, Sara almost talked him into growing his hair out. Two months barbershop free and an inch of new growth was all he could take. The close cropped style suited him perfectly fine.

The union between him and Olivia would be his second marriage. At age twenty-five, he married his college girlfriend, Beverly. She wanted so much to have children, and after two years of unsuccessful attempts, they consulted a doctor. It was determined that Chana suffered from the common cause of male infertility, a low sperm count. The doctors were unable to give a specific reason why this relatively healthy young man had this sperm disorder, except genetics. Devastated, Chana was determined to have the family they desired. Beverly, listening to the counsel of her family and friends, rejected all of his alternative solutions.

She came from a strict Catholic background and her mother convinced her that since God wanted couples to have children naturally, Chana was being punished for some wrong doing in his past. So, Beverly's priest annulled the marriage and by twenty-nine, Chana was single again, very hurt and bitter towards women. Over the next ten years, he did not date anyone, gained about fifty pounds and kept to himself socially, except for Krista and Sara.

Years later as Chana and Sara were strolling around the Taste of Chicago Festival, they came upon Beverly, her husband Mitchell, and their two children. It was a tense encounter as they had not spoken since the divorce. Introductions were made and Mitchell tried to be as friendly as possible and engage in small talk, but, Chana wasn't interested. Sara had forgiven Beverly for wrecking her best friend's life, but still didn't want to know about her new one. Everyone said goodbye and Chana immediately left Grant Park in silence with Sara close behind. She knew from experience how difficult it was to truly forgive someone from a hurt or harm they afflicted upon you, intentionally or not. But a sure way to be healed of an unforgiving heart was through prayer. On the drive home she opened the small Bible he kept in his car and read out loud Mark 11:25, *" But when you are praying, first forgive anyone you are holding a grudge against, so that your Father in heaven will forgive your sins, too."* Chana just smiled and let go.

Two years later Chana ran into Mitchell with the newest addition to their family. The two of them had a chance to talk, face to face.

"Charles, I think this meeting is not coincidental, but a divine intervention. That chance encounter in Grant Park was really awkward for Beverly and me. She had said many times that she wanted to talk to you, but didn't know how to go about it. I'd heard so much about you, good things I might add, that I wanted to meet you myself. Beverly and I have a strong marriage because we communicate openly and honestly. You may not know, but Bev spent the next three years in counseling after your divorce, both spiritual and emotional. She was trying to understand if what she did was the right thing and what effect it would have on any future marriage and family of hers. I attended some of the sessions with her and I know she grieved heavily over how she ended your marriage. Don't get me wrong, brother, if she hadn't, I wouldn't be married to her today. I know that sounds selfish, but I think you know what I'm trying to say. She even regretted her mother having had so much influence on her while you were married. Trust me, I had to put my foot down and make her mother leave us alone, God rest her soul. She died before our last son, Joshua, was born. Anyway, my wife is not some self- centered crazy woman. It would mean a lot to Bev and our family if you forgave her. Besides, when little Joshua Charles gets older, he'll want to know how he got his name."

"Come on, is his name really Joshua Charles?" replied a surprised Chana.

"Yes, it was therapeutic for Beverly, not to just have another baby boy, but to name him after you, and she got no objection from me."

Chana grinned from ear to ear as he said hello to his playful namesake.

"Thanks, Mitchell, for sharing that with me. By the way, I truly forgave Beverly after I saw how happy she seemed with her new family. If you ever need a babysitter, call me after he turns thirteen," smiled a proud Chana.

After that, Chana's heart was opened and his blessings were immediately unblocked. A few months, later he met Olivia Hope Brownlee and now almost three years later and forty pounds lighter, they were about to become husband and wife.

Saturday, February 11th

Everyone had been keeping their eye on the weather, confirming the meteorologist report that a snow storm was heading their way, the day before the wedding. Olivia had picked the month of February not because of Valentine's Day but in honor of her parents. The Brownlee's were celebrating their forty-fifth anniversary and the Nash couple aimed to go the distance as well. We were praying the weather would help the Nash couple get off to a good start.

Waking up that Saturday morning and finding five inches of snow covering everything, meant people would have to dig their way out of their homes. On the upside, the sun was shining brightly, skies were clear, and the temperature was expected to stay above freezing. The streets would be mostly clear by the start of the evening ceremony. *Good, I can handle this!*, Sara thought. Jed Hemings had started clearing Sara's driveway and sidewalks with his snow blower before she crawled out of bed.

"Good morning, Jed. Thanks for coming to my rescue. I'll give you a hand with the sidewalk and steps," she said as he was working up to the garage.

"Get back inside the house. This is a man's job. You gotta get pretty for that wedding later. Make sure you take notes." He thought he'd slip in that jab without her noticing. "When I go to Miss Lizzie's house I'll get the boys to help." That's typical Jed. He would do anything for people in the neighborhood, especially those he considered his women.

"How about a cup of coffee to help keep you warm?"

"Make it hot, black, with a little sugar, just like my women," he said as he waved her back into the house.

"Oh, by the way, what do I need to take notes for?" Sara remarked.

Jed's only woman was his wife of many years, Rhoda. They have raised four children and were enjoying eleven grandchildren. He considered Sara one of his and she proudly acknowledged being a member of the Hemings family. She was happy she landed a home in this community with neighbors like the Hemings and Miss Lizzie. Just as she stepped back inside after delivering the hot coffee, the phone rang.

"Good morning, beautiful. Put the coffee on, and I'll be over to shovel you out from the small blizzard we had last night," said Jonathan.

"Good morning to you also. However, you're just a little late for that. Three of my favorite men have already taken care of my snow," she teased.

"Oh, so it's like that. I've got competition right outside your doorstep. Looks like I'm going to have to move closer to you to stay on top of my rivals."

"Nonsense, sweetie. There's enough of me to go around."

"So I guess I'll just have to get up much earlier to beat out the others?"

"Something like that, but not to worry. You have something they don't have."

"And what might that be?"

"I'll tell you later," she said with a little laughter in her voice.

"I can't wait to hear this! I'll be ringing your doorbell at five o'clock."

"Please make it four-thirty. I need to be there a little early since I'm one of the host and to help Krista with the girls, if necessary."

"Your duties at the wedding won't keep you from me all night, will they?"

"Not a chance, Jonathan. Not a chance." She'd definitely see to that.

Rev. J.C. made sure the parking lot and sidewalks to Rosebrook were cleared well today. When Sara arrived, the bride and groom were in their rooms getting dressed. In Chana's case, he was sitting down, calm and relaxed, like it was just another Saturday. Sara tipped in his room briefly, giving him a final hug and kiss as a single man and whispering in his ear how proud she was. Jonathan kept Chana company as they were laughing and talking when she left to check on Olivia.

A short time later, Krista and Bradley arrived with the flower girls. The twins were so bubbly in their matching lavender and cream color chiffon dresses, accented by a purple ribbon at the waist forming a big bow in the back. Their hair hung down below the shoulder in large curls while lavender ribbons provided the finishing touch. Sara and Krista greeted each other with hugs and kisses as if it had been months since they last saw each other.

"You girls are so lovely. The guests won't be able to take their eyes off of you strolling down the aisle," Sara said to them.

"They can look like this again when it's time to strut down that aisle for your big day," Bradley said as he nudged Krista. "I hear that might not be so far away since you met this Jonathan. By the way, where is he? You know he has to get my approval."

"Don't you two start anything in here. I don't want to get ugly in church," she replied to both of them, trying not to blush. "You'll meet Jonathan in a minute. He's back there with Chana. And like I said, behave yourselves."

It was good to see the Cunningham family together. Krista was all smiles as she took her husband's arm to take a seat. Sara took the girls where the other ladies in the wedding party were waiting.

Olivia only wanted a small, intimate affair, consisting of about seventy friends and family. It was close with about one hundred guest in attendance. The small wedding party was made up of her sister as maid of honor, Rev. J.C. as best man, Autumn and April, and two of her nephews as ring bearers. Olivia's sister, custom designed her absolutely gorgeous wedding gown. Long, cream colored, silk, plain and flared from the waist down with a six-foot train. The fitted sweetheart neckline and long sleeves were made of a very fine lace. Her veil covered her face extending to the neckline. There were shimmering gold strands of thread woven throughout the netting and trimmed the bottom of the veil. Radiating a glow that said," This is my day", everyone could tell this was a marriage made in Heaven. Chana punctuated that notion with his ear-to-ear smile as he watched his bride ascend the aisle to her groom.

The adult reception was held a few miles away at a country club in Indiana. The twin lakes that gave the club its name, were visible in the summer. From every view on this night was a blanket of pure white, untouched snow that glittered in the moon-light.

Inside, the guests dined by candlelight to baked fish and prime rib. Bradley and Jonathan talked like they had known each other for years. That's a characteristic Sara always admired in Bradley. He was a charming stranger to no one, carrying on a conversation about anything and nothing particular. Krista whispered to Sara, "Don't you wish it could be like this forever?"

"Slow down a little, Mrs. Cunningham, and let's just enjoy tonight. You and Bradley have a history of years. Jonathan and I can only count our days."

"Well, I can wish, can't I? Or as you might say, visualize," she said with a chuckle.

"Okay, score one for you. Yes, Krista, I do wish you and that handsome man much happiness, and that tonight's happiness could last forever and a day." Sara smiled sincerely.

Weddings seemed to bring out the best in people. Krista and Bradley looked like a pair of newlyweds themselves, hugging and kissing throughout the evening. Maybe Sara's prayers were being answered and he was being drawn back to the closeness and love of his family. Jonathan seemed to think so.

"They look like two lovebirds rather than a married couple of ten years," he said on the dance floor, moving to Luther Vandross', "Always and Forever".

"Yes, they do, and I pray they'll continue to be that way."

"Is there trouble in paradise?"

"No, sweetie, everything is fine."

"Good. So what do I have that your other men don't? You have something to tell me, right?" he asked, recalling what she had told him that morning.

"They don't have my attention and interest like you do," Sara hesitantly said.

"That's what I'm talking about!" he replied as he held her a little closer and finished off the dance with a forehead kiss.

A good dancer and soft light kisses. Sara felt Jonathan could make a woman melt in his arms. However, she fought hard not to be one of them.

Rev. J.C. joined them at the table as they lingered on in the comfort of the reception hall, admiring the lovely winter-land through the windows.

"What happened to Taylor today?" Sara asked regarding her obvious absence.

"Taylor woke up yesterday morning feeling like she was coming down with flu symptoms," the reverend answered. "She only got worst as the day went on and when I checked on her this morning she was too sick to talk. I'll call her tomorrow and see if she needs anything."

"I'll have to check on her also. Other than a visit from you, maybe some chicken soup will serve as a cure for her ailment." Sara hadn't spoken with Taylor in the past week. *As soon as she sees these pictures of the good-looking best man, her recovery will no doubt kick into high gear.*

"Goodnight everybody," Mr. and Mrs. Charles Nash waved as they made their exit to begin life as one.

Chapter 4

Saturday March 10th

CLEAR was having its monthly reading discussion at Erin's house that Saturday afternoon. They had not gotten into their assigned book when Gloria brought up the news headline about the young school teacher and mother of two who had been killed last week by her boyfriend. Nia had been acquainted with the woman through her sister, also a teacher at the same school. Upset and hurt, as many people were, she needed to vent and they let her.

"I've had enough of this! When are more of us African American women going to stand on our own and not put up with these so called men. Strong, educated, independent women really don't need a man in their lives that bad. Look at Mae Jemison, Condoleezza Rice, Oprah, Taylor, Sara and me. We're doing it and none of us are married. To heck with all men, that's what I say!" cried Nia. "Why do woman find it hard to leave a no good man? Even though he is the father of those kids, she should have left his sorry, worthless butt a long time ago. She put up with his beatings like it was his right to discipline her as he saw fit. I'm just so tired of hearing about this mess over and over again," she continued as tears fell down her cheeks.

"Nia, we are still living in times where we're teaching our little girls to grow up, get a nice job, get married, have children, and her husband will be the head of the house and her faithful partner. You know it's still more acceptable to be married than not. How many times do people ask you that dreaded question, when are you going to get married?" Gloria said.

"Take us for an example. Taylor, Sara nor I have ever stood before God and country and said, 'I do' to any man, and we're doing just fine for ourselves. Tell them, girls, is it that hard to be by ourselves? NO!"

Put on the spot, Sara let Taylor answer as she repositioned her body and reached for her water bottle. Although she was single, there was a time about ten years ago when she didn't act like it. Taylor, on the other hand, was still a virgin and proud of it. So hopefully, she could cover for the both of them.

"You know I was raised in a very strict Christian household with my father and grandfather being Baptist ministers. From my early Bible school days, I was taught to save myself for the man God has planned for me. My parents taught us all about the male and female bodies and how sex was suppose to be between a husband and wife. I never had the desire to experiment with sex. Because of that, I've never been in a serious relationship and this single life is all I know and it works for me," Taylor said, adding a smile at the end of her statement.

"Good for you, Taylor," Erin said. "That's how we are raising our daughter because it's the right way and I was a virgin when Pierre married me. I'm glad I waited and if I had to do it again I wouldn't change a thing."

Serena joined in, "I lost my virginity in college to one boyfriend in my second year. After we broke up I didn't date until I met Derek. It's been all about him since. Yes, I talk to my daughters about the virtues of being married and waiting on sex with their husband. However, all I can do is teach by example and pray for them and their choices."

"Well," sighed Gloria, "I admire all of you women and the way you live your lives. That ex-husband of mine was my first lover, even before we tied the knot, and the only one until the divorce. But I'll admit, I've sworn off marriage, not sex. There have been men who come over occasionally, take care of business, and go home. I don't want anything more than that. Yes, I know I'm not exempt from celibacy and I shouldn't be using men as toys. Shall we say I'm still a work in progress!"

"Please don't think I'm trying to sound as if my life is perfect because it's not. And by no means am I passing judgment on anyone in this room. We're all adults who have the same freedom to choose what we do and why. The only person any of us has to answer to is God, not each other," Erin said. If was she saying that to make Sara feel comfortable enough to add her testimony, it worked!

"Although I'm single, I'm far from a virgin. Ten years ago I was living worldly and all I can say is that I thank God daily for leading me back to my Christian upbringing. I was in love with a married man for two years, thinking he was going to leave his wife and family for me," Sara had to stop and collect herself. "I know God forgave me as soon as I got the strength to wake up and break it off, for good. But I've had the hardest time forgiving myself. Even today," then she stopped, sat still and quiet.

"Like Erin said, none of us are perfect in God's eyes or, if we're honest, not even our own. Let's not be hard on ourselves and each other as women. Please open your bibles to Isaiah 40:31 and let's read it together. *'But those who trust in the LORD will find new strength. They will soar high on wings like eagles. They will run and not grow weary. They will walk and not faint.'* I started reciting this verse to my daughters when I taught them the Lord's Prayer. My desire is that they will be strong women who will make a difference in this world. I pray that they will marry a wonderful man like their father and not be trapped like this woman was."

"I'll drink to that," said a more cheery Nia. So they lifted their juice, water, and coffee in a salute to women everywhere.

"Ladies, I have a special request. Join me in praying for my sister, Teena, and her son, Adrian," Taylor started the conversation again. "She broke my parent's heart when she got pregnant. We still love her very much and have never done anything but overwhelm Adrian with love and attention. What continues to cause pain to my parents though, is that we don't know who the father is, not even a name. My guess is that he's married or shacking up with another woman and his other kids. She moved to a community over two hours away from my parents. Of course that's how this mystery man wants it. Unfortunately, we don't see them that often. She appears to be doing alright, at least financially, and says he supports her and Adrian all the way. But after what just happened to this woman the other night, she probably thought her man would always be there for her and take care of the kids. Look what it got her. Another sad thing is Teena believes this will never happen to her. I pray she's right, although my main concern is for her to start living the way we were raised and to please God, not this man."

"I'm proof it's never too late to turn to God," Sara responded.

"Even I know the Lord will be there for me when I decide to act right. I know He will prefer it be sooner than later," Gloria said adding a little humor. "You want us to be serious about praying for your sister don't you Taylor?"

"Absolutely!"

"Fine, then I have to cleanup my life and heart if I'm going to act as an intercessor for her. So, as of today, I'm giving up my PTL's and will pray for Teena to do the same."

Erin broke down in tears of joy. Serena lifted her hands in praise shouting "Hallelujah!" Nia had a quizzical look on her face then finally asked, "What's a PTL?"

"Part-time lover. Don't you remember that song by Stevie Wonder?" Gloria responded.

"Helloooo, I'm the kid of the group remember!" Nia smirked.

"Welcome to the been-there, did-that, not-going-there-again club," Sara said, giving Gloria a high-five. "Unless the Lord sends a husband our way, we'll stay sex free, for as long as it takes."

"Well, Sara, I guess I'm going out like a virgin because I'm not going down any aisle again. One husband was enough for me and he wasn't even a good one!" Gloria remarked.

"Ladies, I think this calls for an impromptu Burn the B.S. right here and now. What do you think?" asked Erin.

"Sounds like an excellent idea to me," replied Taylor. And they all shook their heads in agreement. Erin grabbed some paper and uncovered her Webber kettle grill that was already on the patio.

Burn the B.S. (Blessing Stoppers) was the ritual CLEAR performed at least twice a year. They came together, wrote down anything that may be hindering them from receiving all of their blessings, and released them by way of smoke and ashes for the Lord to handle in His way and time. At first, it was an annual event. Then every six months as they saw their paths to the Kingdom become clearer when they let go and let God handle things. Usually, a burning ceremony was planned in advance, but today, Erin got the revelation to act now. For the next fifteen minutes they jotted down their burdens to make way for exceeding and abundant gifts.

"Why do we have to do this, anyway? I was always told that good girls, which is what my Granny called Christians, would always live a good life. This life isn't all that good. Admittedly, I'm not exactly living like some of you," said Nia.

"Nia, we're only human and for that reason we're also sinners by nature. I consider a Christian life to be a good life even though no one said it would be easy. As sinners we all do and say things that we sometimes regret. That's why we pray daily and ask for forgiveness. As long as we're alive we'll keep coming across situations that will test our strength and faith. We may slow down, get discouraged or knocked off our feet, but whatever happens, we should never give up or lose faith," answered Erin.

"Okay, give me some more paper, please," Nia said showing her sense of humor.

They took their written confessions and convened on the patio around the kettle. As the fire burned away their burdens Erin suggested, "Let's join hands and pray for Teena, Adrian and for whatever you penned on the paper that is now destroyed. And let's not forget our sister, Cecily, who couldn't be with us today."

On that chilly March afternoon, they got a little closer to God and each other, burning away their blessing stoppers. It was not necessary to reveal anything that had been written but Nia decided to open up and talk more about what was on her mind. This led to more interesting discussion and secrets revealed. The ladies moved back into the warm living room.

"The people in my family seem to get married just to get divorced. There are more divorces than there are couples who are still together. So what's the big deal with being married? Then you tell me I shouldn't have sex as a single person although it is in our nature to want to love, be loved, and make love. Right? Then why is this man-woman, husband-wife thing so difficult? I'm confused!"

Gloria raised her hand and shouted, "Join the club!" She spoke for more than herself Sara thought.

"Nia I wish I had an easy answer for you, but I don't. Nothing in life comes easy and I can say from experience, having a family of my own has been the most difficult. Everyday I'm confronted with decisions and concessions, but I do it with my husband and children in mind, not just for me. The reason is, I made a conscious decision a long time ago that this is the life I wanted then and still do. Recklessly, I almost blew it about twelve years ago. I felt I was in a rut with going to work, coming home, fixing dinner, making sure the kids did their homework, you all know the drill. Some of the women in my family decided we needed a mini vacation just for ourselves. So off to Jamaica we went for four days of fun in the sun. I took off my rings and tried to pretend like my family didn't exist. You know how some of those island men are? They were all over the hotel waiting to be of any service. To make a long story short, I was intimate with one man the first night and regretted it for the rest of the trip. When I came home I could have been wearing guilt on my forehead. I confessed my sin to my pastor and we prayed together. He left it up to me to talk to Derek. When I finally got my nerves up, since I was having sleepless nights, I approached my husband. All he said was, I don't want to hear everything that happened in Jamaica.' To this day, we have never discussed it and cheating on my husband and family is still not an option. For me, the rewards of being a wife and mother outweigh anything else that could give me temporary pleasure. So if that helps you any, that's my testimony!"

"Good for you, Serena. You just proved to me that you're human and even married women can lose their groove every now and then. Now if Mrs. Perfect over there has a testimony similar to this, I'll probably faint," said Nia, referring to Erin.

"Well, get the smelling salt handy. The Gordon household has had its share of problems and at one point when the kids were young I moved back home , thinking our marriage was over."

"This I've got to hear!" said Nia getting comfortable on the floor directly in front of Erin.

"Be quiet!" Gloria scolded her playfully while hitting her with a pillow.

Erin continued. "Before my son was born I started reading every magazine I could find on motherhood and parenting. I wanted to have the picturesque family life and thought I'd find the answers in these publications. After my daughter was born a year after him, I doted on the two of them every minute of the day. What I didn't realize is that by trying to be the perfect mother and have the perfect home I forgot how to be a wife as well. I was too busy with the children and too tired for Pierre. Besides, I was naïve and thought he was satisfied with being the breadwinner, having two beautiful children, a clean house, hot dinner, and a June Cleaver type wife to come home to every day. Little did I know that my husband was feeling neglected and although he tried to tell me, I just thought he was being jealous of the babies. Well, he wasn't and it wasn't long before he was made to feel good again in the arms of another woman, an attorney straight out of law school. Pierre ended their brief affair after she showed up at church one day. At the time, I didn't know who she was, but two weeks later as part of his forgiveness process, he confessed everything to me. I ran home only to have my mother and aunts tell me I had to balance my life between mother and wife. We started seeing a counselor and attended a marriage enrichment group. Well, as you can see we made it through that. We were actually one of three couples that started our marriage ministry at church. And to this day, we still do some kind of annual retreat or exercise to keep our marriage strong and happy. Like Serena, I wouldn't trade this life for anything."

When Erin became silent, they applauded her as Nia fell back on the floor feigning passing out.

"I know my ex-husband wished I had known you ladies while we were still married. Maybe he wouldn't have lived his last few years with me scared out of his mind," Gloria said as they braced themselves for another one of her experiences. Now, they all knew there was absolutely nothing hilarious about domestic abuse and it wasn't her situations that made them laugh. It was her animated way of sharing those dreadful times that were part of her past life. "Back in those days, wives were supposed to always submit to their husbands. There was no such thing as a husband raping his wife. One night in particular, he came home after being out drinking, probably with one of his sluts, oops, I mean lady friends. I didn't want to be bothered with him and he told me I'd better turn over. Well, that old fool forgot he had told me a long time ago where he hid his gun. Little did he know that I had moved it to within arm's reach if I ever needed it. That night, I pulled out that revolver and held it next to his balls. I told him if he ever put his hands on me again, I'd blow them off and he'd better not bloody my sheets. Girls, I got loud and crazy, but I was serious and made my point." Gloria had the floor as she demonstrated how she held the gun and squinted her eyes, reflecting her madness. Then she lightened up a bit as she finished recalling one of their many altercations. "He never touched me again without asking and most of the time, I told him no. Part of his niceness was because I never gave him the gun back or told him where it was. Of course, he wasn't smart enough to find it either." While Gloria poured herself a new cup of coffee, Nia and Sara tried to stop laughing, but neither of them could hold back the tears.

Taylor didn't laugh as hard but appreciated Gloria's sense of humor. "I'm taking notes. Thanks for letting me know that life isn't as green on the other side as I thought it was," spoke Taylor.

"So Sara, why didn't you go knock on the door of your married boyfriend and have it out with his wife like one of my cousins did?" inquired Nia.

"I'll admit I was stupid, but not that crazy. She was his wife, I was the intruder. Besides, it didn't take too long before another man came along and wanted to pick up where the married man left off. I was still in rebound mode when I met a man at a singles dinner club I had joined. The second time I saw him we went back to his house and hit the sheets. About two weeks later, he called, wanting to get with me again. However, I had the good sense to tell him that's not what I wanted. Never saw him again and that's been my last fling. That's been over ten years ago, with a man whose name I can't remember and a face I forgot. Nia, this man-woman relationship thing is a test for anyone," Sara remarked.

"Did you remember anything else about him?" instigated a devious Nia, only to be hit again with the pillow by Gloria. "What! We know who Erin and Serena's husbands are. I just thought Sara wanted to reveal who her men were, especially the married one."

"That's fair game. I don't have anything to hide anymore. Marcus was the married man, now divorced. I honestly don't remember the one from the dinner club. Nor will I try," she replied.

By now, CLEAR's meeting had extended far beyond the regular two hours and it was time to bring the heartfelt meeting to a close. Too bad, of all days Cecily had to miss this one!

Chapter 5

*Wednesday March 14*th

Gloria had the phone resting on her shoulder while talking with an attitude. "Well, it's about time. If I didn't reach you today I was on my way to your house and would've knocked down the door if I had to. Where have you been? Are you alright? What's going on girl? Talk to me."

"Slow down, Gloria! You're grilling me like I'm on trial or something," responded a defensive Cecil

"Saturday night when you hurried me off the phone you told me you'd call back the next day. Don't say you tried to call. That doesn't work anymore with caller ID. Did you get my message on Monday?"

"Yes and I'm sorry I didn't return your call. I didn't mean for you to worry." "I'm just glad to finally reach you even though today's Wednesday. Tell me, girl, is everything okay with you and Mario?" Gloria still didn't let up.

Cecily fumbled over her words a little, then took a deep breath and said, "Ramon has been acting a fool lately. He's accusing me of all kinds of stuff like seeing someone behind his back and hiding money from him. Gloria, you know I'm not doing any of that. I'm really getting sick and tired of this man and this time when I put him out it's for good."

"You just tell me when you're ready and I'll be over to help. I've never liked him and been waiting for the day when you get serious about letting that good-for-nothing jerk go. He's not Mario's father and he definitely ain't doing nothing for you! Listen girl, Saturday I vowed to give up my old boy toys and pray for Taylor's sister. I'm adding you to that list to give up Ramon. Like Nia said, we women have got to quit letting men ruin our lives. So just say the word and I'll be right there."

"Gloria, you know you're my girl and I love you!" Cecily cried.

"Let's celebrate our men-free lives and go shopping on Friday. The Lighthouse Place mall is having a midnight madness sale. We can do some serious damage and I'm ready to wear out some credit cards."

"Sounds like a plan. Count me in," said a happier Cecily.

"Good, I'm planning to take a half day off work for this sacred event," said a playful Gloria. "Listen, I'm serious, if you need me don't hesitate to pick up that phone. I'll be there before you can hang up."

"Thanks, Gloria. I'll be just fine," said a somber Cecily.

Sara picked up the phone to make contact with Nia before she turned in for the night. It was her intention to get to bed a little early since she put in some time on the forest preserve walking path and her leg muscles were feeling the results from the winter's inactivity.

"Hi Miss Nia, how are you feeling today? I saw on the news that the teacher was buried today."

"Yes, as much as we tried to celebrate her life, it was still hard since she lost it too early and at the hands of a fool. I hope he never sees freedom as long as he lives," said a still grieving Nia.

"Is there anything I can do other than lift you and her family up in prayer, which I did tonight at Bible study?"

"No, I'll be fine. Thanks, Sara, for being so thoughtful."

"Don't thank me. That's what sisters do for each other. You know that."

"Gloria left a message on my voicemail about going shopping on Friday. That'll be therapeutic for me so I'm in. How about you?" Nia asked, sounding like her spirits were on the way of being raised to the next level.

"Now, you ladies know getting me to go shopping is as appealing as watching a foreign subtitled love story. No thanks, I'll pass."

"Got a date with Jonathan?" pressed Nia.

"No I do not!" Sara said, still blushing when his name was mentioned. "I wouldn't hide that fact from you or anybody else."

"I hear you. He must really have you hooked? That's good, if, in fact, he's the real thing," cautioned Nia.

"I know you're looking out for me and I appreciate that. But, I'm still grounded where Jonathan is concerned. Trust me!" Sara insisted.

"It's your word and I believe you. If you ever feel like you're drowning in his love, give me a call. I will be there post haste and throw you a personal flotation device."

"Thanks for having my back. Don't spend too much money tomorrow. Goodnight!" she laughed and hung up, saying to herself *thank God for girlfriends!* Although she was ready for bed it was apparent others were not. Right after she put the receiver down the phone rang again.

"Good evening, beautiful. How is my favorite girl doing?" inquired Jonathan.

"A little sore, but otherwise I'm great. Thanks for asking. And how are you?"

"Everything's copacetic, but what's got you so sore?"

"I enjoyed a walk in the woods today for the first time this year and I guess I over did it. I took a warm shower and some of the stiffness seems to be dissipating. I'll be fine in the next couple of days."

"Did you stretch before you went out? What you could use right now is a nice massage to relax those muscles. These hands have been known to soothe away pain and stress, even knock a couple of ladies out for the night," he boasted.

"Thank you for the offer. I can only imagine the pleasure your hands can provide, but I'll have to pass this time. I'll probably be asleep no sooner than we get off the phone."

"Just thought I'd ask. Keep stretching those muscles even though they maybe a little sore. You'll be ready to walk even further next time, pain free," he said, sounding like a fitness expert

"Did you call to give me fitness tips or what?"

"My main reason for calling, other than to hear your voice, is to see if I can talk you into having dinner with me tomorrow evening. There's a nice restaurant down your way that plays live jazz on Thursdays. Besides, I might have to go out of town on business this weekend and I don't want to wait until next week before I get a chance to see you again.

So, how about it? You'd really make a brother happy!"

"Well, since you put it that way I guess I can clear my calendar to have dinner with you," she said, trying to masquerade her joy.

"Good, I'm smiling already. We can make it an early one. I'll pick you up at five o'clock."

"Sounds good to me. See you then."

That call seemed to dispel all tiredness and soreness she was feeling. That brief phone call from him was euphoric. Sara replayed the conversation several times in her head and began to visualize the next night. Sitting across the table, looking into Jonathan's mesmerizing eyes, watching his mouth form just the right words that she wanted to hear, his voice being in perfect harmony with the soft jazz that filled the air in the background. She was tastefully attired in a little, revealing dress but nothing that would suggest a take-me-I'm-yours type of reaction. Similar to the little black dress she wore the night they went dancing. It was just enough to feed his eyes but still leaving a lot to the wonderment of his imagination. It would be another night in utopia with... with... who? The man who runs from a totally committed relationship? The man who may just be a platonic friend forever? The man who frequently goes out of town on weekends for some sort of business? Whatever that business was remained unknown to her. Once again, she was going off onto a tangent where she didn't need to go.

Sara picked up her book of twelve extraordinary women of the bible and read again the story of the redeemed life of Rahab. These sojourning minutes into the life of a once worldly wild woman who was transformed into a blessing for many generations, was what she needed to bring herself back to the here and now. She finally let go of the "what ifs" and breathed a sigh of relief because she knew to let God handle it.

With those thoughts, she was ready to cuddle under the covers and get a good night's sleep. However, the phone rang again and interrupted the tranquility of her bedroom.

"Girl, I'm bored. The twins are asleep and Bradley is at work, although he said he'd try to get home early tonight. I'll believe that when I see him walk through the door. I hope I wasn't disturbing anything, was I? If it's Jonathan, then just hang up. If it's anything else, too bad. I need someone to talk to." Krista said all of this before Sara even whispered hello in a partially sleepy voice. Krista normally didn't bother her during the week unless it was an urgent matter. The truth is Krista would do the same for her. So, she sat up, knowing she'd do more listening than talking. Sara just hoped it wouldn't be a marathon phone event.

Chapter 6

Friday March 16th

Friday was ushered in with the pleasantries of a Spring day. Temperatures reached the low sixties by early afternoon to compliment bright sunshine and beautiful, clear blue skies. During the lunch hour Sara opted out of the usual fish fry in the cafeteria and decided to walk around the building, exercising her mind and body. It was especially needed after another perfect evening with Jonathan. This was a good time to clear her mind, visualize, and let the Spirit speak to her. Both of her good friends were now married. Would she be next? Was Jonathan her Heaven-sent man or was he commitment phobic for life? Had she gotten too comfortable in this job to look for something else? Maybe even step out as an entrepreneur and be her own boss? How much longer would she want to live in Illinois? Where else would she go? These were the type of questions she searched deep within her soul and waited for the Spirit to answer. Long walks, especially in the forest preserves, rendered the court where the informal conversation between God and Sara was uninterrupted.

As she was about to reenter the building, her cell phone rang. It was one of the shopping gurus, making a final pitch for her to join the mall excursion.

"Sara, this is your last chance to join the party before we raid the mall. Are you sure you won't change your mind? Even Serena is going to spend some of Derek's hard earned money," pleaded a persistent Gloria.

"No, ladies, you enjoy yourselves. They need me to work overtime today since we are a little shorthanded. It sounds like you aren't the only ones playing hooky on this fine day. Please, don't hesitate to bring me something back."

Maybe saying that she was needed to work was a bit of a stretch. The overtime was voluntary and she had said yes. However, after one hour of overtime they were dismissed. Thank goodness sighed Sara!

Her agenda for the weekend was to simply finish redecorating her two bedrooms, a process she had started the year before by painting the walls. She had now saved enough money to complete the project. Nia, a Feng Shui enthusiast, stopped by one evening, and talked to Sara about applying this technique, of bringing harmony to her and her surroundings by balancing time and space. Sara wasn't sure what any of that meant, but she appreciated the help in her quest to obtain a new look. They had moved some furniture around and Nia made suggestions on plants, flowers, pictures, and color coordination that would create an atmosphere for more than sleeping. It was up to Sara to finish Nia's 'interior experience', as she put it.

Unlocking the door, stepping into her quiet haven, the Feng Shui thing was going to have to wait until tomorrow. Her mind and body went into complete shutdown mode, deciding she would do absolutely nothing tonight but enjoy total solitude. At least that was the initial plan. The voicemail indicator let her know someone had reached out to her.

Hey, baby, it's Jonathan. Just wanted to let you know I'll be out of town on business after all this weekend and won't be back until late Sunday night. I'll be thinking about you the entire time. Have a good weekend, as difficult as it will be without me. Miss you already.

This was his third trip out of town on business since she met him. What's on his plate other than being a real estate agent and mortgage loan officer? *Leave it alone!* She only asked him to share whatever information he wants as long as he's truthful. Therefore, it was none of her concern, she convinced herself. So Sara smiled at the telephone and prepared to have a quiet evening, until the next two messages were played.

Sara, where are you? You're the most difficult person to reach. I'm coming to Chicago next month and would love to take you to dinner. I'll call you back soon. Take care!

Again she saved this to the archives. She was now becoming annoyed by this mystery man and was ready to let someone else know about these calls.

Click, dial tone.

Sara was tired of these calls too!

Dinner would be a chicken Caesar salad, garlic toast, and iced tea. After the table was set, including lighting two, long silver candles, and the CD compartments were filled with music of The Whispers, the atmosphere assuaged the anguish of the phone calls.

All seemed perfect. Then, the doorbell rang, several times, followed by a rhythmic knock with two hands, and then the doorbell again. Would it be one, two, or all three of the T's?

"Good evening, Trent, and to what do I owe the pleasure?" she said as she forced a smile when she answered the front door, finding him standing there solo.

"Huh? Whatcha mean by that?" replied a not so jovial Trent, dressed in baggy jeans and an extra large #23 Chicago Bears jersey, bouncing a basketball.

"In other words, what do you want?"

"Nothing much. I'm just hanging out," he answered. The last thing anyone in the neighborhood wanted to see was Trent or any of the young people just hanging out, doing nothing. So she opened the door and invited him in.

"What's wrong? You don't seem to be your usual energetic self. Mr. Hemings must not be home or you'd be over there with him."

"I'm just bored, tired of doing the same ol' things, day in and day out. No, Mr. Hemings ain't home either."

Sara couldn't imagine how he felt and what he went through sometimes. It'd been over a year since he'd seen his parents, and the grandfather who'd spoiled them was now dead. Rayanna, the three T's mother, was the only child born to Grayson and Elizabeth Payne. They doted on her and saw to it she that wanted for nothing. Rayanna was an ideal daughter and student, always on the honor roll and dean's list while she kept busy in many activities including cheerleading, her first love. She could be seen on national television whenever the North Carolina university she attended, was in the NCAA basketball tournaments. She went on the get a master's degree in Biomedical Engineering, then accepted a job with NASA in Houston. She married classmate Matthew Miller in a lavish ceremony that was the buzz of

Rosebrook Community Church for years. That was as much of the story as Sara knew. What happened in the subsequent years was still not known for sure. The bottom line was that, Rayanna was in a drug rehab program for a second time and Matthew was serving a jail sentence for possession and distribution of illegal drugs. The first time Rayanna entered a rehab program, Miss Lizzie went down there and stayed with the children. Today, she has legal custody and moved them in with her.

Looking into Trent's sad eyes tonight, Sara wondered if he is feeling abandoned or betrayed by his parents. That's what he told her one day shortly after he came to live in Glynnwood. At twelve-years-old, he was experiencing emotions that many adults never had to deal with. She could only encourage Trent to talk to God when he felt this way and it was why her door would always be open to him and his siblings whenever they came knocking. Tonight would be no different.

"Would you care to join me for dinner?" she asked.

"Sure. Whatcha having and why do you have those candles? Is Mr. Jonathan on his way over? What's that music you listening to?"

So ended her romantic night of solitude and serenade by one of her favorite singing groups. Instead, she made another salad plate, blew out the candles, and adjourned to the living room where one of their favorite movies, *Finding Forrester*, would entertain them. First, she had him call Miss Lizzie so she would know exactly where her grandson was, something all the neighbors did when it came to the Miller children.

"Hey, Granny, it's me. I'm over at Miss Sara Smile's house, be home later. See ya".

"Hold it," Sara said reaching for the phone.

"Whaaat? I did what you told me to do, didn't I?" And he did, just not quite the way she wanted him to.

"Hello, Miss Lizzie. How are you this fine evening?" Sara spoke into the phone.

"Doing good, Sara. How about you?" she replied.

"No complaints, just enjoying life, especially with a gorgeous day like today."

"Well then why would you want to end the day with Trent getting on your nerves like I know he can? Where is that handsome Jonathan?" Miss Lizzie quizzed.

"Jonathan is out of town. Even if he wasn't, you know your grandkids are no trouble at all and they're welcome anytime. That's why I'm calling. Do you need a break from the other two as well? They can join us watching..."

"Noooooooooo!" Trent cried out loudly. "I don't want those two following me everywhere I go." Sara was not totally surprised at his outburst. Being a preteen he didn't always want to be part of the threesome and needed time to display his unique individuality. Maybe this was contributing to the sadness of his eyes.

"I hear him yelling in the background. It's alright this time. Tamala is napping on and off and Tyree is entertaining himself on the computer. You just send Trent home if he starts acting up," she said.

"He'll be fine. As soon as the movie is over he'll be home," she stated, winking at Trent and watching his face soften up a bit.

"So, Miss Sara Smile is this like we're having a dinner date?" he asked managing to crack a smile.

"No, it's like we're eating a salad and watching a DVD, that's all!" she responded, amused by his comment.

Time went by quickly since they talked and munched on potato chips throughout much of the movie. Having seen this particular movie at least a half dozen times, it wasn't as if they missed anything.

"Miss Sara Smile, how come you never had kids or a husband?" Trent worked up the nerve to ask that question, again. She knew she had entertained this discussion before. Of course, she also recognized this as a stall tactic.

"Trent Miller, are you about to ask me to marry you?" she playfully responded.

"No, not me. I'm never getting married or having kids," he seriously said.

"You're still very young with a lot more living to do before you think about something like marriage and a family. Why are we even talking about this tonight?"

"Cause I don't know why my mom got married and had us if we're just gonna live with Granny. And, why did my daddy have to do something so stupid like get involved with drugs, only to go to jail? He should have been in the D.A.R.E. program at school instead of me." So the sadness was uncovered.

"Trent, first, both of your parents love you, Tyree and Tamala very much. Don't think any of their problems are your fault because it has nothing to do with you. Adults make mistakes all the time, including me, Mr. Chana, Mr. Hemings and Rev. J.C. Some of our mistakes aren't as costly and can be fixed without a lot of punishment. Unfortunately, your parents mistakes were a little more severe, but, they have a chance to make things right and correct their problems. You know how we can help, don't you?"

"No."

"Sure you do. We can pray that they will turn to God for guidance and wisdom to make better choices. I know it's difficult for you to understand because it's not easy for me. Maybe God used them to help show you, your siblings and cousins the consequences of making bad choices such as getting involved with illegal drugs. It has helped you, hasn't it?"

"Yes, ma'am! Even before I graduated from D.A.R.E., I knew I didn't want to use or sell any kind of drugs. You know we got kids at school that do drugs."

"I know, sweetie. Drug use is a big problem for people of all ages. We've got to continue to do the right thing and say no when people approach us about drugs, no matter what others are doing. Trent, since you're the big brother you've got to keep being a good example for your little brother and sister," Sara said, putting her arm around him.

"I know. I'll bust 'em out if I ever catch either one of them with drugs. Then I'll find out who gave it to 'em and get that guy too."

"Hopefully it'll never get to that point. You know you're quite a young man and I'm very proud to be your neighbor and friend," she said, giving him a hug. At this point, Sara got up so he'd get the hint it was time for him to go. Also, she avoided answering his original question. Trent had perked up by now although he was traipsing about the living room, kitchen and towards the bedrooms while running his mouth about anything that came to the tip of his tongue. Sara asked him to help check all the windows and close the blinds and curtains. He was more than happy to oblige.

"Miss Sara Smile, the window in your other bedroom doesn't lock but all the rest of them do," he announced coming back in the living room.

"I know. I keep forgetting to get it fixed. Thanks for reminding me. I'll put it on my to do list." Sara had truly forgotten to repair that rear window.

She opened the front door, but before he walked out the door she gave him another big hug and thanked him for being her company tonight. As always, Sara stood on the porch to watch him dash across the street. Darting off the steps they heard someone yell, "Hey, boy, where are you going?" It was Jed, standing in his front yard.

"Hey Mr. Hemings, I was looking for you earlier," Trent slowed down to acknowledge him.

"Well, son, it looks like you were in good company without me," Mr. Hemings said.

"Yeah, me and Miss Sara Smile had dinner and watched a movie," Trent proudly announced.

"Hi, neighbor, and now he's on his way home" she announced.

"Bye, everybody!" Trent shouted, running home. Sara watched and waved to Miss Lizzie when she opened the door for him.

"Hey, Miss Sara Smile, was that your date leaving?" Jed joked.

"Yes, it was and we had a good time."

"Where's that man you dragged into church?"

"Oh, you mean Chana's friend, Jonathan."

"Then how come he wasn't with Charles? I bet Charles doesn't receive flowers on his birthday from Jonathan," said Jed as he laughed and she tried not to blush. "You know he's got to get my approval before he gets too serious. I will get him alone and give him the treatment. Not every man passes the test at first. Some, not at all. Just ask my daughters about the treatment."

"Sir, when I get serious about any man I'll be sure to send him your way first so he can get the treatment. If he fails then I'll just have to wait on the next serious man who comes my way. Is that fair enough?"

"Sounds good to me. But please, make it sooner than later. I want a reason to wear my tux again before they bury me in it," he laughed.

"Goodnight, Jed," she said waving and closing the door on the world.

Contrary to her earlier attitude about a do-nothing evening, she now had a small burst of energy that she would expend in the bedroom on the 'interior experience' project. But, before she could leave the living room, the phone rang.

"Hey, girl, you missed a shopping trip to beat all others," said a tired sounding Gloria. "We shopped until we dropped, then got up and shopped some more."

"I know the credit card companies are happy tonight after all the damage you four did," Sara said.

"Yes, and it was well worth it. We almost had to rent a U-Haul to bring all the packages home. We combined for a little bit of this and that, from household items to everything for the body from head to toe. We can always go back and help you spend some of that overtime money you made today," laughed a cynical Gloria.

"That money is already spent redecorating my house. Let Nia tell it; she's costing me more than I would have put out on my own."

"Then in that case you need to put in some extra overtime. That girl almost had me beat tonight, but I'm still the queen, followed by Serena. Derek's going to take away her shopping privileges for the entire summer!"

"No, he won't. It's not that bad," shouted Serena in the background.

"Maybe on your next trip, I'll join the fun."

"We'll hold you to it, Sara. I'm pulling up to Serena's house now so I'll let you go and get ready for bed. Say goodnight to Jonathan for us," she said and quickly disconnected.

These ladies already had any and everything they would need to wear for the next several years. Gloria and Cecily made a fashion statement wherever they were. Serena loved to redecorate her house according to the seasons. Nia used shopping as a stress reliever, especially when men got the best of her in some way or the other. She wasn't discriminate in her purchases, she just spent money. Sara would rather spend her small disposable income on traveling. Clothes to her represented a necessity to cover the body. Designers and famous brand names were foreign to her, and her house. She just lived the simple life.

Turning the CD player back on, she danced her way into the bedroom, getting back to this Feng Shui phenomenon. Trying to remember what Nia had said, she picked up one of her favorite vacation pictures. Chana and Sara had flown to California one long weekend seven years ago, rented a red convertible mustang and drove the coast from San Francisco to San Diego. It was a blast! One minute they were sitting in her living room talking about how short life was and how every second counts. Three hours later they were on a late night flight to the west coast. The most memorable part of the trip for her was their overnight stay in Morro Bay, the little seaside fishing village north of Los Angeles, known for the famous big rock located in the ocean, simply named, Morro Rock. Tranquility surrounded them with breathtaking ocean views, mild temperatures and some of the best tasting seafood she had ever consumed. With the sun starting to set and mild waves crashing against Morro Rock, this was the background for the picture showing two happy care-free Midwesterners celebrating life. Chana almost had to lock her in the trunk just so they could be on their way the next day.

Grinning from ear to ear at the memories she hung the enlarged photo on the wall that welcomed the early morning sunlight. Nia said the sunlight would give the effect of the waves in motion and make the picture come to life, depicting happy times that would help keep her daily mood on a natural high. Okay, whatever, Sara thought!

Another photo that would grace a wall was that of family, sprawled out on a green field, next to a small stream on a campground site in

Alabama. Twenty years ago her family reunion was held at her great grandmother's birthplace. Nearly three hundred relatives were wearing navy blue and white tee shirts designed by a cousin. That precise moment captured by the photographer showed them appearing as a happy family in perfect harmony, (*at least on that day)!* Since this picture revealed her love of family and welcomed people to her world, it was hung where it could be seen upon entering the room.

Everything was removed from the round bedside table except the vase that held a single, fresh rose and one scented candle. The smell of a single rose tickled her nostrils on those rare mornings when she awoke, not having to hit the floor running, or at night before her head hit the pillow. Nia said this was a reminder to relax and appreciate simple things. Sara had begun this pampering treatment about six years earlier. She had attended a seminar on finding the perfect mate, led by a psychologist who specialized in love therapy. Today, she continued to pamper herself, the only real advice she gained from that day-long session.

There were still a few more artifacts and plants that needed to be situated, but that would wait until the next day. As the clock chimed the one o'clock hour, her body was ready to shut down for a good night's rest. Before retiring, Sara picked up her Bible and read Psalm 91:1-2:*Those who live in the shelter of the Most High will find rest in the shadow of the Almighty. This I declare of the Lord: He alone is my refuge, my place of safety; he is my God, and I am trusting him.* Her day was now complete.

Suddenly, the phone rang, scaring her out of a comfortable sleep! After the third ring she became coherent enough to eye the digital clock and see 3:35 in red lights. Before she could get a complete word out Taylor frantically shouted, "Ramon was killed tonight!"

Chapter 7

Emergency lights flashing, news crews mingling about, police officers, men, women, and children standing around whispering, waiting and wondering what had happened at 1021 Popular Drive tonight. Late comers such as Sara had to park a block and a half away because Cecily's street was blocked off. Approaching the house, she saw Taylor talking on her cell phone. She began to ask herself, *Why did I come here? Did I hear Taylor correctly? What really just happened here? What could I do for Cecily in a time like this?*

"Sara, thanks for coming. Nia is so upset and angry that she couldn't bring herself to meet us here. Actually, it's better that she stay home and calm down. You know how she can go off on anyone at any time and now is not a good time for that! Erin and Pierre are on their way. Pierre is going to handle things for Cecily."

Pierre Gordon, the husband of CLEAR member Erin, was a prominent attorney specializing in criminal defense. Among his many successful cases included having charges dropped for a twelve year old boy accused of raping and killing a nine-year-old girl. Because this was such a horrific crime, the public's outcry pressured authorities to make an arrest. The suspect was seen with the girl on the day she died. The police tried to make it an open and shut case, using aggressive tactics to get the alleged offender. However, according to attorney Gordon, it would not be his pro bono client, and less than a month later, he proved it. Further DNA testing and other evidence from the crime scene led to a twenty-three-year-old man with an arrest record since age fourteen that included two other attacks on young girls.

Sara and Taylor knew Cecily would have the best legal care in the area. Erin and Pierre showed up less than five minutes after Sara arrived. Erin stayed outside with her friends as her husband went to work.

"Gloria is in there with Cecily. She was the first person Cecily turned to, even before calling police. Then she called us and we got here as soon as we could," explained Erin. "My husband told her to let him handle everything. You know he's going to defend our sister as if she was his own. Thank God Mario was not at home tonight. He is spending the weekend with Cecily's sister."

The three of them stood in front of the house in the chilly morning hours, embracing each other for comfort and warmth, and did the only thing they knew to do to bring some peace to this quiet chaos. Pray.

Inside, attorney Gordon was now in control as Gloria and Cecily found some solace with his presence. He first came upon Ramon, lying face down on the living room floor. He was dead from what appeared to be a single gunshot to the chest, as stated by an investigator on the scene. In the bedroom were the ladies with two police officers watching over them. Pierre later said the officers were glad to see him so they could be relieved from the wrath of Gloria. Apparently, Gloria had given the police officers a hard time when they arrived. She told them she shot Ramon and would shoot them as well if anyone bothered Cecily. Gloria had even picked up the gun and squeezed the trigger just to ensure her fingerprints were on the weapon to shift suspicion her way. Pierre reminded her that her hand would be checked for gunshot residue where she would fail as a potential suspect.

Cecily was sitting on the bed, discombobulated, holding an ice pack on the side of her bruised face and swollen, discolored eye. Gloria showed Pierre her cell phone displaying the pictures she had taken of Cecily when she first arrived. Pierre, the consummate gentleman as well as lawyer, sat next to Cecily, put his consoling arm around her, assuring she had nothing to worry about. He asked Cecily for the truth about what happened earlier and she gave it to him.

Cecily arrived home about eleven-thirty after spending the afternoon shopping with Gloria, Serena and Nia. She had made Ramon aware of her plans on Thursday. Mario had gone to her sister's house for the weekend after school. Ramon was sitting on the couch, drinking a beer watching something on ESPN when she came in the house with three shopping bags. Ramon said nothing while Cecily greeted him and briefly spoke of her shopping trip. She put the bags in the spare bedroom and began to get ready for bed. Shortly after midnight, he came in the bedroom, walked up to Cecily, and hit her across the face with his fist. He began to accuse her of being out with another man and having her friends cover for her. Realizing he was drunk, she yelled at him to get out of the room and leave her alone. This only angered him more and he started hitting her repeatedly. She managed to get away from him and make it to the bathroom. Ramon yelled obscenities through the locked door that he wasn't finished with her yet. He remained at there for several minutes before he stumbled back into the living room. Cecily remembered a gun she kept in a sanitary napkin bag in the linen closet, a tip from her uncle before Ramon had moved in. Hoping she would never have to use it, she took her uncle's advice anyway and the gun had remained there. Secretly, she would check it every few years, just in case. Tonight would be that dreaded case. She retrieved the gun, removed the safety lock, and hoped she could get back to the bedroom without another confrontation with Ramon. It proved to be an infelicitous moment as he must have been standing in waiting for the sound of the door to unlock. He pushed open the door, hitting her in the face with it, unaware of what she had in her hand. In an instant, she raised her hand, fired one fatal shot, sending him stumbling back into the living room where he dropped to the floor, ending years of physical and emotional abuse. In shock, Cecily called her confidant and best friend, Gloria, who expeditiously came to her aid. The level-headed Gloria immediately summoned the police and her attorney.

Pierre convinced Cecily that as part of the investigation she would be in police custody, needing first to go to the hospital to be examined for any possible head injuries. He kept reassuring her that he would be by her side and have her back home as soon as possible.

Outside, everyone watched, as the sun was starting to rise, Cecily was being escorted away in a police car with criminal investigators still swarming in and out of the house. Pierre tried to comfort the four of them, insisting they go home and get some sleep while he did what he did best. Without saying anything, his demeanor gave an unequivocal assurance that her actions were in self-defense. The ladies knew it could not be anything else.

Taylor drove an emotionally perturbed Gloria home while Sara followed. Already daylight, sleeping was just not an option right now. For Cecily and Gloria's sake, they switched to prayer warrior mode. Taylor, very sagacious at her young age, also prayed for Ramon's family, who would soon learn their son and brother was dead.

"Why didn't she listen to me? I should have stayed on her until she left that no good man a long time ago. If I had gone in the house if only for a few minutes tonight, maybe this wouldn't have happened. I knew I should have taken Ramon out myself when I had the chance last year," Gloria cried non-stop. They knew she needed to vent and release some anger and frustration, so they let her. Pacing the floor, Gloria continued to talk about Cecily and Ramon. "His abuse has been going on for some time now, too long if you ask me. I suspected it even before she confided in me. Although Ramon never touched Mario, which is a good thing, because, she would have surely killed him for that. But, in recent years, he has been treating her like she was his personal punching bag. And for what? This alcoholic was just crazy, jealous, and insecure. It all started when he got laid off from the Ford plant and could only find lower paying, laborious jobs. We all know Cecily never looked at another man since Ramon came into her life. She thought she needed him to help raise Mario and validate her as a woman. Girls, is that bizarre or what? She could have easily gotten a better man than him any day."

Taylor sighed and began to speak while Sara was bringing in a pot of freshly brewed coffee from the kitchen. "Violence against women has been going on almost since the beginning of time. Thank God we have not allowed a man to break our self-respect and confidence down to the point that we don't know if we're crazy or not. Battered women syndrome is very real, I'm afraid. My research shows that after a while, a woman experiences a helplessness, and psychologically, her beliefs about the abuse are irrational, believing it's all her fault. And if he has threatened her or the kids, she fears for them. This is all too real for women who are suffering from violence, especially physical abuse. I wish there was a way I could convince women that life doesn't have to be that way. Not dismissing my own family, I can't get my sister to leave her mystery man. I don't know if he's physical with her, but the fact that she keeps him a big secret from our family is indicative of the control he has on her life, which is just as bad."

"Girls, my ex-husband and I use to have knockdown, drag out fights," Gloria added. "He finally stopped jumping on me when he realized I wasn't going to put up with him treating me like he had the right to put his hands on me. The worst part is that the kids witnessed most of our fights, resulting from his drinking. All the love between the two of us was long gone and he just stayed around until the first one finished high school. I was one happy sister the day he moved out! I actually use to pray that my daughters would never get married. Maybe that was selfish of me, but I don't want them to go through what I experienced in a so-called marriage. I'd kill any man who put his hands on my girls like their daddy did me. I also prayed that my son would not turn out to be like him!"

"I'll admit, I've only experienced what I know now to be minor abuse by one man but I know what it can do to a family. My father's youngest sister killed her husband of sixteen years. We later found out he abused her all those years and threatened their six kids if they ever told anyone. It must have been extremely horrible to be so scared of their own father that they tried to keep it a family secret. Eventually, my father knew something was not right and offered to help her and the kids get away from him, but she refused. One night, the beating was so bad that despite a slight concussion, she pulled out his gun and blew him away with the three youngest in the house. My aunt died seven years later, broken-hearted and dispirited," Sara added, pausing to take a sip of coffee, recalling some of her family history. "Today, two of her sons are in jail and one girl died from a sexually transmitted disease after years of prostitution. The other two girls and one boy have struggled to live normal lives in the wake of their tumultuous upbringing. It's so sad how one person's deportment can affect so many others. When is it ever going to stop?"

Taylor spoke up again. "I heard it's been proven that battered women often become a generational thing. As sick as it sounds to us, abuse is the norm for some and they pass the behavior on to their daughters and sons. When men think women will tolerate their violence, that's when the Cecily's of the world prove them wrong. Ladies, we can't keep letting it get to the point that abuse will only end with the death of the abuser or abused."

"Like Sara said, when is it going to end? When are women going to wake up and realize that life doesn't have to be that way? Some of these people need to quit looking at television, thinking they're going to find Mr. or Mrs. Perfect and live happily ever after," said a calmer Gloria.

"I know," responded Taylor. "That's one of the reasons I'm a coordinator with the Roses. We teach the teenage girls about everything from dating to marriage, and what's appropriate behavior for Christian women, including how to dress, good hygiene, healthy eating habits, exercise and most importantly why they should remain sexually inactive until marriage. We had a seminar on date rape and teenage violence sponsored by the local police department. Even I learned a few things from that session."

The Roses was a program, initiated four years ago by Portia Stevens, for girls between the ages of thirteen and seventeen. Membership at Rosebrook was not a requirement to participate since her aim was to reach all girls in this vulnerable age group. The program was designed to nurture these young ladies to live a life of purity and pride as the Lord intended. Many of the girls came from broken homes or didn't have a female to help lead them into Christian womanhood. The program also emphasized the importance of striving for academic excellence and to live out their dreams. The Roses have proven to be a successful investment of time and resources. Out of their success grew the Blossoms, for younger girls preparing them to enter the teenage years. Similarly, Rev. J.C. was heading up a group of men developing a much needed program for teenage boys in addition to engaging them in sports activities.

"Well, ladies, you know I'm so very proud of the two of you and think you are good role models for women of all ages. You give so much of your time to your church and don't seem to let men get in your way of doing what's right. Sara, my hat goes off to you for not touching Jonathan by now. I hear he's really good looking and obviously treating you like he's had some kind of training or you would have kicked him to the curb by now," Gloria commented. Finally, a reason to laugh in the midst of what just happened earlier to one of CLEAR's sisters.

"Gloria, I'd rather accumulate 'good 'n faithful servant' points than score some meaningless points with some good looking or well behaved man. And yes, the women in Jonathan's past did teach him a thing or two," Sara replied lightheartedly.

"Good 'n faithful servant' points, that's a good one. Maybe I should try earning some of those myself. I'm sure I have a long way to go to catch you in the rankings."

"Don't worry about any rankings. Let's just stand on faith, stand on commitments, and stand our ground when it comes to men," Sara said.

"Amen!" Taylor responded.

They laughed a little more as the climate in the house started changing, becoming more subdued. It was well into Saturday morning and the reality of the very early morning hours was this; Cecily killed Ramon.

Several knocks at the front door roused them from their sleeping positions on the floor, on the couch, and on the lounge chair. The clock on the DVD player read 1:15 in bright blue digits. Gloria answered the door to find a weary, but smiling Cecily, accompanied by Pierre Gordon. Taylor and Sara sprang to their feet and joined in a group hug.

"Looks like you ladies had a sleepover this morning," said a professional- looking and wide-awake Pierre. They guessed he was use to calls in the early morning hours summoning him to work. "I told you I'd take care of Miss Cecily, didn't I? Here she is, in need of plenty of sleep and much love. That's why I brought her to your house Gloria."

Pierre had called in a couple of favors to some colleagues in the Prosecutor's office to expedite the investigation. He persuaded them that the evidence would clearly point to Ramon's death as a result of self-defense. Even though the investigation was ongoing, she was released pending the outcome. They knew the outcome would be in her favor, so Taylor and Sara followed Pierre and left Cecily with Gloria to get some much needed sleep.

Entering her home, Sara was engulfed in serenity. She thanked God for delivering her from some of the evils of the world. For some reason, He spared her from a life like Cecily's, not that she deserved to be that chosen one. However, reminded of His grace led her to cry out loud, "Thank you Jesus!"

She headed straight to the bedroom with the intention of getting a little more sleep so she could muster up some energy to do more redecorating later. Before she laid down she knew Chana needed to be inform of last night's event. She caught him on his cell phone at the grocery store with Olivia. Briefly giving him the highlights, he would call back later in the evening when they were able to hold a conversation. For now, she just wanted to rest and forget about all things violent, and concentrate on all things related to love, peace, and hope. As an added measure of not being disturbed, she turned off the ring tone on all phones. Hopefully, no one would make an attempt to drop in on her this afternoon even though she probably would not hear them. A couple hours to herself was all she wanted.

The afternoon had turned into evening by the time Sara woke up. With the digital clock brightly displaying 7:20, she, was somewhat disappointed that she had slept so long. *Oh well.* She had learned not to fight her body when it needed to shut down. The uninterrupted sleep was exactly what her body and mind needed. Realizing she hadn't eaten since yesterday evening, she prepared another salad and sat on the couch watching, another Law and Order rerun. During a commercial, she glanced at the telephone to see the red light blinking, jolting her memory to turn the ringers back on. Calling voice mail she had three messages.

Hi, Sara. It's me Taylor. I couldn't sleep so I thought I'd give you a ring. Maybe you're not having my same problem. Call me back if you feel like talking some more.

Taylor sounded like she needed a listening ear. Sara would give her hers.

Sara are you still asleep? Wake up and fill me in on all the details. You know the story is on all the local news.

Chana had been waiting patiently to learn what she knew firsthand.

Sara, you are the hardest person to reach. I'm beginning to think you really don't live at the house where this phone number is connected. Anyway, I hope you're getting my messages. I'll be in Chicago in three weeks and I'm looking forward to actually speaking to you in person. Be sweet until then.

Mystery man strikes again. After what just happened she had to inform someone about these disturbing calls, soon.

"Sara, you are so blessed to have had the revelation and let go of that mess you were involved in a few years ago. I had prayed so much for you to let go and move on. Thank God He answered those prayers. That could have been you last night," said Chana when she spoke with him again.

"I know, which is why things are vividly clear today as far as my relationship with men are concerned. Thanks, again, for helping me get through that dreadful time."

"That's what true friends are for. You know that," he stated.

Cautiously, she informed him of the phone calls and he was glad she did. Actually, Sara sighed a feeling of relief that someone else knew about this mysterious man from her past. Chana insisted he would find out who he was and what he wanted

Once again, she felt blessed to have Chana as a friend. So she passed on the blessing and called her friend Taylor. She thanked Sara for calling her back but they didn't talk very long. Taylor had been on the phone for hours with Nia, who was still ranting about everything. Also, Rev. J.C. had stopped by to console her, so Sara didn't want to impede any progress there.

Sara turned off the television and went back to the bedroom, inspecting the progress and making a mental note of what remained to be completed. However, one look at the bed and she was soon sleeping comfortably until the next morning.

Sunday March, 18th

Rev. Stevens delivered a spiritually powerful homily that Sunday entitled 'What's Faith Got To Do With It?' Using as the main text 2 Corinthians 5:7: *For we walk by faith, not by sight.* Faith was the word he repeatedly emphasized. "Faith has everything to do with it!" exclaimed Rev. Stevens as he concluded and called for non-members to join the family. Eleven people accepted the invitation to join Christ and hopefully join the growing Rosebrook family. As Rev. J.C. led the final altar prayer, he made a plea to the congregation that if they believed in the power of prayer, they should open their hearts to forgiveness, patience, understanding, kindness, and love. He especially petitioned for two families who were dealing with a very difficult situation, that being Cecily's and Ramon's.

Later that day, revitalized, Sara completed redecorating the second bedroom, with its hunter green and peach color scheme. Nia had suggested some low maintenance plants, especially since Sara's green thumb was a bit discolored. A sales person at the nursery helped her pick out a small Fern and Chinese evergreen. Dressing the walls were pictures depicting some travel adventures in Paris, Montreal, and Sedona, Arizona. The futon and computer workstation completed the 'multi-functional arena', as Nia put it. New futon covering, curtains, and an area rug were the finishing touch. Canvassing the room brought a smile of satisfaction to Sara's face. Perhaps it would do the same for Nia if she knew how much Sara admired their work. Dialing Nia's cell phone she was prepared to leave a message. *Surprise*!

"Nia, you should see how lovely our redecorating project turned out. You missed your calling as an interior designer. I feel like I'm living in a new house."

"Well, I'll just have to come over this week and check out the final results. Perhaps you should hold an open house or something," Nia replied.

"I wouldn't go that far, but my friends will see the difference and I know they'll like what they see."

"I'm sure Jonathan liked what he saw before now," she giggled a little. "Has he seen the new look yet?"

"No, he's been out of town this weekend. Besides, he doesn't spend time in my bedrooms when he's here anyway, thank you very much!"

"Whaaat? I wasn't implying anything," she said non-convincingly.

"Right. Stop by soon before I mess things up. Goodnight," Sara laughed and hung up the phone. Nia sounded like her old self again and that was music to her ears.

Suddenly, Sara began to think about Jonathan. The past forty eight hours was a sinusoidal wave of emotions. If there was one stabilizing force that could have eased the ups and downs, it was him. Knowing he was out of town, she saw no sense in her calling him and interrupting his business activities. No way was she going to interfere with a man and his line of work, possibly coming across as an emotional cripple. Instead, she'd just wait until he informed her of his return. Then Sara would fill him in on what occurred in his absence. Yes, Jonathan would be proud of how well she was able to handle herself. Sure he would be, she hoped. Can't let him think she's so much in control that she wouldn't need him if the future brought on another devastating event. Realizing she was getting way ahead of herself, Sara took several slow deep breaths until she was relaxed. Then she was able to spend a few moments *visualizing.* She felt good again.

Monday's workday went by fast and uneventful. At lunchtime, she overheard a conversation by three people sitting at a table nearby discussing Ramon's shooting. She quickly tuned them out and finished her food while entertaining the thought of getting to bed early tonight.

No sooner had she walked into the house with the mail in her hand, the phone rang.

"Hello, sweetie. Did you miss me this weekend?" inquired Jonathan.

"Good afternoon. I'm so glad to hear your voice. I take it you're back in town?"

"Yes and I'm looking forward to seeing you when you're up to a few hugs and kisses from a brother."

"Jonathan, you don't know how much I could use some hugs from you right now."

"What's wrong, baby?"

"It's a long story and I'd rather tell you in person."

"I'm on my way," he said and hung up.

Fifteen minutes, later Jonathan was knocking on the door. He had to be somewhere in the neighborhood to get there so quickly. Regardless, he was a welcome sight and Sara immediately dismissed any thoughts from last night as he embraced her when he stepped into the living room. For about two minutes, it seemed, they said nothing, just enjoying each other's company. Finally he cupped her face in his hands, kissed both cheeks and planted a longer one on her forehead. She melted ever so slightly further into his arms, squeezing him a bit closer. "What happened this weekend baby?" he spoke up. She led him to the couch and spent more than two hours talking about the shooting, her redecorating efforts, and her dinner 'date' with Trent. The latter brought a smile to his face as he approved of her choice of male companion, in his absence. They engaged in dialogue about the whole issue of violence against women for the next hour. Sara was relieved to hear him say he never had nor would he ever hit a woman. He said he wouldn't consider himself a man if he physically assaulted a female, no matter how angry he was. She exhaled a sigh of satisfaction.

Grateful that Jonathan changed the subject and asked to see the newly decorated rooms, she put on her tour guide hat and proceeded to show off her and Nia's artistic ability. He smiled and complimented their endeavor. Then he offered his help with anything around the house she couldn't handle on her own. Teasing, he said, "Experience has taught me that women like to change the appearance of their home on a regular basis. I wouldn't be surprised if they looked different this time next year."

YESSSSS! He just validated some of her earlier thoughts. She kissed him on one of his cheeks saying, " I can appreciate this new look for more than twelve months. I promise!" *Who knows what the next few months have in store. Maybe the rooms might look a little more masculine or maybe the house would be empty with a sale sign in the yard. Visualizing!*

Back in the living room, the clock chimed for the eight o'clock hour. The evening had rapidly faded into night.

"I'm so sorry I haven't offered you anything to eat or drink since you've been here. Please forgive my manners. Can I get you something from 'Sara's Kitchen'?" she asked.

"Let me see, how about a medium fillet mignon, baked potato with melted cheese, bacon bits, sour cream and chives, broccoli and your finest house wine."

"Would you settle for a frozen dinner and Diet Pepsi?"

"Sara, I'd settle for popcorn and water as long as I'm sharing it with you."

"Good! Popcorn it is," she stated with joy. Actually, she grabbed two frozen entrees and placed them in the microwave.

"That's one of the things I like about you, Sara. You don't try to put up a front and be somebody you're not," he said, laughing at her kitchen preparedness and reaching for the diet drink.

"Jonathan, that's what I expect out of everybody. Just be yourself. Trying to live a lie will only catch up with you sooner or later and the results won't be pretty. So just like Flip Wilson use to say, what you see is what you get."

"And you ain't seen nothing yet," Jonathan joined in with a little dance.

They both laughed and felt even more comfortable in each other's presence. She told him to make himself at home and turn the television on if he wanted. No sooner than said he was laughing at a popular sitcom when she brought in the steamer dinners. They ate, including some freshly popped cheese popcorn, and talked a while longer, not paying much attention to anything on the tube. Before long, they were both starting to yawn and fight off sleepiness.

"As much as I hate for this night to end, I have to say goodbye so that both of us can get some sleep and be ready to tackle another day," Jonathan said standing to his feet. He took her hands and helped her up off the couch, which was a good thing because she could have fallen asleep right then and there.

"Thanks for keeping me company tonight," Sara remarked.

"My pleasure, sweetheart; but please, don't ever feel you can't call me if you need me. I'm never too busy to hear from you. If I can't take the call immediately, I'll call back as soon as possible. That's a promise!"

"Thank you and I promise to call if I need you," she said with another sigh of relief. Then they hugged and ended the night with a friendly peck on the lips.

Before Sara went to bed, she was led to read 1 Corinthians 13:4-7: *Love is patient and kind. Love is not jealous or boastful or proud or rude. Love does not demand its own way. Love is not irritable, and it keeps no record of when it has been wronged. It is never glad about injustice but rejoices whenever the truth wins out. Love never gives up, never loses faith, is always hopeful, and endures through every circumstance.* With a thankful heart, she promptly fell asleep with a smile on her face.

Chapter 8

April tendered picturesque Spring days of blossoming trees, flowers, and, light rain followed by beautiful blue skies with rainbows that seemed of a paradisiacal future. Weekend lawn mowers humming, driveways transformed into basketball courts and kids racing about the street on bikes and skates, all signs that the Winter hibernation had ended.

Saturday, April 21st
Late in the month the Hemings' hosted an afternoon game party to jump start the Summer. Jed mentioned to Sara twice to bring Jonathan. She thought he wanted to start the treatment process, whatever that entailed. Nonetheless, she came to the potluck affair equipped with a seven layer salad, another limited recipe favorite committed to memory, the fun card game, Phase 10, and her date, of course. Throughout the day, they would also engage in other board games as well as Jed's favorite crowd event, karaoke.

Playful repartee accompanied every game regardless of who the players were. A steady stream of people flowed throughout the house going from table to table with everyone claiming to be the master of that particular game. Gloria arrived with Serena and Derek. She whispered to Sara that her main reason for coming was to finally meet Jonathan. Jed and Derek happened to be cousins, as Serena learned one day after a CLEAR meeting at Sara's house. With a variety of good food and background music, a fun time was be shared by all.

As the evening was drawing to an end, Jed began to hand out to their guest what he called door prizes. In a decorative tin can on the mantle, he had several dollars in uncirculated new nickels, Thomas Jefferson's side profile on the front and Monticello on the back.

"This is a parting gift from my great-great-however many greats Grandfather, President Thomas Jefferson. May he rest in peace," said Jed. Turning to Jonathan, he continued. "You probably don't know I'm a direct descendant of ol' Tom and his longtime squeeze, Sally Hemings."

"You don't know that either," said his wife Rhoda, who had heard him tell this story all of their married life. Sara had heard it since she lived in the neighborhood. Neither Jed nor anyone in his family had traced his name back to Sally or her lineage. He wasn't even sure which of the many versions he'd seen, is the correct spelling of her last name. Admittedly, he had no real interest in finding out. He said he got a kick out of upsetting some conservative white folks when he made this claim.

"Thanks, man. I'll cherish this nickel, knowing the history behind it," joked Jonathan.

"If I saved every nickel he gave me in honor of his descendants, I'd be lying on a Caribbean beach, getting a serious tan right now," Sara remarked.

"Me too," laughed Rhoda.

As Jonathan and Sara left, he appeared to have fit right in with her neighbors as well as Serena and Derek. Gloria said she'd get back with Sara after she totaled all the points she was using to size him up. Once again, Gloria made the comment that she thought his name and face looked a little familiar, but she couldn't pinpoint from where. Overall, Sara was pleased that her newfound friendship left a favorable impression on everyone.

Each passing day seemed to just get better and better. The Nash newlyweds were settling into the life of happily ever after, Cecily and Mario were attempting to put their lives back together after she was not charged with any crime, Jonathan and Sara were not stressing, letting nature run its natural course, and Krista was not complaining as much about Bradley.

Friday April 27<u>th</u>
The next Friday night, Sara took Krista for a girls' night out. She wanted to show her married friend that what she thought she was missing was just not happening. Also, Sara couldn't take too much more of hearing how tired she was of her mundane marriage. So Krista rang her doorbell early that evening, excited not to be watching the Disney channel for a change.

"You're dressed to kill and looking a little hot," Sara said as she admired Krista, attired in a blue, gold, and white sequin strapless top, blue tight fitting, soft lambskin leather pants, a jacket, and four inch stilettos. She was also sporting a new shoulder- length weave with blonde highlights that framed her pretty face.

"You're not doing too bad yourself," Krista responded to Sara's conservative designer jeans, and burgundy lace camisole with matching sheer blouse. She maintained her short, rinse the gray out of her hair, cut that Jonathan admired at the wedding. "Are you ready to drop it like it's hot?"

"I'll let you drop whatever you want tonight, just as long as you behave yourself, Mrs. Cunningham."

"Mrs. Who? I'm Krista White tonight," she laughed.

Their first stop was dinner at the Iceberg Restaurant, the south suburbanites' destination to be seen and treated to great food and music. They toasted with a glass of the house white wine although Krista enjoyed two more glasses during dinner. The atmosphere was festive as the dining room filled up with all of those taking a break from a home cooked meal. Oblivious of the time, the ladies ate, talked, and laughed until the restaurant was about to close. The bar and dance floor in the adjacent room was starting to come alive. And so was Krista. It took some coaxing, but Sara got her out of the door before the DJ turned up the volume and the crowd got younger.

Jade Association was hosting a line-dance party at Prairie State College. This group of women was known to have some of the best dances that drew a large number of line dancers and steppers. Since line-dancing doesn't require a partner, this was the reason Sara opted for this venue.

"All I see are women. Where are the men?" Krista inquired, scanning the room.

"Welcome to the new nightlife for a lot of women. Especially, those of us who can't honestly claim to be thirty-something anymore. Come on and loosen up. You'll have fun and a good workout, too." Since they were not up on the latest dances, they stayed near the back of the room and joined in when they could. Watching Krista laugh, sing, and dance was priceless. They were some of the last people to leave when the party was over.

Making their way back home both ladies kicked off their shoes and fell onto the couch, exhausted and exhilarated. Sara relieved her ears of the dangling earrings that emitted various colors when hit by light and movement, adding a clinging sound mostly heard by her ears only. She removed her sheer blouse and had gotten so comfortable stretched out on the couch she thought she had fallen asleep.

"Sara, we need to do this more often. I haven't had this much fun since I don't know when, except the wedding."

"My days are a little too involved for a lot of night activities. Even Jonathan and I don't spend much time at dances and he's never even suggested we go to a night club. I'd like to attribute that to his respect for me knowing that I prefer the home life, such as when we had dinner at his sister's house."

"How serious are you two? You seem to mention his name quite a bit. Do you think he's the one?"

"It's only been a few months since I met him, although I'll admit, I'm very attracted to him and he's the only man who I want to spend time with. We're not rushing into anything and I believe he's comfortable with that as well. There's still a lot about each other we need to get to know."

"I'm convinced you never get to know everything about anyone, especially a man, no matter how long you spend time with him." Sara knew this would lead to Krista unloading her frustrations about Bradley, so she sat back and did a lot of listening and little talking. "What am I doing wrong? I'm trying to be the perfect wife for him, working hard not to gain weight, keeping the house spotless, and the girls are his little angels. I give him space, don't nag him about anything, which is what Winston used to accuse me of doing. Rarely do I question his long working hours. Besides, he had two jobs when I met him so I can't complain now. One thing for sure, he gives me money every week and doesn't question me about my shopping habits. However, I'd give up a trip or two to the mall if it meant he'd be home more often. You can't imagine how lonely I feel sometimes."

Sara had to be careful and chose her words as she attempted to respond just to assure her she was listening and empathized with her plight as the lonely housewife. "You aren't doing anything wrong. Bradley is lucky to have you as his wife and the mother of those adorable twins. At the wedding, you two looked like newlyweds yourself. I have no doubt that he loves you even more now than he did ten years ago." Hopefully, Sara had said the right things.

"There are times I wish I could be absolutely sure of that. Yes, Chana's wedding brought back some happy memories of the way we started out. I want some of those days back, now and more often," she said, fighting back tears.

"I know you'll do whatever it takes to keep your marriage together. I've got a feeling you two have at least another thirty years together. Bradley will probably get tired of looking at you by then," Sara said, trying to lighten the mood.

"No, I'll be on husband number four by then," she joked with a smile. Sara took a pillow and hit her in the head and they got off the subject of their men and chatted on about a little of everything, just like they did in their college days. Unaware of the time, it was Krista's cell phone that broke up the fun and sent her home to her husband.

Later that early morning, when Sara's body succumbed to another long day, her mind refused to let her sleep. Krista's unhappiness was on her thoughts. Bradley had never been one of Sara's favorite persons, but she tolerated him due to friendship's sake. After they married, he moved into a large, expensive home in the Main Gate subdivision of Olympia Fields. Eyebrows raised as to how a delivery driver turned supervisor for a national company could afford such luxury. His explanation was a winning lottery ticket several years before they met. If it required him to work two jobs to maintain this lifestyle, what was the point? None of Krista's family or friends placed any value on the dwelling. But, that's her life and everyone loved and supported her and the twins unconditionally. As far as Sara was concerned, Bradley just came with the package.

Tossing and turning, trying to get her mind off of them, Jonathan's face kept appearing. She was getting more curious about his home life since she had not been officially invited to the Bronzeville neighborhood where he resided, although he had mentioned his address once during a conversation. It had crossed her mind to drive by even before Gloria suggested it, but, that definitely wouldn't gain her any 'good 'n faithful servant' points, and would probably even subtract a few. *Patience Sara, patience,* she thought. Minutes had turned into hours of unrest. Thank goodness it was Saturday and she could sleep well into the afternoon hours, so she thought.

Saturday, April 28ᵗʰ

Completely startled, she sat straight up when the doorbell rang several times, followed by a rhythmic knock with two hands, then the doorbell again, at eight thirty-one. *Lord, now what?*

Entering its sixth year, the youth fitness program at Rosebrook continued to grow in popularity and participation. This program was launched with the intent to teach discipline, sportsmanship and promote physical fitness while giving God the glory. Initially, it started out being a five-week basketball fundamentals camp for boys. Now, more than one hundred boys and girls participated in an eight-week activity camp that covered basketball, baseball, golf, tennis, and the latest cardiovascular exercises. It was a highly anticipated event that had also proven to be an outreach mechanism that helped Rosebrook maintain its vibrancy and community appeal.

Answering the early morning call of Trent, Tyree and Tamala jogged Sara's memory that registration began at nine o'clock. She thanked them for the wake up service and scurried to get dressed.

Rosebrook's activity center, Palmer's Place, named for its first pastor, Elliot Palmer, was a seven-year-old, twenty-five thousand square foot, one and a half story facility annexed to the existing structure. It housed a gymnasium which doubled as a banquet room, a commercial kitchen, a computer learning center and library, a conference room, and a day care program for children and mature adults. Palmer's Place was maximally utilized by the church and south suburban community.

"Good morning, sleeping beauty," Chana said as he gave her a hug when she arrived forty minutes late. "Trent told me they woke you up this morning. Did you tie one on last night?"

"Give me a break. I haven't had a wake up cup of tea or coffee yet so excuse me if I seem a little out of it. The only thing I tied on last night was a lot of line-dancing and gabbing with Krista until the early morning hours."

"Ladies' night out! Did Bradley approve of this or did my girl sneak out on him?" he teased.

"He let her out for a while, but was on the phone summoning her to come home so he wouldn't be alone in the house. She mentioned something about husbands being big babies who can't sleep in a dark house by themselves," Sara responded with a smile.

"Olivia has no desire to be without big daddy any night," he said with a wink. Just then, a nice looking man approached them and shook Chana's hand.

"Hi, Sean. I'm glad you could make it," said Chana.

"I didn't have a choice. My kids were up earlier than usual this morning, even made breakfast. Since they seemed to be interested in something other than computer games and movies, I'm more than glad to support something that's good for them."

"Sara, meet Sean McKnight," Chana said, making the introductions.

"It's good to meet you, Sean."

129

"Likewise. I just moved to Lindwood back in January. My kids are with me on most weekends. We visited Rosebrook a few weeks ago and heard about this program and they've been talking about it non-stop. So here we are."

"Good. I hope you'll be a part of the program and consider making Rosebrook your church home as well," she replied. Chana excused himself and joined another family standing nearby.

"Thanks, Sara. I'm giving it thought. I really haven't been going to church much since I got divorced two years ago. The kids still belong to a church in the city with their mother. They like it there. I don't have any excuse though."

"Let the Lord lead you, Sean. I'm not passing any judgment."

"I know. I'm still getting used to being alone after being married for fifteen years." Sean started opening up and sharing more information than she was ready to receive, especially after lending an ear to Krista last night on the topic of marriage. She felt she was the last person that needed to be engaged in a conversation on a subject she knew nothing about. But, it seemed Sean wanted to talk, so once again, she just listened and said very little.

"The kids are adjusting well to the divorce. I talk to them every day by phone and email. We usually get together one night during the week and go to dinner. I pick them up after work on Friday and they go back home on Sunday mornings in time for church. Sometimes my son hangs out with me and we watch football or basketball; you know, guy stuff." As if on cue, a teenage girl and boy approached. "Here they are. Nikki, Sean Jr., say hello to Ms. Sara." And the two well-mannered teens shook her hand with their greeting. While the four of them conversed for a few minutes, Sara was sizing up Sean Sr. with Nia and Gloria in mind. No intentions of trying to be a matchmaker, simply picturing good people coming together for good times. Her thoughts were temporarily interrupted when her help was needed at one of the enrollment tables. A few hours later, before the room was completely empty, she left to get some much needed sleep.

Returning home early in the afternoon, she headed straight for the bed. But before her head hit the pillow the phone rang.

"Hey, baby. How's my woman doing this afternoon?" Jonathan asked.

"A little tired, but otherwise I'm feeling great."

"What are you so tired from this early in the day?" She laid across the bed and told him about the events of the past eighteen hours. "So you and Krista went out last night and broke some hearts?" he teased.

"I wouldn't say all of that. Besides, she has a husband at home and I have a…..," then she paused, trying to pick the right words to say.

"You have a what?" he asked.

"I have a very good friend in you and no desire to touch any other man's heart, not even to break it," she laughed.

"That's what I want to hear. Now I know my heart is safe. I'll let you get some more rest and I'll talk to you later."

"Thanks for checking up on me. Enjoy this lovely day, Nate." They both laughed and hung up.

She laid on the bed a few minutes, wondering how safe her heart was at this time. It must be quite secure because when she turned over again it was after five o'clock and all seemed well. Slowly moving about the house in an effort to do something productive before she went back to bed, the phone rang again.

"Hey, girlfriend. How did you sleep this morning?" asked a spirited Krista.

"Not long enough. Where were you this morning? We started registration for the youth fitness program."

"Girl, my mind was far from a youth fitness program. Bradley and I had a mini honeymoon since we didn't have the twins to get us up. As a matter of fact, I didn't get up until shortly after noon when I fixed us something to eat and served my hubby breakfast in bed. I told him we need to do this more often and he agreed. Sara, I'll give it all I've got."

"I know you will, Krista and I'm sure Bradley will once again start appreciating what he has at home. Soon you'll be complaining that he doesn't give you enough space," she teased.

"That'll be the day. Can I still sign the girls up for the program?"

"Of course, and you can be a part of it also," Sara reminded her.

"If all goes as planned, the girls can be exercising with the fitness program while Bradley and I are working out at home," Krista said, laughing.

"Get off my phone. I'll talk to you later," Sara replied smiling. This was a praise report of sorts, although she would continue to pray for strength and fidelity in their marriage.

Two weeks into the fitness program, the staff of volunteers held their most successful fundraiser, a get acquainted night at Beggins Pizza. This drive netted enough money for each participant to receive tee-shirts, hats, water bottles, and trophies at the recognition banquet. Sara was able to rally Nia and Gloria to support the cause and the opportunity for them to meet Sean McKnight.

As hoped, Nia and Sean seemed to hit if off well while Gloria teasingly flirted with both Sean and Jonathan, saying it was her way of checking out the men in her CLEAR sisters' lives. Bradley, Krista and the twins strolled in hand in hand, giving the appearance of a Hallmark-card family. The twins darted off to be with the other children and their parents joined the table. Sara soon spotted Adelaine Richardson coming in the door, escorted by her son Marcus, his lady friend, Brianna and their son Marc. Marcus and Sara briefly caught each other's eye when he shot her one of his famous winks. She immediately turned all her attention to Jonathan who didn't notice anything since he was rooted in a humorous conversation with Bradley. However, Krista looked at her when she spotted him being seated at a table nearby. Sara's facial expression told her to leave it alone, which she did.

Shortly after the Cunninghams, left she noticed a young man heading their way. Looking up as he stood at the table, Jonathan spoke to him. "Well it's about time you showed up. This place might be out of food by now."

"Nah, it's still early for Beggins. I've walked in just before they closed and walked out with a pizza in one hand and cheesy chilly fries in the other," said the young man.

"Sara, meet my son Johnny," said the proud father.

"It's a pleasure to finally meet you, Miss Sara," said a charming Johnny, who planted a kiss on the back of her hand. *Like father, like son.*

"Johnny, I'm so glad to meet you at last. This is my friend, Miss Gloria," she replied, smiling while he kissed Gloria's hand also.

"This looks like a family affair," she whispered to Sara turning to invade Nia's conversation.

"You two get acquainted while I order you a pizza," Jonathan said to his son.

"Make it a deluxe and don't forget some cheesy fries too. I would have been here sooner, but I worked some overtime today. You know how bad traffic is on Fridays," Johnny remarked.

"That's okay because your dad didn't tell me you were coming. This is quite a pleasant surprise. Do you live with Jonathan?"

"No way! Me and one of my buddies got a place in Presidential Towers. It's pretty cool living near downtown with so much going on all the time."

"Well I really appreciate you sharing some of your time with us down here in the suburbs."
"Yeah, Dad said this was a fundraiser for the young people at your church. I use to do things at my mom's church when I was young."

"Please feel welcome to visit Rosebrook at any time. You might just find we have things that might interest you in church again."

"I'll have to come and check it out. It must have something of interest, besides you, to get Dad there more than once," Johnny said, laughing. Just then, Jonathan approached with a plate of hot cheese covered French fries. "What did I miss?" he asked, placing the food in front of his son.

"Nothing!" they both replied simultaneously.

The three of them continued to talk while Johnny cleaned the plate of fries just as his pizza arrived at the table. Sara watched and remembered how she use to eat junk food like that when she was his age. Jonathan must have been thinking the same thing when he spoke up and said, "To be young again and eat any and every thing your eyes can see and stomach can hold."

Sara just shook her head and said, "That was then and this is now," picking up a carrot stick that was left on her salad plate.

"Enjoy it while you can, son," Jonathan said as Johnny didn't appear to even take a breath between pizza slices. "So where else are you going, son?"

"Me and the guys are going to check out a new club in Riverdale. I won't be out all night because I'm working tomorrow."

"You sound like a young man who seriously handles his financial business," Sara commented.

"He'd better because he's not moving back in with me," Jonathan jumped in, playfully nudging his son.

"Dad, you know I take care of myself and have no intentions of invading your space, old man."

"Good, then we'll continue to get along fine," replied Jonathan giving his son a fist bump. All the while, Sara was admiring their loving interaction. Johnny had his father's handsome looks with his smooth, dark complexion and a deep dimple on this left cheek. He sported a short designer hair cut and a small diamond earring in each ear. He was about an inch taller than Jonathan and had an athletic physique. When he stood up and patted his stomach, it was to show off his flat abs which he attributed to daily workouts.

The ringing of his cell phone indicated he was ready to get with his boys and get the party started. They all walked out together and said their goodbyes.

"Johnny, please don't hesitate to visit Rosebrook or me anytime you want. Be careful and have a good time tonight," Sara said while giving him a hug.

"Thanks, Miss Sara, I will." Then Johnny turned to his dad and gave him a handshake and hug, touching Sara's heart.

"Thank you for inviting him. I enjoyed meeting Johnny," she said kissing Jonathan on his cheek.

"I thought you'd get a kick out of him. He's really a good kid despite his job jumping, and I'm very proud of him."

"As you should be," she said, still smiling.

By now, Gloria, Nia and Sean emerged from the restaurant. Nia and Sean gave the appearance they were being enthralled by this chance encounter. Gloria put her arms around Sara and Jonathan, shook her head, then chuckled. "Nia has met her match. Sean can talk as much as, if not more, than her. Both of them have an opinion on any and every thing."

"Come on, Gloria, you know how it is when you meet someone for the first time, especially if you have the slightest interest in them. Maybe Nia and Sean have a mutual attraction," Sara said.

"Yeah, Gloria, Sara didn't shut her mouth the first night I met her," Jonathan spoke up, giving them something else to laugh at.

"Whatever I had to say obviously interested you enough to keep you coming back again and again," was her cavalier response.

"Oh, cut it out, you lovebirds," Gloria said.

Sean called out to them, saying goodnight as he motioned for his kids to follow him to the car. Nia sauntered over their way with a slight smile on her face, but did not utter a word. The three of them just looked at her, then each other, not quite sure what to say or who would speak up first. Never the shy or cautious one, Gloria broke the silence. "So, when is the wedding?" she joked.

"Pleeezzz! He's definitely not for me," Nia flippantly replied. Jonathan and Sara looked at each other and just shrugged their shoulders. Gloria kept grilling Nia.

"You two just laid out your life history. Did he say something to turn you off? Could have fooled me."

"I know, but he did most of the talking and it was all about him and what women say about the way he looks, how he walks, what he wears, how he's so sensitive, yadda, yadda, yadda! I started to ask him if so many women think he's all that, why is he divorced and not hooked up with one of those bimbos?"

"Now why they got to be bimbos? Maybe he's just letting you know how he likes his women, so the next time you two get together, you'll be the one telling him how he looks and walks and talks," Jonathan said, trying to keep a serious look on his face. However, Gloria and Sara couldn't keep it in and burst into laughter.

"Trust me, I am not the one!" exclaimed Nia with a finger snap and neck roll.

"Chill out, Nia. I can tell you're not the type of woman to feed a brotha's ego."

"You got that right, brotha."

"Nia you've got a lot to learn about men. I'll give you a few tips as I drive you home. And calm down. You know we're only teasing," Gloria said, trying to put Nia in the same playful mood as the rest of them. Sara could tell their drive back home would be a spirited one. Jonathan made a peace offering by giving Nia a hug, then Gloria, as they all departed the successful event.

They arrived at Sara's house, still laughing and talking about the evening. For her, it was one of those nights she never wanted to end, not at the restaurant or at her home. However, as the expression goes, all good things must come to an end. Jonathan pulled her into his body and held her very tight before planting a passionate kiss on her lips. "It's late and I've had a long day. Hopefully, I'll make it home alright tonight."

"You'll be just fine. Can I get you anything before you go?"

"You!"

"That's not an option and you know it."

"Wishful thinking, that's all. Thanks for the offer, but I'll be fine. Now, you get some sleep so you can be ready to handle all those kids in the morning. Did you know I told Charles I'd help with the golf instruction?"

"No, I didn't know you're a golfer. How long have you been playing?"

"I'm just a weekend player but I'm not all bad. I got into the game ten years ago and have grown to love the sport. Can I interest you in coming out on the greens with me one of these days?"

"Yes, you can. I've got a set of clubs in the garage that needs to be dusted off. I have to warn you, my irons aren't the only things rusty."

"Don't worry, I'll teach you what you need to know," he said with another kiss. "Okay, it's a date!" he said, backing off as the heat was on.

Standing on the steps, she watched as he slowly backed out of the driveway, almost as if he wanted her to signal for him to come back. Little did he know that she was waging her own internal battle between right and wrong. The wrong side wanted to holler out his name and wave him to come back into her arms and unleash his passion. But the right side was telling her to get in the house and leave him to drive home. The latter won.

The African proverb, *"It takes a village to raise a child"*, was a reflection of the evening. The villagers really came out in full force to raise up the children. Sara wished for many more nights like this. She wished she knew what the future had in store, not only for the children.

Sunday, May 13th

Once again Jonathan surprised her Sunday morning arriving in time to take her to church. She was running late from turning the alarm off, opting for a few extra sleep minutes. The few turned into forty-five. When he called from her driveway, she calmed down, got dressed, and prepared to walk into the sanctuary on his arm. That's what they did, precisely at ten-thirty.

After another Spirit-filled Sunday service, Jonathan treated her to brunch at the Oaks of Glynnwood, known for its grand buffet. Offering a variety of salads, breads, meats, seafood, and side dishes, including a large dessert table, the selections seemed endless. Sara took pleasure watching him fill up on a little of everything. Over dessert he teased, "I'm looking forward to the day you lay out a spread like this prepared by your hands in your kitchen."

She took this opportunity to speak what was on her mind. "I'm looking forward to the day you let me see your kitchen."

"And what is that supposed to mean?"

"At least you have had pizza at my house and you know I can make a seven layer salad. I don't know how you live on a daily basis since I've never been invited to your estate."

"Sara, you aren't missing anything. I live like a bachelor. But, I'll make a deal with you. I'll invite you over for a home cooked meal and you'll have to do the same for me. Is that a plan?" he said. extending his hand.

"You're on," she said, accepting his offer and sealing it with a handshake. Just that quick her mind started to wonder what was she getting herself into. Whatever it was, she knew this competition would be fun while giving her more insight into the world of the man who was starting to occupy a larger portion of her heart.

Back at her home, he turned on the television to an NBA game while Sara changed into a comfortable pair of pale blue leggings and a colorful shirt. She joined him on the couch, pretending to be interested in the game .By the fourth quarter, she was napping on his lap when the phone rang and made her sit up. The caller ID revealed that familiar 'Unknown Name, Unknown Number'. Could this be the mystery man that has annoyed her for the past several months? Hoping that it was, she grabbed the receiver and answered in a very serious voice.

"Well, Sara, I can't believe I'm finally hearing your voice instead of the machine I've gotten to know," he said.

"Who is this?" she shouted as she turned down the volume on the game and placed the receiver between her and Jonathan's ear. She put her finger to his mouth indicating for him to just listen.

"This is Zach Lewis, but you probably remember me as Moose. That's what everyone called me when we were growing up. How have you been all these years?"

The combination of the puzzled look on her face and the shrugging of her shoulders let Jonathan know this was not a call from an old friend or even someone she wanted to talk to. "Yes, Moose, I mean Zach, I remember you. After all, we did go to elementary and high school together. I'm fine. What can I do for you?"

"I know it's been a long time, but I was surfing the internet one day, looking up people from Dayton and I ran across your name. I figured there was only one Sara Joy Deyton from Ohio in this world. So tell me, do I have the right person?"

"Yes."

"Good, I'll be in Chicago in two weeks on business. I'd love to have dinner with you and talk about the good ol' days and new ones. I'm kinda surprised your last name is still Deyton. You haven't made some man the luckiest person on the face of the earth?" he asked. Jonathan attempted to speak, but she placed her finger back to his lips.

"I wouldn't go so far and say all that. Yes, we can arrange dinner," she said as Jonathan pointed to himself implying he was included. This made her laugh, but she knew she needed to control herself. "But let me ask you, why were you so mysterious instead of identifying yourself at first?"

"I didn't think you'd remember me, so I thought I'd spice up your life a little bit." After that comment, she had to fight Jonathan for the receiver and remind him to be quiet since he wasn't supposed to be on the phone anyway.

"I'll admit, it was more annoying than flattering, Moose, or shall I call you Zach?"

"Whatever you're comfortable with is alright with me, Sara. I can't wait to see you again. Take care of yourself and I'll be back in touch soon. Be sweet." On that, he hung up.

"What was that all about and who is he?" Jonathan asked. She let him listen to all the past messages Moose had left on her voicemail, then erased each one. They had gone to the same school since the first grade. He was, a big boy, not very outgoing, got average grades, had one or two male friends who he was with much of the time, and more importantly, not more to her than a boy at school. Everyone, including teachers and his family called him Moose. He didn't have a humongous nose or ears so she guessed Moose was just a loving nickname that described a slow-moving boy who was bigger than most kids his age. What they'd find to talk about over dinner escaped her since he was slightly more than a stranger to her.

"Why didn't you tell me about these phone calls? I would have put a stop to them after the first one," Jonathan said.

"He didn't sound threatening and I could tell he knew me, I just didn't know from where. But now I do and I, or shall I say we, agreed to have dinner with him."

"You got that right. We'll have dinner and it will more than likely be the last time you'll hear from him. The nerve of him thinking he's adding some spice to your life, like you need any more sweetness than what I'm giving you," he said while tickling and wrestling her on the couch. Then the pillow fight was on.

"Thanks for wanting to be my knight in shining armor," she said, claiming victory.

"I'm supposed to be. You know how special you are to me, don't you?"

"No, you've never told me," she said, totally flattered.

"Sara, you must be a special lady, and a very exciting girl. Because, you got me sitting on top of the world."

"Which one are you, Ray, Goodman, or Brown?" she asked to keep the conversation light, not wanting to open her mouth and let her heart come out.

"I'm going to make this an early night so that you can have some time to yourself. I know my ex use to love to have time to pamper herself and Sunday was usually her day for that," he said in an effort to show his sensitive side.

Sara's first misguided thought was she was being compared to one of the women in his past. But not to make a fuss over nothing, she thanked him for being considerate. Not wanting another situation like the other evening, they made sure this departing moment would be less intimate. So at the front door, he kissed her forehead and made his exit.

Chapter 9

Taylor had always been a source of spiritual assurance and positive energy. She was a prayer warrior and the one Sara turned to when she needed an intercessor. They formed a sisterly bond four years before when Taylor joined CLEAR at Erin's request. Although she wasn't a member of Rosebrook Community Church, Taylor volunteered her time and talents to help build up the Roses. Her membership remained at the church her family has attended for generations, Greater Fellowship Baptist, where her father remained senior pastor for the past thirty-eight year. She spent most Sundays at her family's church and at least once a month at Rosebrook or whenever Rev. J.C. delivered the message.

Thursday, May 24ᵗʰ

When Taylor phoned Sara on Monday night excited to extend an invitation to her nephew's third birthday celebration that Thursday, she was equally excited to accept the offer. Lake in the Hills, a northwestern suburb, was about a two hour drive from the Chicago southland, if traffic moved at a reasonable pace. Taylor was still feeling abandoned by Teena, her younger sister. They had been very close growing up, only eighteen months separated their ages. Both girls were very active in church, outstanding academic achievers and professionally accomplished. Taylor was the human resource director of an established black-owned company on Chicago's south side. Teena was working in a family clinic and had

145

started on her doctorate in child psychology. That all ended when Adrian was born.

Taylor was glad to get the opportunity to see her sister and nephew on this special occasion, but, she still wasn't sure why her parents were not invited, knowing that they would have jumped at the chance to spend time with their only grandchild. Teena said she'd bring Adrian to his grandparent's house for the weekend. Taylor jovially drove them to the North Woods Eatery and Saloon with Spiderman gifts in their hands, his latest craze. The two hour drive seemed like a breeze as the after work traffic flow was smooth and without incident. In good time, they pulled into the parking lot just ahead of Teena's blue Toyota Land Cruiser.

Even though Sara had never met Teena, she could be easily recognized due to the resemblance of the two sisters. Both women were attractive with their light brown complexion and naturally sandy colored hair. The very noticeable difference was their taste in fashion and appearance. While Taylor was quite the conservative one, with short hair, very little make up, and a basic solid-color wardrobe, Teena tipped the scale in the other direction. She had light green contact lens, blonde streaked extensions that hung perfectly straight midway down her back, designer, long sculptured nails, flawless makeup, tight fitting jeans showing her curves, and a low cut print top revealing cleavage under a fitted leather jacket. Sara applauded her ability to walk in four inch ankle boots and keep up with her son. Her trendy appearance was immaculate and probably quite time consuming.

At first sight, Adrian was the kind of kid anyone could just fall in love with. He had his mother's skin color and a head full of big, dark sandy curls. His big brown eyes lit up when he spotted his Aunt Taylor crossing the parking lot headed in his direction. He ran straight into her open arms as she swung him around, kissing his dimpled little cheeks. Meanwhile, Sara approached Teena to introduce herself.

"It's a pleasure to finally meet the sister I've heard so much about over the past couple of years," Sara exclaimed, extending embracing arms.

"You too, Sara, and thanks for coming to our little celebration."

"There's no way I would have missed the fun. I can tell those two get along very well," she said, pointing at Adrian, still in Taylor's arms.

"Say hello to my friend, Miss Sara," Taylor told Adrian. He did so and they shook hands while Sara was able to sneak a quick kiss on his cheek, causing him to wriggle more.

"Com' on, let's go see my friend the bear," Adrian insisted even though they were walking towards the door, obviously not fast enough. Inside, he darted directly to the taxidermy black bear that stood in the corner behind a thick red rope. A sign on the rope read BIG BENJAMIN DO NOT TOUCH as Teena called out, reminding her son again of what not to do. Taylor and Sara joined the birthday boy and met Big Benjamin.

Teena spoke to the hostess, who led them to a reserved table near the rear of the dining room, complete with a setting for five. The special spot at the head of the table for the birthday boy was marked with a hat, noisemaker, and booster seat. Although Adrian didn't seem to comprehend the extra place setting, Taylor and Sara noticed it immediately. Teena whispered to them that Adrian's father, BJ, was planning to surprise him. She also had an unintentional surprise for his father, not mentioning that Taylor and Sara were joining the family fun.

"Well, at least I'm closer to knowing his dad's name," said Taylor. "I'm anxious to know who turned your life upside down."

"Taylor, please don't start. This is my son's day. Let's not spoil it for him."

"You're right, I'm sorry sis. I love you and Adrian too much and I don't want anything to ruin his celebration. I'm glad you invited us so let's enjoy ourselves."

"I second the motion," Sara said in an effort to bring them back to all smiles. It worked, even if they were superficial and only for a brief period.

Teena sat facing the door next to the empty plate so she could see when BJ entered the room. The other two ladies sat on the opposite side. Appetizers helped ease the wait and get them back to laughing and talking.

Scanning the dining room, this place had more of a family atmosphere than its name implied. There was a bar in another room that was also the designated smoking area. In the center of this rustic dining room was a double-sided fireplace with a ledge where people sat and talked over a drink or took pictures. The white tablecloths, china and silverware were about the only items that didn't represent a cabin in the woods like the wooden tables and chairs suggested. Along the walls and beamed ceilings were other taxidermy animals, including the head of a deer and elk, a squirrel with a nut in its paws, and wild birds. These were not Sara's ideal dinner companions but, Adrian was really enjoying himself, pointing out the dead creatures that she tried to ignore.

From the corner of Sara's eye, she saw a man get up from a table he shared with a young woman, not far from theirs. It wasn't until he walked towards them, passing en route to the men's room, that she caught a glimpse of his face. As he got closer, Sara had no doubt who it was. For the third time in less than six months, she crossed paths with Marcus Richardson; first the car accident, then the pizza fundraiser, and now the birthday party. Hoping not to be noticed, she turned her attention back to the conversation of the table, but no such luck. Not only did he acknowledge her with his signature wink, but he spoke to everyone, including wishing Adrian a happy birthday. Curiosity overcame Sara as she put forth an effort to see who his dinner date was. For sure, she knew it wasn't Brianna, not this young white woman with long blonde hair. Marcus, Sara concluded, without any substantiating facts, was still quite the womanizer. At age forty-six, he maintained that athletic body he developed in high school and college as a football player. Combined with his attractive facial features, big dark eyes with naturally curly eyelashes, (the kind women regularly spend money on), and straight white teeth, that he and his dentist took very good care of. His face formed a killer smile that could warm the coldest heart. He maintained a clean shaven face and short hair cut in line with the standards for a law enforcement official.

Sara met Marcus when she was twenty-eight, living worldly as part of the sexually uninhibited population. She and Krista were at a club one night in between her marriages. Ladies' heads turned when he strutted in the room. Bodacious Krista sent him a drink but told him it was from Sara. He joined them to say thanks. That started a two-year affair that had Sara doing things she never thought she would do, mainly getting involved with a married man. For months Marcus said what she wanted to hear, how much he loved her, and as soon as he could, he would divorce his wife for a life with her. Foolishly, she believed him and held on to a shallow, one-sided, going nowhere relationship. Chana, pleaded with her to get away from Marcus, but she was too much in superficial love and too far removed from God to heed his advice. Even Krista thought six months was long enough for her to love him and leave him. But, Sara was determined to prove her friends wrong. Like a well behaved mistress, she never told her family about him, never went to the precinct where he was assigned, never called his house and never looked at or spoke to another man. She was available whenever he wanted to see her and pleased him how and when it suited Marcus. And that's how it was for two long, painful years.

Finally, Sara had an awakening that told her Marcus wasn't going to leave his wife, and the past two years were spent being nothing but the other woman. She'd never forget the night she told him it was over. He behaved in a way she'd never seen nor did she want to experience again, from any man. He grabbed her arms and pinned her against the wall. With a fierce look in his eyes, he told her that no woman broke up with him and the relationship wasn't over unless he said it was. He started trying to rip off her jeans when his pager went off, summoning him away. Sara felt that buzz spared her from being raped by her former lover.

Over the next few weeks, he called and came by her house day and night. Sara refused to respond. The harassment finally wore her down and she cried to Chana about the ordeal. Being the protector that he was, Chana told Sara he'd take care of everything. To this day, Sara still didn't know what was said or done, but the relationship with Marcus had finally ended. It took her almost a year to move on with her life and keep him in the past. To her dismay, when she joined Rosebrook one of the first persons she met was Adelaine Richardson, his mother. To this day, Sara doesn't know what, if anything Adelaine knew about their involvement. It was through her that Sara learned of his divorce and new live-in situation with Brianna and Marc.

"Sara, who is that?" Teena said snapping her back to the present.

"His name is Marcus Richardson. His mother is a member of our church."

"You've mentioned him before during some of our open discussions at CLEAR. You two used to be...," then Taylor abruptly stopped. "Ooooh, that's Marcus. I know his mother Adelaine." She remembered Sara mentioning him during one of their Burn the B.S. ceremonies. That was the time Sara burned the names of her past sexual partners and reaffirmed her vow of abstinence.

"Yes, that's him. Maybe you recall seeing him at the pizza party. He was there with his family," Sara said in a way that hinted she wanted to drop the discussion.

"There were so many people at the restaurant that night I don't remember seeing his face. Besides, I only stayed for a few minutes. Not even long enough to eat," replied Taylor.

"How could you not remember seeing a face and body like that!" Teena said, much to Taylor's surprise. Sara wanted to agree but sat in silence and waited.

Twenty minutes passed and still Adrian's dad was a no show. Marcus and his lady friend left, but not without bidding Sara's table good bye. Adrian was getting a little restless so Taylor suggested they order. Confident that BJ was on his way, Teena ordered a dinner for him. *(She must really know her man)*, Sara thought. Taylor apparently had similar thoughts as she looked at her with raised eyebrows and hunched shoulders. They had just finished eating their salads as the waiter was removing those plates making room for the entrees, when Adrian looked up and squealed, "Daddy! Daddy's here!" He darted from his seat and jumped into the arms of his proud father. Turning her head to finally get a view of Teena's baby's daddy, Sara almost couldn't believe her eyes. Approaching the table to join his family was none other than Bradley Adrian Cunningham, Jr., BJ.

Thank goodness she was already sitting down because Sara felt a little faint. She immediately and silently called upon God's grace to get her through this evening. And judging from the look on Bradley's face he was equally shocked and didn't know how he'd get out of this either.

With Adrian hugging him so tightly, thrilled to see his dad, Bradley knew he couldn't disappoint his son, so he kept his attention on him and Teena. He'd just have to deal with Sara later.

"Daddy, I didn't know you were coming here too," said an excited Adrian. Bradley put him back in his booster chair and sat next to Teena, kissing her lightly on the lips.

"I wouldn't miss my big boy's birthday for nothing in the world," he replied. Then turning to Taylor and Sara, he continued, "I didn't know we were expecting company. Ladies, I'm glad you joined us on this special day."

"BJ, this is my sister, Taylor, and her friend, Sara." Teena had a glow on her face, expressing pride and love for the two men in her life.

"It's my pleasure to meet you," he said, doing a very good job of pretending not to know Sara.

"You look familiar, but I can't place where I might have seen you before," said Taylor. Of course Sara wanted to tell her that he's the husband of her best friend and father of her goddaughters. But she had the good sense to sit quietly and just get through dinner without losing it, food and all. Taylor turned to Sara and raised the question that caused her to squirm a bit. "Sara, doesn't he look familiar to you, too?"

"Yes, he does," was her only comment without looking his way. She kept her focus on Adrian who was all smiles and acting like he was on top of the world seeing his mother, father, and aunt all together for this happy occasion. However, this was no easy task. Before the dinners were served Sara excused herself and made a mad dash to the front door for some fresh air. Krista's smiling face dominated her mind as if she was right there in front of her. Tears swelled in her eyes and a lump developed in her throat from the pain that ripped through her heart. This type of thing only happened to other people, not someone who was as close as family. Maybe she did have her suspicions about Bradley, but nothing quite this dramatic. She didn't know who to feel bad for, Krista or Teena. There was one man between two women who obviously loved him very much. And what made matters worse, he appeared to be happy and in love with both of them. Sara's natural instinct was that she couldn't, nor should she, be the one to tell Krista about this. But how could she live with his lie? How could she pretend that life was great when indeed it wasn't? What would she do or say the next time she saw her girlfriend? Fighting back tears, she looked up to the heavens and cried for help. *Lord, now what?*

The food had arrived and the others were enjoying their entrée when Sara returned. Adrian innocently spoke up first, "Where'd you go?"

"Just to get a bit of fresh night air and to give you a chance to tell your daddy all about your birthday so far," she said, trying to conceal her aching heart.

"Well hurry, up before your food gets too cold to eat," Taylor replied. Then she took a closer look and noticed that her friend was having a difficult time shielding her pain. "Sara, are you alright?"

"Yes, I'm fine," she said, believing that the Lord would make everything alright.

154

They watched Adrian open his gifts after the servers gathered around and sang the restaurant's version of happy birthday. His excitement and joy saved the evening for her and his dad, who did his best to avoid looking towards Sara. They were relieved when Taylor made the first move to bring the celebration to an end.

Outside the restaurant, Sara went straight to the car, allowing Taylor time to say good-bye to her loved ones. Then she watched as BJ, Teena and Adrian disappeared into a starry night, just like a real family should.

Before Taylor started the ignition, she turned to Sara, knowing that something happened in the restaurant to change her mood. "Sara, it's just us now so tell me what's wrong. What happened tonight that has you looking like your world has just been turned upside down? Was it seeing Marcus again that upset you so much?"

"No Taylor, Marcus had nothing to do with it," she answered with tears falling down her cheeks again.

"Then what is it? One minute you were all smiles and the next minute you disappeared and came back an entirely different person. Please talk to me."

It took a few minutes to gather her thoughts and speak the right words. Slowly, Sara began. "Taylor, when you said BJ looked familiar to you and asked me the same, all I could do to keep his secret was say yes. The truth is, there's a good reason why he seems like someone you've seen before because you have. He was also at the pizza party with his family."

"His family? Who, Sara, who?" Taylor begged, becoming upset herself.

"My very good friend, Krista and their twins, Autumn and April."

A stunned Taylor just sat behind the wheel, frozen in time at the news Sara blurted out. Shaking her head in disbelief, her eyes began tearing also. They sat in silence with sincere thoughts for Krista, Teena and women everywhere who were betrayed by the men they loved.

Knowing they had a long drive ahead, Taylor wiped away tears and asked, "Sara, what are we going to do?" And for once, Sara didn't seem to have any answers and words completely escaped her. "I don't know," was all she could manage to say. Instinctively, Taylor grabbed her hands and muttered a quick prayer, which was all they could do.

After a long and silent trip back home, Sara threw herself across the bed, still in denial about what had just taken place. With the message indicator blinking, she was hoping the answer for what she needed would be on the machine.

Hi, baby. I hope you are enjoying the birthday party. Just wanted to let you know I'll be leaving tomorrow afternoon for business, but I should be back by Saturday evening. I'm already looking forward to seeing your lovely face or at least hearing your sweet voice. Have a good night.

Normally, Jonathan could always put a smile on her face but tonight she was numb to his words. Maybe his business trip would give her time to figure out what, if anything, she would do to come to grips with this new, but sad revelation. She saved the message just in case

156

she wouldn't have remembered it by tomorrow evening.

Hi, Sara. I hope you and Taylor had a safe drive home. Thanks again for helping us celebrate my son's birthday. We're having a time getting him ready for bed. Anyway, Sara, please let me handle this my way. I know you were shocked by my presence but the truth is, it-is- what-it-is. Please, Sara, if you are Krista's best friend, I know you don't want to see her hurt. Let me do this when the time is right.

The nerve of him. How could I hurt Krista? The damage is already done, Bradley, thanks to you! Delete.

Sara, there's a lot you don't know about me and this situation. Give me a call on my cell phone anytime and let's talk. You don't know the half of it. Please, Sara, you need to know would never intentionally hurt my wife and daughters. I love them very much. Give me a call anytime.

Another call! What is he talking about? I only know half of what? The only way he could have not hurt his wife and daughters, was to not have a relationship with Teena, unintentional or not. Delete.

Before Sara went to sleep her mind kept racing over the recent events she encountered. She thought about Cecily, Marcus, Moose, and now this. With no malice intended, she let out a deep breath and loudly signed, "Lord, now what?"

Friday, May 25th

Friday dragged on, the result from lack of sleep and a wounded heart. With Jonathan out of town, there was only one other person who could help her make sense of adulthood. When she got home from work, she phoned her dear friend and confidante.

"Chana, I hope I'm not disturbing a romantic evening for you and Olivia?"

"Well, if you call my wife's hair appointment and me doing yard work romantic, then yes, you're calling at a bad time. Otherwise, what's up with you and why aren't you and Jonathan getting ready to work a dance floor tonight?"

"He's out of town. Besides, you know we don't get out that much. Been there, did that, not now."

"You know I'm just kidding. But I did want to know about the two of you and you sort of answered my question. So, what can I do for my old friend? You sound kind of serious."

"It's very serious, Chana, and I really need to talk to you whenever you get the chance. I don't know what to do," she sniffed back tears.

"I'm on my way." He must have dropped everything because he was at her front door in twenty minutes.

"Hey, girl. What's wrong?" he asked, holding her tightly allowing the release of anger through tears, hoping they would finally dry up. She knew Chana had the answers. When he had heard all of her details he cupped her face in his hands and kissed her forehead, knowing this would bring a little smile to her face. And it did.

"Sara, listen to me, you have to let go and let God handle this just as I had to do."

She was taken aback by his comment and asked for clarification. "What do you mean by that?"

"I've known about Bradley and his son for two years. And yes, I confronted him, man to man. The biggest surprise to me was finding out the other woman is Taylor's sister."

"Charles Nash, I can't believe you've kept this secret to yourself all this time!"

"I haven't held it in. My spiritual advisor helped me to do what was best. That is to let Bradley handle his mess. I knew better than to mention anything to you because I knew you'd behave this way. It's difficult for me pretending he's the husband and father Krista dotes over while he splits his time between his two families."

"I'm sorry, Chana, I didn't mean to take it out on you. And you're right, I don't know if I could have kept silent all this time, especially since I feel like I'm caught in the middle. I have a strong bond with Taylor, you and the world knows Krista and the twins mean the so much to me. Chana, what am I going to do?"

"Sara, I know you've prayed about this. Am I right?"

"Yes."

"Then let go and let God work it out."

"Chana, how can men live with themselves in a situation like this? Do they know how wrong this is? Do they think they can live a lie forever where nobody gets hurt, or do men even care?"

"Sara, you're hurting, but you know what it's like in the world today for a beautiful black woman. There are far too many of you and not nearly enough God fearing men who are willing to commit to a monogamous life. You'd be surprised at how many women have seriously approached me just in the short time I've been married. My gold ring doesn't deter some desperate woman at all. Because I know the Lord put Olivia in my life to be my one and only love, I can ignore all other women, no matter how good she looks or how much money she's willing to dish out. Men who live by their own rules take full advantage of the opportunities that are thrown in their face." Chana paused for a moment and gave Sara a look as if to say 'you know I'm right.' "According to Bradley, he met Teena, who was counseling one of his nieces after she had been molested by some boys at school. He picked his niece up a few times after her sessions, immediately drawn to Teena's good looks. She gave up her phone number as soon as he asked for it. He claims he told her about his family early on, but they kept seeing each other. You know the rest."

"What do you think is going to happen now? You know how crazy in love Krista is with her husband and family," sighed Sara.

"Yes, I do and I try my best not to think about it. As hard as it will be, that's what you need to do as well," he said, laying her head down on his lap and massaging her shoulders. "Everything's going to be alright," he said, with a measure of assurance that lifted some of the pain. And that's the last thing Sara remembered about Friday. Again, as many times in the past, Chana comforted her to sleep, then quietly let himself out.

A little dazed at first, she finally woke up to realize it was late Saturday morning. Having slept on the couch in her work clothes, she was happy no one disturbed her much needed rest. Missing the fitness program she pondered for several moments what she would do today. Changing into jogging wear, the fresh air and sounds of nature found in the forest preserve is exactly what she needed. She warmed up by

160

stretching while her mind started chanting *(walk, release, forgive, let go, walk, release, forgive, let go.)* As soon as she closed the front door and commenced the journey, with water bottle in hand, she was greeted by three youthful voices. "Hi, Miss Sara Smile. Where was you at this morning?" they seemed to ask in unison.

"I had something else to do today."

"Where are you going now?" inquired Trent.

"For a walk."

"Can we g"

"Nooooo!" she quickly snapped back before they could finish the question. "Not today kids, I need this time to myself." *Walk, release, forgive, let go. Walk, release, forgive, let go.* She picked up the pace as the cadence ran through her head. *Walk, release, forgive, let go.*

One and a half hours later, she returned home, elated and feeling free. Freedom from worries and anxieties about consequences that were not in her control. Free to live and enjoy today and not merely exist. Freedom to let tomorrow come while faith would prepare her for whatever it would bring. Free to just be Sara! This day, albeit well into the afternoon, was off to a wonderful start and she wanted to keep it that way!

A soothing lavender bubble bath and a delivery order of Chinese food nourished her body and soul. If she just had a large piece of decadent double chocolate cake with scoops of vanilla ice cream she would have experienced Heaven on earth. This visualization humored her to the point she laughed out loud. But with no dessert, the ringing phone brought her back to real time.

"Hi, Sara. What are you doing home on this lovely Saturday afternoon? You should be out shopping with me and the girls. Last night my adorable hubby came home and dropped two grand in my hands and told me to buy something for me and the all kids. I haven't blown it all yet and I'm sure you can find something new that'll please your man. Come on and join us. What do you say, Ms. Deyton?"

That Bradley, dropping cash in her hands before dropping something else on her. Those negative thoughts told Sara not to go there and remembered her conversation with Chana. "Krista, as good as that offer sounds, I'm going to have to pass. I need some time to myself and that's exactly what I'm going to do, just stay home and chill out."

"Is everything alright with you and Jonathan? There's no trouble in paradise, I hope?"

"No, nothing like that. If you see something for me, don't hesitate to get it. Whatever it is will be highly appreciated," she managed to say lightheartedly.

"Sara, you know me. I promise not to bring back one pretty penny! Smooches."

Sara had passed the first test, keeping her mouth closed. A little painful but she did what she had to do. Now she was beginning to understand what Chana had been going through. Sara quickly returned to watching the Lifetime movie in her humble abode, one victory under her belt.

As whatever movie she was watching ended, she phoned Taylor. They had not spoken since Thursday night. To their delight, both ladies had freed themselves from the situation. As an added comfort, they agreed to a fast from solid foods on Mondays' for the next seven weeks, from midnight to six o'clock in the evening and pray for something positive to happen, much sooner than later. This phone call was revitalizing. Early evening drifted in and the ringing phone lighted her eyes.

"Good evening, Ms. Sara. I'm somewhat surprised that I caught you at home. How's my favorite girl doing today?" asked Jonathan.

This time, she was more than glad to hear his voice. All smiles, she responded, "I'm doing great. How about yourself?"

"Other than missing you, I'm glad to be heading back home earlier than I expected. Do you want to do anything tonight? Dinner, a movie?"

"Thanks for the offer Jonathan, but I just want to stay in and relax, like I've been doing all afternoon. Besides, you could probably use some time to yourself with all the traveling you do."

"You know, you're absolutely right. See, it takes a good woman to help a man out with his own life. I just haven't seen you in several days and I miss you."

"I miss you too and I'm looking forward to us getting together again soon, just not tonight. Is that okay with you?"

"Sara, anything for my queen."

"Thank you, your highness."

"By the way, has that buffalo or Bullwinkle fellow bothered you again?"

"No," she laughed, "and you mean Moose."

"Whatever. Just remember, I'm in on any meeting, right."

"I wouldn't have it any other way." With that, they ended the call. For the remainder of the evening, she focused on thankfulness and forgiveness. This had turned out to be a glorious day after all. The kind that she would long for again in the weeks ahead.

Chapter 10

Jonathan phoned Sara as soon as she walked in the door from church.

"Hey, baby, you were right. I slept straight through the night and half of the morning. I'm sorry I missed church today. I'm sure it was inspirational as usual. Have you made plans for dinner today?"

"Other than eating something, nothing special. Why do you ask?" she replied, trying to contain the anticipation that dinner would include him.

"You'll be dining with me today. I'll be there to pick you up in one hour."

"Sounds good, but may I ask where are we going?"

"We won't be dining at Beggins Pizza nor will it be the 95th Floor, if that will help you decide what to wear."

"Could you be a little more specific, please?" she begged.

"It's a surprise. You always look good whenever we go out. But, I'll give you a little hint. You may want to bring a sweater or jacket. I'll see you in an hour," Jonathan said and hung up before she could say another word. Truthfully, she was flattered by his take charge gesture.

Sara refused to spoil his plans, so when Jonathan came to pick her up she just jumped in the car, enjoying the drive and conversation. Her pastel multi-color sheath dress and sky blue sweater, complemented his cream color double-breasted jacket, navy blue slacks and light blue silk shirt. Their color coordination was purely coincidental.

She talked about the birthday dinner, purposefully declining to mention the biggest surprise of the day. He was all smiles when she told him how she had spent Friday and Saturday at home alone, relishing the time to herself. More of her feelings were being exposed as she revealed to him her desire to spend time with only him. Jonathan's smile spoke volumes that he was pleased to hear this non-coerced confession.

The further they drove, the more talking Sara seemed to be doing. However, she attempted to open the door for him to speak up about his business trip without appearing to be prying. But, as with the other trips, he was very elusive so she other topics to share even as they pulled into the Navy Pier parking garage. Jonathan led the way to their destination.

"Good timing," he commented, glancing at his watch. "They have just started boarding." They strolled hand in hand along the pier's walkway until they reached the Anita Dee II, a luxurious private yacht. "A buddy of mine had purchased these tickets to Dr. Eli Spencer's birthday party. He had to make an emergency trip out of town and didn't want the tickets to go to waste. So, I assured him I'd make good use of them. Besides, he cut me some slack on the price."

Dr. Spencer was a well-known and highly respected plastic and cosmetic surgeon in Chicago. He was one of few African Americans in the field. He was celebrating his fiftieth birthday with a two hour cocktail cruise. Judging from the crowd of party goers, this should be a memorable occasion for him. The man of the hour stood at the top of the loading plank, greeting all of his guests.

"What's up, Doc?" Jonathan said as he and Eli greeted each other.

"Look at you, Nate, looking good and obviously doing well enough to be able to afford to pay this beautiful woman to hold onto your arm," he teased, taking her left hand and kissing the back of it. After Jonathan made the introduction, Eli held up Sara's hand and stated, "No ring yet? Don't wait too long or I might move in and take care of business myself."

"Keep dreaming," Jonathan shot back quickly.

The couple made their way inside the main deck where there was food galore, an open bar and a small jazz ensemble in the corner providing smooth sounds for sailing.

Eli was considered to be a very sought after bachelor. However, unlike other social affairs Sara had attended, his guest list appeared to be a reasonable balance of men and women, although the scale tipped towards men. *A rarity!* Jonathan kept her close by his side as they mingled about the crowd. He seemed delighted to introduce her to the people he knew. Even when they came upon his former girlfriend, Candace, he was just as cordial as with everyone else. So, finally Sara was allowed another glimpse into the private life of the man who was threatening her singleness.

Candace was an attractive woman who boldly wore confidence and success in her demeanor. "So, Sara, how long have you been dating the man who had once stolen my heart?" she opened her conversation.

"I've only known Jonathan since Christmas. We're still becoming good friends," was all she wanted Candace to know.

Then she leaned in towards Sara and whispered in her ear, although it was loud enough for him to hear. "Be careful and guard your heart. He's not the marrying type."

"Thank you for that piece of advice, but we're not at the stage in our relationship where marriage is a topic of discussion," Sara whispered back with a crafty smile. She really wanted to tell her, no, they weren't sleeping together and they definitely wouldn't be living together either. But her better judgment took charge of her mouth and Sara said no more.

Candace was ready to move on after that encounter. "It was good to see you again, Nate. Nice to meet you too, Susan."

"Sara," Jonathan spoke up quickly.

Sara's first impression of Candace was lessened by a few degrees at that point. But, she was still in control and hanging on to Jonathan's arm tighter. "It was my pleasure to meet you too, Candace. I'd heard so much about you that I was actually looking forward to this opportunity," Sara said, slightly exaggerating. Jonathan saw someone else he knew and quickly moved in that direction.

Two hours vanished quickly. Based upon all the smiles, hugs, and kisses being shared as they disembarked the yacht, a good time was apparently had by all. Not ready for the date to end, Jonathan and Sara lingered around the famous pier, admiring some of the shops and the many visitors. They joined another couple on the 150-foot-high Ferris wheel. The four of them hopped into one of the slow moving cars and admired the early evening view of Chicago's famous skyline and lakefront, both men holding their woman close to his side. *What a perfect day!*

Back at Sara's house, they settled on the couch, talking non-stop about a little of everything. She let him open the door regarding Candace.

"That was some dialogue you and Candace had. I'm surprised she made that marriage comment to you."

"It was just her way of trying to find out what's going on with the two of us."

"All she has to do is ask me. It's not like I don't run into her from time to time. Lately, she's never mentioned anything about my personal life except to ask about the kids," he said nonchalantly.

"I didn't know you still see her?"

"I don't except if I happen to run into her out somewhere like today. This is really her type of crowd. I met most of them while we were together and haven't seen them since then. Some of the people you met are into money, expensive cars, and owning the latest electronic gadgets before they hit the market. I'm not mad at them, but that's just not me. Doc Eli is cool and I make it a point to give him a shout every now and then, but that's about all. Have I really talked about her that much like you said?"

"Of course not, but she doesn't know that," Sara said with a wink. "Today gave me a chance to get to know a little more about you and I appreciate that," she said giving him a peck on the cheek. "By the way, did she ever get married?"

"No and she still blames me for wasting six years of her life. I hesitated about going because I was sure she'd be there. You know how territorial you women can get about your man. I didn't want a cat fight to break out although you two were getting close." Sara acknowledged his comments by slapping one of the throw pillows upside his head.

At that moment, the clock chimed, indicating that it was now late evening. Too bad the day was coming to an end. It had been a consoling way to calm a mini turbulent wave over the past three days, of which Sara still chose not to share with Jonathan at this time. But, the day was not over yet! As the clock quieted, the phone rang. *Who's calling at this hour?*

"Hello, Sara. Once again, I'm honored to hear your voice instead of the recorder. How are you this evening?"

"Hello, Zach," she coldly replied while mouthing the word 'Moose' to Jonathan.

"So you know my voice now. That's good."

"Well, my friends don't usually call me this late unless it's a matter of extreme importance."

"I'm sorry I didn't mean to be rude. I'll make this quick. Can we get together this week for dinner? You can name the place and time."

"Dinner this week will be fine," she said while her facial expression was asking Jonathan if that was okay with him. He nodded in approval. "How about Thursday at The Flavor Restaurant in Matteson. Are you familiar with that place?"

"Yes. As a matter of fact, I had dinner there a few months ago with some business associates. That will be fine with me. What time?"

"Let's make it seven o'clock. By the way, you won't mind if my companion, Jonathan, joins us, will you?" There were a few seconds of silence.

"I'm just a little jealous to hear you mention some man in your life. Is this a serious relationship you're in?"

"He is the man I've been seeing for a while now and we don't have secret dinner meetings with other men and women and not inform or invite the other. I'm sure he'd like to meet a former school mate of mine. Besides, I'd expect you to bring your significant other." This exchange was pleasing Jonathan. She had to remind him to be quiet since it wasn't respectful for him to be listening.

"Of course your boyfriend is welcome to come. And you're right, I'd bring my woman if I had one," Moose commented.

"If we're just going to socialize over dinner, maybe I can bring one of my girlfriends and we can make it a foursome. What do you say to that?"

"Sara, whatever makes you comfortable and happy is alright with me. I'm just looking forward to seeing you again after all these years," he said to her disbelief.

"Great, Thursday night it is. See you then," she said and hung up before he or Jonathan said another word. "I have no idea why he wants to see me. Like I told you before, it's not like we were good friends in school. All of these phone calls are still a mystery to me."

"Don't worry, baby. After he pays for Thursday's date, I'm sure all of these calls will end and maybe he'll just have to find another high school sweetheart to look up. You know, it sounds to me like he had a crush on you," Jonathan remarked.

"No way! Let me show you what he looked like back then." She went into the bedroom and retrieved her yearbook. "See, here he is." Zach's face was the biggest picture on the page. Wearing dark rim glasses, a bow tie, plaid sweater vest, close cut hair, and a blank expression on his face. This was the Zach Lewis she remembered.

"I don't know, Sara, I might have to ask Johnny to get me outfitted for this date so I can hopefully beat out my competition," he said, bursting into laughter. Once again, Sara took the pillow to his head all in fun.

"He didn't interest me then and I seriously doubt I'll have an interest after Thursday. So you can save your new threads for another time."

"If you say so. But, I'll have something to back me up, just in case."

"Alright, then you'd better get ready to go and work on your game plan," Sara replied, getting off the couch and extending her hand for him to do the same.

Walking to the door, they both reiterated what a good time they had today and she thanked him again for treating her to a wonderful dinner. Then Jonathan turned to her and looked straight in her eyes with a hint of seriousness.

"The last time we were standing in this position, I got too aggressive and I'm very sorry I did. You are a woman of your word. That's one of the things I respect about you. So, sweetie,

I'm going to say goodnight the way a gentleman should." He kissed her forehead.

"Jonathan, it takes two and I hope I didn't mislead you."

"No, Sara, a real man should always be in control of himself. It was nothing that you said or did. I just lost my head for a minute. Now, sweet dreams and I'll see you on Thursday." With a second thought, he continued, "By the way, who are you going to get to be Moose's date?"

"I'll see what Gloria is doing. Maybe she'd like to join us. She'll know I'm not trying to set her up and the table will never be at a lost for words with her there."

"Good. He probably wouldn't be Nia's type anyway," he said, laughing.

We'll see.

First thing Monday evening, Sara was on the phone with Gloria. "Hi, Sara. How are you? Or better yet, how is that fine man you've been kickin' it with?"

"And hello to you to, Ms. Gloria. I'm blessed and taking life one day at a time. Jonathan is doing the same. What's been going on with you lately?"

"Nothing much, just working and trying to live the single life like you and Taylor. I don't know how you do it with a man like Jonathan. If it were me, I'd be begging the Lord to forgive me on a regular basis!"

Sara couldn't help but to laugh out loud. Gloria wasn't one to hold her tongue when she wanted to say something. Over the last few years, she had really cleaned up her mouth and was careful to be more respectful and savvy with what she said. Sara really liked the new

173

and improved Gloria. "Remember, 'good 'n faithful servant' points! That's how I do it. You know you can too. Listen, Gloria, what's on your calendar for Thursday evening?"

"Let me think, CSI and The Mentalist. Why, what's going on?"

"How would you like to have dinner at The Flavor with us?"

"Sara, what's up? Are you two making some kind of special announcement?"

"Gloria, please! It's not that serious. Actually, we're meeting someone else and I'm just making it a foursome. No, I'm not making an attempt to set you up with anybody." Then Sara went on to tell her about what led up to this proposed dinner meeting. "So what do you say? A good meal at his expense and you get to drill Jonathan a little more, if you aren't too intrigued by Zach."

"Well, since you put it that way, count me in. Who knows, maybe Zach might be the one to help me get my groove back," she said, laughing.

"Behave yourself, Gloria! Yes, if nothing more we'll have a good time spending Zach's money." Gloria and Jonathan would see to that.

Chapter 11

Thursday, May 31st

Wet, windy, and whirly best described the first three days of that week. The rain started early Monday afternoon, continuing into late Thursday morning, although not as heavy. Wednesday was the worst weather this area had seen in years. Tornados were spotted throughout the Chicago area with reports of touchdowns in the villages of Plainfield, Aurora, and Kankakee .Fortunately, the damage to these areas was minimal. Widespread flooding was reported in parts of Lake County that closed many roads and stranded motorist who had to abandon their vehicles before they were fully submerged. As of Thursday afternoon, power had still not been restored to several far southwest suburban communities and parts of northwestern Indiana.

All of this added to the gridlock of daily commutes. Sara's usual thirty minute drive was extended to seventy-five. The local radio stations deviated from their regular formats to keep the listeners updated on weather related conditions, including the numerous auto accidents coming from every part of the city and suburbs. Meteorologists were predicting the rain, becoming light drizzle by Friday, would continue until early Saturday morning.

The news reports were filled with stories that were sad, depressing and humorous. Sara turned the radio off and opted for silence except the sounds of nature. Her mind was filled with anticipation about this evening's mystery date.

Gloria had already left her a message asking if dinner was still on. Before Sara called her back, she checked with the restaurant. The manager said she was forced to close early yesterday due to a power outage, but today was business as usual. So she returned Gloria's call and phoned Jonathan as well that the date was still on. And once again, Jonathan had her beaming from ear to ear when he told her there was no weather bad enough to keep him from getting to her. Although this was a line very similar to an old favorite Diana Ross song, Sara was still engulfed by those simple words and loved hearing him say it.

The ringing of the phone snapped her out of her *visualization* and back to the present. She just knew it was Zach inquiring about dinner, so she picked up the receiver before the second ring.

"Hey, sweetie. How's my favorite-waiting-on-the-Lord-to-send-me- Mister Right, girlfriend doing?" said a bubbly Krista.

"Great! How's my favorite goddaughters momma doing?"

"Wonderful! What's up with you other than staying dry?" Krista inquired.

"I'm getting ready to go to dinner with some friends. What's on your agenda?"

"Friends, does Jonathan know about this?"

"Yes, Mrs. Cunningham, he's picking me up in about an hour."

"Sara, when are you going to grab that man and make him yours for good? If I were you, I'd be Mrs. Tate by now."

"When the Lord puts it on both of our hearts and gives us His green light. No sooner and no later than that," Sara quickly answered.

"I hope it's sooner before I get too old to strut my stuff down the aisle and stand next to you. I wouldn't be surprised if some hot mama isn't trying to move in on you as we speak. Maybe you should help speed up the Lord's decision."

"Krista, you know me better than that. If Jonathan wants someone else, he won't get a fight from me. That just means he's not the one. I'd rather be single and happy than with someone and worrying if some hot mama is turning his head or anything else for that matter. Now, did you call me to get all in my business or what?" Sara said with sisterly love.

"I need a babysitter this weekend. My darling hubby wants to spend some time, just the two of us. I'm planning a quiet riot myself, if you know what I mean? Can you keep the girls any time this weekend? I know its short notice, but when my man wants me all to himself, I jump to it. My mom hasn't been feeling well lately and the twins are getting to be a little too much for her to handle. Please Ms. Deyton, please?"

"Quit begging. You know I'll always make time for my girls. I have a CLEAR meeting on Saturday, but I'll see if Chana can take them for a few hours."

"Thanks so much, Sara. You're my she-ro."
"Save it. I might need a favor from you in the near future."

"I hope it's throwing you a bridal shower. Smooches."

All of a sudden, it hit Sara as to why Bradley wanted to spend some time alone with Krista. GUILT. Remembering that Chana told her to let go and let God, she looked up, closed her eyes and said, "God, You've got this!"

Making her way to the bedroom, Sara stood in front of the open closet trying to decide what to wear. She wanted to look good for Jonathan but not appear that she was out to impress Zach. By the time she had sized up the fifth ensemble to her body and danced around in the mirror, she picked the second outfit, orange pants and matching spaghetti strap tank top with a multi-color sheer duster. Nothing too dressy or flashy, she felt, just comfortable. It took her longer to decide which pair of earrings to wear due to her vast collection that spanned over thirty-five years. She had earrings dating back to her high school days, everything from costume to diamonds, big and small ones. Some women love shoes, others handbags, but earrings were Sara's favorite things.

When Jonathan came to pick her up, he planted a light kiss on her cheek and commented that she looked nice, as usual. And he was just as hand-some in black pants and silk T-shirt with a tan silk jacket. Jonathan had mentioned that Candace used to dress him from head to toe. He chuckled when he said one of the things he got from their relationship was a closet full of clothes.

"I hope Moose brings his own date because you two ladies are mine tonight," Jonathan said after he escorted Gloria into the car.

"What do you say about that?" she teased.

"For you Gloria, I'll share this handsome gentleman, but only for tonight," Sara replied.

Gloria loved to shop and had enough clothes in her closets for any occasion imaginable. When she described herself, she stated that she can easily fill out a size fourteen and maybe a sixteen. Nia told her she should be a plus size

AARP model. Jonathan remarked that she was a fine healthy woman that had something for a man to hold on to. Her various accessories also included wigs and weaves. Tonight, she chose a nautical look consisting of yellow pants with a matching yellow and blue navy jacket. She pulled her hair back, sporting a shoulder length wavy ponytail, taking at least ten years off of her age. Her shoes, purse, and jewelry were a complementary combination of blue, gold, and white. When Sara got a better chance to see the complete outfit once they entered the restaurant, she whispered to Gloria, "Girl, you know you've got it going on!"

"We both do!" she whispered back.

The host seated them at a reserved table as they ordered drinks while waiting on the man of the hour to arrive. Gloria sipped a martini cocktail, a Chardonnay for Sara, and Jonathan drank a scotch on the rocks.

"Sara, maybe you should be facing the door so you can spot Zach when he arrives," said Gloria.

"I hope he recognizes me because I have no clue what he might look like after more than twenty years."

"I'll be on the lookout so he'll see me first. Then he might leave when he sees the look on my face that suggest he's not welcome here," boasted Jonathan.

"Well, Sara, based on what you told me, all we have to do is look for the biggest thing walking through the door. And, Jonathan, behave yourself. He just might turn out to be the man of my dreams," Gloria said, trying not to laugh at her own remarks.

About fifteen minutes into the cocktails and conversation, their young waiter came and asked if they were ready to order appetizers, but they decided to wait a while longer. "We'll let him see what he's paying for," Jonathan said

Amidst their laughter, a man appeared at the table from out of nowhere, it seemed. "I'm sorry I'm late and missed the joke," he said. Then looking directly at Sara, he continued, "Sara, you look the same as you did in high school only more beautiful. May I?" he asked as he looked to Jonathan while lifting Sara's hand to his slightly bowed head, planting a kiss. Jonathan rose to his feet as Zach introduced himself. "I'm Zach Lewis. You must be Jonathan?"

"Yes, Jonathan Tate and this beautiful woman is Gloria Wells. Have a seat. We've been waiting for you."

"My pleasure, Ms. Wells," he said while giving her hand a kiss also. "Again, I apologize for running late, but I don't have to tell you what the weather is doing to traffic out there. Anyway, I wasn't going to let a little rain keep me from seeing Ms. Deyton again."

Never in a million years would Sara have recognized Zach Lewis, a.k.a. Moose. He looked nothing like he did during the school days. The man with a medium brown complexion who was now seated at their table was tall, about six foot three, medium built, maybe two-hundred twenty pounds, had a clean shaven head, and was impeccably dressed in a tailored, light brown, double- breasted Calvin Klein suit, shoes, crisp white shirt and silk paisley tie. His accessories included a diamond ring on each hand and a gold watch that sparkled, shimmered, and shined. This charismatic man looked good, smelled good, and seemed to know it as a fact. Of course, as far as she was concerned, he still didn't hold a candle to her man. Gloria, on the other hand, had different thoughts.

"Zach, it's good to see you. I must admit, you're not the same person previously known to me as Moose."

"You're right about that, Sara. I've changed a lot since then. For the better, I hope."

"I'd say it was for the better and I didn't even know you back then," Gloria spoke up, giving them a laugh.

When their waiter came to take Zach's drink order, he announced, "May I order a bottle of Dom Perignon for the table?" They nodded their heads in agreement. "And please, order whatever you'd like, dinner is on me tonight. Let's see your appetizer menu please." Gloria seemed delighted, Sara was cautious, and Jonathan was not impressed.

While munching coconut beer shrimp and quesadilla crabmeat, they all engaged in small talk about a little of everything, but nothing particular. Zach seemed to be at ease around the three of them. To Sara, he was just as much of a stranger as he was to Gloria and Jonathan. However, she remained somewhat reserved since his motivation behind all the mysterious phone calls was still questionable. And his flair for spending raised an eyebrow as he ordered another bottle of the expensive champagne to go along with their entrees. He, Gloria, and Jonathan indulged but Sara had her share of alcohol after the first glass.

"Come on, Sara, let your hair down a little. Jonathan is our designated driver tonight," teased Gloria, knowing Sara's alcohol consumption, rare as it was, was always minimal at best.

"None of you need to worry. I'll make sure each of you get home safe if I have to call three taxi's," stated a flamboyant Zach.

"That won't be necessary, bro. My baby knows I'll always take care of her and Ms. Wells too," responded Jonathan, then leaned over and planted a soft kiss on Sara's lips. Gloria and Sara were flattered by the high level of testosterone flying back and forth across the table.

The live Brazilian jazz band pleasured them with festive and mellow sounds throughout their dining experience. The foursome was never short on conversation and they had totally forgotten about the pluvial weather that had accompanied them to this place. It was already half past the ten o'clock hour and The Flavor was closing, although the manager told them there was no need to be in a hurry to leave. The truth was Sara had been ready for the evening to end an hour ago but she had no intention of ruining everyone's enjoyment. Gloria and Zach seemed to be engaged in their own getting-to-know-you session. Jonathan was into the music, rocking his head and swaying to the beat. At one point, he pulled her close and whispered in her ear, asking her if she was having a good time. With him by her side, most definitely, even if he was showing out just a bit.

When their waiter presented the tab, Zach spoke up. "I'll take that." He pulled out a wad of bills from his inner jacket pocket, flipping through them until he counted out five one hundred dollar bills. Again, Jonathan was not impressed, Gloria didn't seem to pay it any attention, and Sara was now more hesitant than before. *What is this Zach character up to?*

"Gloria, would you like for me to see to it that you get home?" Zach asked.

"Thanks, man, but like I said, that won't be necessary. The ladies are in my hands and they'll get home as safe as they arrived," Jonathan snapped back.

"Brother, I have no doubt you'll take good care of these ladies. I just thought maybe Ms. Wells wanted to continue our conversation and give you and Ms. Sara some privacy."

"Thanks for the offer, Zach, but I'll go back with Jonathan. Besides, it might be out of your way."

"I'd go anywhere for you, Ms. Wells, that's not an issue. But, I respect your decision and I bid you all a good night. Sara if it's alright with Jonathan, I'd like to keep in touch from time to time."

"Well, Zach, you found me after all these years so I'm sure you'll know how to reach me again. Take care of yourself and thanks for a very nice evening," Sara indirectly answered.

"My absolute pleasure," Zach pleasantly said.

"Yeah, man, you can take us out to dinner again, no problem," Jonathan said, with a hint of sarcasm.

Gloria and Sara waited for Jonathan to pick them up at the front door. Zach dashed to his car, a shining S-class silver Mercedes-Benz. "So what does money-bags do that has him rolling like a millionaire?" asked Gloria as he drove by and waved.

"You tell me, since he held you as his captive audience."

"Sara, I wasn't impressed. He never said anything specific about his line of work, but he kept bragging about how successful he was. He rambled on about houses he owns, places he's been, and toys he has, including women. I'm like Jonathan, he can treat me to dinner anytime but that's about all. Believe me, I'll never have dinner with him alone."

"Me neither," Sara replied

Friday, June 1st

Friday afternoon seemed to drag on and on. Sara had little pep in her step and the only thing on her mind was what she would do with the twins all weekend. Being a little tired from last night, she was hoping to get in a quick nap before the girls arrived. So she dashed home and laid down, only to toss and turn until the doorbell rang at six o'clock sharp.

"Hi, Auntie Sara," the girls sang as they stepped into the house.

"Hello, my little angels. It's so good to see you. Come on in and get comfortable. We're going to have a good time this weekend." She gave all three of them a hug, then asked Krista, "Are you going to stay for a while?"

"No, I can't. Bradley is in the car and we're headed to dinner. Thanks again for your help and we'll have to talk later."

"Enjoy yourself and don't worry about hurrying back. The girls and I will be fine." Krista hugged her daughters and left, smiling and dancing like it was a first date.

"Auntie Sara, do you think Trent is home?" asked Autumn.

"Probably. Do you want me to see if they can come over and play with the two of you?"

"Yeaaah!" they exclaimed in unison. Ten minutes later, there were five kids in Sara's house, laughing and playing while they waited for the pizza to be delivered. Afterwards, they'd be entertained by watching the DVD's the girls brought with them. Despite all the noise those five generated, she was starting to fight sleepiness. Luckily she heard the phone when it rang.

"Hello. May I speak to Sara?"

"Jonathan, it's me," she said recognizing his voice immediately.

"With all that noise in the background, I thought I had the wrong number. Sounds like a party that I wasn't invited to."

"It's just the usual suspects, the twins and the three T's. Do you care to join us?" she asked, knowing what the answer would be.

"Only if you absolutely need me. Otherwise, I'll pass on all the fun this time."

"Okay, but don't say I didn't ask," she remarked.

"Sweetie, I'll be around all weekend. If you need anything, I'm just a phone call away. Have fun and don't stay up too late."

"I'll probably be the first one to fall asleep. Thanks again for the offer and for last night," she said, hanging up the phone just in time to hear something crash to the floor in the guest bedroom.

Saturday, June 2nd

Chana and Olivia were more than happy to have the girls spend Saturday with them. They even insisted the twins stay overnight and go to church with them. Sara had no objection and neither did Autumn and April. Their Uncle Chana spoiled them just like their daddy did; non-stop playing and agreeing to whatever they wanted to do, or eat, or had to have.

Although the CLEAR meeting started at noon, Sara arrived a little late because she had taken the kids to the fitness camp. Uncle Chana took all five home with him since they didn't want to leave each other. Miss Lizzie and Sara gladly turned them all over into his willing and capable hands. By the time she got to Serena's house, Gloria had told them about the dinner date. Sara didn't know what all she said, but she could tell from the questions and comments that Gloria exaggerated the truth.

"So, Sara, you had two men fighting over you the other night. You go girl!" Nia blurted out first.

"Sounds serious to me," replied Serena. "I mean Jonathan must really want you to himself and I say good for you!"

"So how serious is he?" asked Erin.

"Ladies, slow down and don't go picking out wedding gifts just yet. Jonathan and I are good friends," she said, attempting to downplay her feelings.

"The way she talked about how good Jonathan looked and how he treats his women so good, you'd better watch out for this one over here," Cecily said, referring to Gloria. They all knew she was just teasing and Sara took the

186

comment in the playful and loving gesture that it was intended.

"Alright, you Divas, let's get to the business of the book," Sara said and they turned their attention to Stephen Carter's *The Emperor of Ocean Park*.

Their discussion had gone very well and the two o'clock hour was upon them. The ladies were going through their prayer request wrap-up when Cecily spoke up in a serious tone. "Ladies, I had to do this in a way that would be easiest for me. I love all of you, especially the way you supported me and Mario during our crisis. But, I need to make a change, a chance to go somewhere and put my life back together. I have to make God and Mario my number one priority. My brother in Dallas invited us to come down there. We can stay with him until I find a job and get settled in an apartment. So as of this Monday, we're leaving for a new life in Texas."

There was silence across the room. They all seemed to have been frozen by her words. Cecily was saying good-bye to CLEAR and Illinois. They were stunned, although not totally surprised, yet happy for her in a bitter-sweet way. Serena was the first to shed tears.

"No, not again!" cried Nia. "Not another sister's life being drastically interrupted because of some no good man. I can't take this anymore!"

"Please, girls, don't start crying. Be happy for me and try to understand that this is best for Mario also. This isn't a bad thing. It's a blessing to have the opportunity to get a new perspective on my life. I don't want any special or long drawn out good-byes. Look at it on the bright side; you have a good reason to come to Dallas at least once or twice a year for a CLEAR meeting," Cecily said fighting back tears, but losing the battle. Then she turned to her closest friend, Gloria, and said, "You understand don't you?" Gloria's answer was grabbing Cecily and holding her in a way that said she was free to begin a new life in Texas. When Gloria released her hold, they all exhaled and let go of any hurt to make room for the happiness they felt for her and her son. Of course, they all cried and hugged Cecil individually. But she couldn't leave like this. Not just walk out of their lives after all the time they had spent together.

"Cecily, I heard what you said about not making a big to-do out of your leaving, but isn't there something small we could do? Today? Tomorrow? Something? Anything?" Sara asked with no disrespect.

"Well, there is one thing I wanted to do before I left Chicago and the only time I can do it is this evening. I've followed the WNBA since it first started. It would be a shame for me to leave and not get a chance to see my hometown girls in action on their own home court. There's a game today at five o'clock if anybody else is interested?"

"Count me in," Sara said, followed by the other women. So they stayed at Serena's house and began to celebrate. Then they piled into two cars and headed to the UIC Pavilion to cheer on the Chicago Sky.

At the game, the ladies felt free to behave like a group of teenagers, something they needed to do in order to handle this loss. They treated Cecily to everything she wanted and they wanted her to have, including Sky T-shirts, basketball jerseys, mugs, hats, posters, and all the hotdogs, chicken fingers, and popcorn she could eat. Three of them bought disposable cameras and took all kinds of pictures, mostly of them, managing to get in a few of the Sky players. In Cecily's honor the team defeated the Los Angeles Sparks in a hard-fought close contest.

Nia returned to her usual playful self as she zeroed in on a nice looking police officer at the door as they were leaving. She immediately went into her flirtatious mode and struck up a conversation with him.

"Nia we're going to leave you if you don't come on now!" shouted Erin, the mother figure. Nia just flipped her hand their way as if she knew they would wait. She was right.

"Let her have fun. She needs it like we all do. Besides, Sara and I got our flirting done on Thursday," said Gloria, who was still feeling the pain of Cecily's announcement.

"Gloria's right. I'll stay and wait for Nia to find fault in that man too and walk away. The rest of you can go ahead home," Sara said, knowing Nia's habits when first meeting a man. And that's how Sara said good-bye to Cecily. A quick hug and off she went with Erin and Serena. Taylor lingered behind with Sara and Gloria, hoping Nia's excitement about this man would help erase some of her pain. So while Nia continued to engage in what appeared to be a very animated conversation, the other three were off to the side, passing time.

"Sara, are you still praying and fasting like I am?" Taylor asked.

"Definitely! Even more now than before."

"What are you two praying and fasting for? I hope it has to do with me living without sex like you two because I'm getting weaker by the day," responded Gloria.

"Hang in there, Gloria. We're proud of you. Remember the 'good 'n faithful servant' points. You can earn them too. You aren't giving thought to hooking up with Zach, are you?" Sara teasingly inquired.

"Zach, absolutely no way. But Jonathan, that's something to think about! Girl, the Lord owes you some major 'good 'n faithful servant' points for not being all over that man by now. I still don't know how you do it. Sara, you have to admit, he's hot!"

"It's easier when you make Jesus your number one priority. Now I won't lie and say I haven't had some serious thoughts about him. *Visualizing* is what I call it. But I know better than to act on it. I've even had to back away from kissing him so passionately. That can get you in trouble also. Remember, I've been there, did that, and I have no desire to go back there again. I stand my ground on that fact!" Sara said, all kidding aside.

"Bravo, Sara," Taylor said.

"I still say the Lord would have scolded me at least once or twice by now and probably deducted a few points," Gloria said, shaking her head and grinning.

"You're one of the reasons we pray and fast on Mondays from midnight until six in the evening," Sara replied.

"Well, if it will help, count me in too!" Gloria sighed.

"Hallelujah!" shouted Taylor. "Sara, I'm proud of how you put the men in your life in perspective. I mean to walk away from a man like Marcus, and now Jonathan. You must come and talk to the Roses one of these days. There are some girls in the group who don't believe women like you exist."

"Where do you know Marcus Richardson from?" Gloria asked Taylor.

"We ran into him at my nephew's birthday party. So you know him too?"

"Yes, who doesn't know Lieutenant Richardson? He's got a reputation as a serious womanizer, but that hasn't stopped women from chasing after that man. I'll admit, he is something to look at, but that's all I'll do, look but don't touch."

"If only I could have been that smart years ago, then I wouldn't have been one of his many bed partners," Sara ignominiously whispered.

"But the good thing, Sara, is that was some time ago. You got away and have stayed away. Back then, his antics were not as well-known as they are today. And that young thing he's with now can't touch you with a ten- foot pole," testified Gloria, comforting her friend.

"Amen to that!" shouted Taylor, applauding.

"Who's preaching the Gospel over here?" asked Nia joining them.

"So did you get his name, number, and a date for next week?" Gloria spoke first.

"Nope, he's not my type. Are you ready to go or is the sermon not over yet?" That's the Nia they all knew and loved!

Ahhhhhh, this felt good! Laying her head back she sank down into a warm, lavender bubble bath, cherishing the peace and quiet of this Saturday evening. With Chana playing host to the children and Jonathan being in his private world, Sara was looking forward to climbing into bed long before midnight. When she felt water in her nostrils, realizing she had drifted off to sleep, she jumped up, dried off, and retired to her comfortable bed.

Startled by the phone ringing, interrupting her much needed sleep, she sat up and looked at the digital display on the clock. 3:10 is what she saw. Who's calling her at this early hour? *Or worse, what's wrong? Who's in trouble?*

"Sara, Bradley's in trouble and he left me," sobbed a barely audible Krista.

"What? Krista, what did you say?"

"Bradley left me," she cried harder and louder. "He's in some kind of trouble. He walked out on me and the girls for another woman and his son. Sara, Bradley has a son! He's gone Sara. What am I going to do?"

"Krista, I'm on my way. Everything's going to be alright!" *Lord, help,* she prayed.

Chapter 12

*Sunday, June 3*rd

Early Sunday morning, the sun shined its bright face and rocketed its rays on the rain-soaked area. Signs of recent torrential rains where slowly disappearing. Dry were the puddles in the grass that had suspended ball playing. Dry were the standing waters that had splashed havoc on pedestrians scampering from place to place. Sprightly activities of those who were confined indoors would soon be in motion.

Dry was not the face of Krista Cunningham, as an endless stream of tears kept pouring down from her eyes. The eight o'clock hour was upon their sleepless souls. For most of the morning, Sara had kept quiet as her arms, surrounding her friend's grieving body, was all the comfort she could provide. Throughout the early morning hours, Krista cursed Bradley in one breath and cried how much she loved him in the next. She hated the woman who gave birth to his son, knowing only that her first name was Teena. In her anger and broken-heartedness, she anathematized Adrian, the innocent victim of adulterous behavior. "How dare she name that bastard child after my husband?" she cried. Sara had already learned that his full name was Adrian Bradley Taylor Cunningham.

Sara was speechless, the way she wanted to be, since there didn't seem to be any words that would bring comfort to this situation. The one thing Sara knew she had to do was not reveal to Krista her knowledge of her husband's infidelity. Although she was upset with Bradley, she knew it was not her place to pass judgment on him or Teena. But pure human nature couldn't understand why Teena, a Christian woman, turned a defiant head to her upbringing, and allowed this to happen, much to her family's chagrin. Based on her own experience, Sara wondered why Teena didn't have the strength to walk away from a relationship with a married man. How could she settle for being the other woman all this time. Teena hadn't asked God for deliverance because, surely, if He did it for Sara, He would have done it for her.

"Krista, let me call Chana so he won't be looking for me this morning. Maybe he should keep the girls until later today while you get yourself together. You don't want them to see you in this state, do you?" Sara finally asked, breaking her long silence.

"No, but what do I tell my babies? They think the world of their daddy and are too young to understand the truth," Krista sobbed.

"I know they do because he really loves those girls... like a father should." Sara started to say, with all of his heart, but now he shares some of his fatherly heart with his son, as he should, but refrained. "You know Chana always knows what to do in every situation we've been in and sought his help. Today won't be any different."

Chana answered the phone after the first ring. Sara briefed him on the call and he took charge. She handed the phone to Krista and he assured her he would be by her side for as long as and whatever she needed. They both had come to know and expect that of him. Chana had a peace and calmness about himself that led Sara to believe he had prepared for this day

194

to come. She didn't know what, if anything, could have spared her from sharing the hurt that had overcome her best girlfriend. Sara just wished there was something more she could do to help erase her pain. Time! She knew for a fact that as hours passed into days and weeks into months, the healing process would turn this into less of a current event and more like a thing of the past.

Sara persuaded Krista to take a shower and let the pulsating hot water soothe her muscles, providing a bit of relief and comfort. Also, it would give Sara a chance to shut her eyes for a few minutes. No sooner had Krista stepped into the bathroom than Sara thought about Jonathan. She hadn't talked to him since Friday evening and a lot had happened over the past thirty-plus hours. She tried his cell phone, only to get his voice mail. With a little disappointment, she left a message that she needed to see him today if possible, emphasizing that she missed him, even more than before.

Once Krista was out of the shower and back in the family room where they had spent the night, Sara lost the battle with sleep. It was the doorbell that got her out of a dismal slumber.

Chana must have made a quick dash for the door as soon as the benediction was said. He entered the house and tightly embraced their distraught friend, who still had more sobs to release. Unhurried and poised he let her unburden the soul that was overcome with grief. Gradually, she was cognizant enough to inquire about the girls. "They're just fine. Olivia is treating her nephews and the girls to dinner and a movie. We're enjoying their company and they can stay as long as you'd like." Turning his attention to Sara, he asked, "How are you, sleepyhead?" A shrug in between yawns was her response.

Krista, picked up a large yellow envelope from the coffee table and handed it to Chana. "He gave this to me before he left. Bradley said he's in some kind of trouble, but really I couldn't concentrate on that. All I remember him saying was he had to leave and he was taking his son and his baby's momma with him. He had the audacity to say he still loves me and the girls. How could he love us and them too?" she cried on.

Chana examined the contents of the envelope. It was the deed to the house in Krista's name along with the title to the minivan. Also inside was a large sum of money, exactly how much they didn't know at the time. "Well, Krista, the house and minivan are yours, paid in full. I guess this money will help you out for a while, a peace offering of sorts."

"I don't want to think about these material things now. I don't know what to tell my babies. He's going to miss their tenth birthday," Krista cried shedding more tears.

"We'll keep everything as normal for them as possible, including their birthday celebration. Who knows? Maybe Bradley will come to his senses and find his way back home by then. But, in the event that he doesn't, let's just tell the girls that he's sick and had to go away to get well," Chana replied.

"Well, that's not too far from the truth. He's sick, that's for sure," Sara venomously mumbled.

"What kind of trouble do you think he's in?" Krista asked regaining some composure.

Chana took a deep breath then began to tell them what he knew about Bradley's part-time employment. "I've always had my suspicions about Bradley's income, but it wasn't my place to question him. I looked up his name among lottery winners and never found it. Then I started hearing some things about that company he works for at night. This private carrier service has been investigated for trafficking drugs and stolen goods like laptops, cell phones, and MP3 players. Recently, there have been rumors about a sex ring involving minors and the company's owner. This man lives in a multimillion dollar mansion somewhere south of Crete. Anyway, my speculation is that Bradley has been involved with moving drugs and hot items around, or even outside of, the state."

A shocked Krista spoke up. "No, I can't believe my husband was trafficking drugs all this time and I didn't know anything about it. He's not that crazy to be doing something that could bring harm to me and the girls. I don't believe you!"

Sara continued her silence. "Krista, you were blinded by love and maybe you didn't want to know the truth. He was gone numerous times a week. Have you ever seen a checkbook or a check from this company? Did he do most of his financial business with cash? You live in a house that's worth well over a half million dollars and both of you drive new expensive cars every few years. A legitimate carrier worker, even with a second job, probably makes about fifty thousand dollars a year. You have always lived

197

on a whole lot more than that," Chana explained.

"To tell you the truth, I have no idea how much money Bradley makes. Our accountant handles the finances and I just take care of him and the girls. It's always been that way. I just put my trust in him, knowing that this is how it would be forever. Yeah, I did complain that he wasn't around enough at night, but I never thought he was keeping another family and definitely not involved with drugs. Am I that big of a fool?" she shamefully sobbed.

"No, you aren't anybody's fool. You were being the submissive, loving wife God wants you to be. Unfortunately, you were deceived by a man who isa conniving charmer. However, there's no excuse for what he did, the way he made his money and his relationship with Teena." Chana got quiet for a few seconds, but it seemed like a lot longer.

"How did you know her name?" Krista asked.

"I'll be totally honest with you." Chana hesitated, but knew he had to be truthful since he just let the cat out of the bag. "I've known about Teena and Adrian for some time now and he never denied it."

"You've known all this time and never told me?" she shouted. "And I guess you've known about this too?" she directed her anger at Sara.

"No Krista, I never mentioned a word to Sara. It wasn't my place to tell her or you, even though you probably wouldn't have believed me anyway."

"Chana is telling the truth. He never told me anything about your husband. Krista, could I have kept something like that away from you?"

Sara said, hoping to drop this part of the conversation.

"I guess you're right because I can get you to tell me anything I want to know," she said, which was partially true.

"Krista, I don't believe you and the girls are in any danger and you've got plenty of time to decide where you go from here. Maybe he'll be back soon after he realizes what he left behind," Chana said, spoken like a man of men.

"I don't know if I could take him back after all this," Krista said.

"Although you have all the love and support we can give, you really need to have the Lord in your life, especially now. He's the only one who can see you through this or restore your marriage. Look at your girl over there. She's happily living a life rich with people who love her and is actively involved with meaningful events. You don't see her obsessing over the fact that she's not married, yet."

"I may be sleepy, but I heard you throw the word 'yet' in that sentence," Sara wearily spoke up, partially smiling.

As the three of them entered into a third hour of dialogue, it was really a two-way discussion. Their voices were heard, but Sara couldn't make out a thing that was said. She was fading back to a sleep that wouldn't be long enough. The ringing doorbell and happy voices of Autumn and April had awaken her. In reality, she had slept for about two hours

"Hi, mommy," they sang as they bolted into the room and bounced on the couch, hugging and kissing her. "Where's daddy?" was the next thing out of their innocent young mouths. Not waiting for an answer Autumn joined Sara in the recliner. "Hi, Auntie Sara. Were you asleep?"

"No, sweetie, just napping a little," she said, trying to regain full consciousness.

"You look like you could use some coffee," said Chana as Olivia took a seat next to him in the family room.

"Yeah, it'll help," Sara responded trying to get out of the chair.

"I'll get it. You just sit there and relax," Olivia, said heading into the kitchen.

The twins were busy telling Krista about all of their activities over the weekend between Sara's house and the Nash residence. Autumn, the more outgoing of the two, did most of the talking. April chimed in if her sister left out any detail. They were now on Sunday's events when Olivia returned with a fresh pot of coffee and cups for the adults. After a little more small talk, the girls came back to their first question which had still not been answered. "Where's daddy?" April spoke up again. "Yeah," said Autumn, "how come daddy's not here with all of us?"

There was silence in the room as all eyes shifted towards Krista. Even she knew the time had come to face the music. But she didn't seem prepared to sing. Their mother wanted to be strong and convincing as she told her daughters that their daddy may not be coming home, for a very longtime. She opened her mouth and tried to speak, but words eluded her and emotions began to take over. Her rapid eye blinking was her effort to ward off tears, but she was losing the battle. Even more unnerving was the look of concern on the faces of the twins. Not wanting to upset them more than they would already suffer, Chana stepped in and took over for her.

"Come here, girls, and sit next to your Uncle," he instructed them, each one happy to oblige, taking a seat on his knees. "Your daddy had to go away because he's kind of sick and he needs to be in a special place where he can get the help he needs."

"Is he in a hospital?" inquired a saddened April.

"Something like that," Chana replied.

"Can we go visit him?" she said.

"Not right now. It might be a while before he's well enough to have any visitors."

"I'm scared and I miss my daddy already," cried Autumn.

"Don't be scared, girls. I know your daddy wants you to do the things you do every day. He loves you very much and he'll miss you too. Remember what Rev. Stevens said today at church about how we should pray for others. That's exactly what you should do every night before you go to bed. Ask God to help your daddy get better so that all of you might be together again real soon. In the meantime, if either of you need anything, and I mean anything at all, you just call Uncle Chana and I'll be here before you can snap your fingers," he said while snapping a finger on each hand. The girls imitated him and he smiled and said, "Yeah, just like that."

Chana's gesture seemed to bring a little comfort to all the Cunningham ladies as each one managed to display the slightest smile on her face. "You know Aunt Olivia and I love you very much," he said squeezing them tighter in his arms.

"Yeeeesss," they sang, planting kisses on his cheeks.

Krista had regained control of herself and told the girls to get ready for bed since they had a busy weekend. The twins were not the only ones who wanted to get ready for bed. Sara sipped the rest of her coffee and started preparing herself mentally for the twenty-five minute drive home. The other three were engaged in a discussion that also included the girls birthday at the end of the week. All Sara knew was she was volunteered to help chaperone a sleepover for about a dozen girls, which she would have had no objections to, even if she did know what they were talking about. One thing for certain, she was ready to go back to her quiet haven where her bed was beckoning.

"Sara, would you like for Olivia and I to take you home?" asked an observant Chana.

"No, thanks, I'm alert enough to find my way home in the few minutes of daylight that's left," she replied, moving out of the chair.

"Sara, I'm sorry I took up your entire day, but...,"

"Honey, please, you know you don't even need to go there with me," Sara interrupted Krista. "Kiss the girls for me and I'll talk to you tomorrow."

"We'll walk out with you, Sara. Krista, you know I'm just a phone call away if you need anything, and don't hesitate, no matter what time it is," Chana said.

"The same goes for me too, Krista," said Olivia with a hug.

"Thanks, you guys. I don't know what I'd do without you," Krista said.

"And you'll never have to worry about finding out," Sara responded with a final hug for the night.

It was about nine o'clock when Sara arrived home that evening. The message indicator light on her phone was blinking. She immediately thought about the message she had left for Jonathan earlier in the day. Dropping her handbag and kicking off her shoes, she listened to the callers.

Hey, baby. Got your message and it sounds like there's something going on. I'll try you on your cell. I've missed you all weekend.

Jonathan! Her cell phone was still turned off.

Hey, sweetie, I tried your cell but it went straight to voicemail. Call me as soon as you get this message. I've missed you and now I'm just a little concerned about you.

The last thing she wanted to do was make him worry about her. She'd call him immediately.

Sara, it's Taylor. Teena and Adrian are gone! They just left sometime over the past few days without saying good-bye or where they were going. Sara, they're gone! Call me, please.

The last tearful message didn't come as a surprise in light of spending the past eighteen emotionally draining hours with Krista. So before she picked up the phone, she called upon the Lord to provide her with the mental strength to offer comfort to her dear friend. Sara was reminded of when Rev. Stevens told them to remember Joshua 1:9 in their time of weakness and despair: *This is my command—be strong and courageous! Do not be afraid or discouraged. For the* LORD *your God is with you wherever you go.* With a deep breath, Sara telephoned Taylor and was caught a little off guard because she sounded like her usual poised and confident self.

"Thanks for returning my call, Sara. I'm sorry if I sounded so distraught, but that's how I was feeling earlier. Jeremiah has been here with me, praying and reading scriptures. Although I'm still saddened from not knowing where they are, I've got a peace knowing that God is with them and they're in the best hands possible."

"You probably have an idea that Bradley is with them, don't you?" Sara said as a comforting fact.

"I assumed he might have had something to do with their sudden disappearance. Does this means he's not with his wife and daughters?"

"Unfortunately, yes! I just left a very bewildered and hurt Krista. He told her everything before he walked out last night. Now, Taylor, I'm even more committed to praying and fasting because we all need the Lord's help to get through this madness."

"Jeremiah suggested we have a special prayer session. How does that sound to you?"

"I'll be the first one there. Say goodnight to Rev. J.C. for me. Taylor, you, Teena and Adrian are in my prayers."

"My prayers are with Krista and the girls too. Thanks Sara and goodnight to you."

Now that phone call had a soothing and calming effect so that she could now get back in touch with Jonathan. Sara had forgotten she turned off her cell phone so she could devote all her time to Krista. Now she definitely needed some of Jonathan's time. Dragging her weary self into the bedroom, she flopped onto the bed with phone in hand. It was truly a pleasure to hear his voice after the first incomplete ring.

"Hello, sweetie. I thought I'd have to send a posse out after you. Where have you been and what's going on? There was a sense of urgency in your voice," he said with some anguish in his.

"Good evening, Jonathan. I'm sorry for just getting back with you but this has been a weekend like none before."

"I can be there in less than thirty minutes if you want my company?"

"Thanks for the offer, but I'll be asleep before you get here and that's what I really need right now. I'll just briefly fill you in on the last forty-eight hours." Sara spent the next few minutes giving him the highlights. All he kept saying in between sentences was, "What? What?" When she finished the weekend in review, the other end of the line was silent. "Jonathan, are you still there?"

"Yes, baby, I'm still here. I'm in a state of shock! Why didn't you call me sooner? You know I'm here for you."

"I know, Jonathan, but everything happened so fast, it was like putting out fires the entire weekend. If there was something you could have done, I would not have hesitated to call for help. But the truth is there was very little I could do myself. Now I just want to get some sleep."

"I hear you, baby. Hey, let me cook dinner for you tomorrow and help you take your mind off of things, at least for a night?"

"I can't wait to get another glimpse into your world and taste your home cooking."

"Don't set your taste buds too high. I'm no great chef."

"Jonathan, whatever you fix will be highly appreciated. I'm already looking forward to just spending some quiet, unemotional time with you."

"Good, then I'll expect you around five o'clock."

"Make it six when my fasting is over. Thanks for your concern, and by the way, I missed you too these past few days."

"If you need me for anything, I'm just a telephone call away. But remember to have yours turned on."

"Okay, I'll remember. Good night," Sara whispered with a genuine smile that had been absent the past two days.

Chapter 13

<u>Monday, June 4th</u>

Monday morning arrived too soon, but Sara managed to roll out of bed and began with a reading from her daily devotional. During the summer her company faced slow periods and most overtime was cancelled. Occasionally, they were dismissed early, to most of the employees' approval. She asked God to let this be one of those days. He answered her prayers.

Sara had been visualizing her dinner date all day. She still had four more hours of fasting so she took a long walk in the forest preserve mainly to help calm her nerves. She was almost as excited as a first dream date. Even when she returned, butterflies were fluttering in her stomach while she was deciding what to wear, practically emptying her summer wardrobe on the bed. She modeled in the mirror skirts, pants, dresses, capris', and anything else she could put together. Finally she settled on a colorful crinkled floor- length skirt with a lime green tank top. Selecting the jewelry added fifteen minutes to the process. After she opened the eighth box, a white seashell necklace and earrings set, purchased on a Caribbean cruise, completed the ensemble. So she retreated to a twenty-minute lavender bubble bath and a fifteen minute power nap.

Sara made one detour stop before arriving at Jonathan's Bronzeville two-flat, fifteen minutes fashionably late. "Well, you were most definitely worth the wait. You look, smell, and feel absolutely beautiful," Jonathan said as he greeted her at his front door with a big bear hug.

"Hello, Jonathan. It's so good to see you. Thanks again for the dinner invitation. I can use a little relaxation and some good food right about now. And to show my appreciation, this is for you," she handed him a small potted Fern she had picked up at the garden center. The look of surprise and smile on his face followed by the kiss he planted on her lips was his way of saying thank you. It was a change to see the usually panache man dressed down in jeans and a White Sox jersey. But he looked out of place in his own home.

Jonathan's house was as clean and appealing inside as it was outside. Sara was pleasantly surprised at the cleanliness and color coordination that greeted her entering the living room from the foyer. The warm earth tones were present from the floor to the ceiling. The adjoining dining room featured a large, maple-colored china cabinet with matching table and chairs. She admitted to herself that she was very impressed and a bit curious.

"So, if I may ask, who's your interior decorator and housekeeper?"

"What, you don't think I'm capable of designing and maintaining my own home?" he responded trying to keep a straight face.

"I don't mean to insult you, but this is quite immaculate, especially for a busy single man such as yourself. So, what's your secret?" she insisted.

"Alright, I can't take the credit. Mrs. Robinson, the tenant upstairs, is a neat freak and she insist, I be one too. She's been cleaning my house and taking care of the landscaping since I moved in here and rehabbed the building after my breakup. I could probably make another three hundred dollars in rent each month if I didn't have to compensate Mrs. Robinson for all of her hard work. I even tried to convince her that I'd be happy with her cleaning this place once a month, but we compromised on every other week. As you can tell, she's worth every penny. You wouldn't believe there are five people who live upstairs as well kept and quiet as it is. Her daughter and three grandchildren moved in three years ago, but you can practically eat off the floor. They are tenants from heaven. As far as the interior, I have to give accolades to my two sisters. The dining room set belonged to Rebecca back when she was living with this guy we all thought would be her husband. After they broke, up she gave away or sold all of her furniture and started over again when she bought her downtown condo. So I inherited this set. And since I don't have any china, this cabinet serves as my bar. Can I offer you a drink?"

"I'll have a glass of Chardonnay, thank you very much."

After he handed her the wine and fixed a scotch on the rocks for himself, he continued to give her a tour of the three bedrooms, two baths, and eat-in kitchen. Each room had its own color scheme and did not have as much as a piece of string out of place. One bedroom had a feminine tone, probably the one Jasmine used. The other served as an office. His bedroom was all male; black, maroon, and a hint of grey. Mrs. Robinson did her landlord a tremendous favor.

Jonathan tuned the television to a jazz station where it could be heard just above a whisper as they engaged in small talk while he worked his majestic hands in the kitchen and on the grill in the backyard. Sara's job was to sit back and relax, which she happily did. As an added gesture of comfort, Jonathan came into the living room, removed her sandals and placed her feet up, elongating her position on the couch. He refilled her wineglass and with a soft forehead kiss, he whispered, "This is your evening."

Sara felt she had found heaven in Bronzeville as she closed her eyes and *visualized!* She must have relaxed herself into a little nap because the sound of the doorbell jolted her back to the present. But before Jonathan made his way to the door, the visitor had opened it and proceeded to walk in.

"Hey, Nate, where are you, man?" hollered the male visitor who was now standing in the living room.

"Hey, Deacon. What's up man?" Jonathan returned the greeting. Noticing Sara on the couch, the man smiled with a nod of his head.

"Sorry to be interrupting. I didn't know you had company."

"Sara, meet a long-time friend, Matt Jones, also known as Deacon. Deacon, please meet a very good and, as you can see, beautiful lady friend of mine, Sara Deyton." Deacon came over and shook her hand then kissed the back of it, something all the men associated with Jonathan were in the habit of doing.

"Ms. Deyton, it's definitely my pleasure to make your acquaintance. I consider any friend of this man's to be my friend too. Deacon at your service," he said while taking a quick bow. The attention and flattery was going to her head and she was loving it.

"I'm making dinner for the lady tonight."

"You're cooking? It must be love. Don't kill her, man. In all the years I've known Nate, he's a great guy, but I've never known him to do anything in the kitchen except eat," said the risible Deacon, giving them all something to laugh about.

"Alright, man, get out," Jonathan said while giving him a playful shove towards the door. "Sweetie, continue to relax. I'll be back in a few minutes. And stay out of my kitchen!" he ordered.

Sara waved good bye to Deacon and obeyed Jonathan's command, quickly getting back into the mellow sounds of smooth jazz. In just the hour that she had been there, the surreal perfection of the evening was almost scary. However, she needed to free her mind of any complicated thoughts and take the evening minute by minute. The past several days had over taxed her brain and she could use the downtime. With the soft music, wine, and ambiance that was straight out of a Lifetime movie, it didn't take long for her to drift back into a nap.

She didn't know how long Jonathan had been outside talking to Deacon, but once again, the front door aroused her to consciousness. Jonathan came over to the couch, asked if she was enjoying herself and needed a refill. She politely replied yes and no. As soon as he made his way back to the kitchen, Sara heard him yell an all too familiar expression, "Oh, no!" followed by the slamming of the back door. Being slightly amused, she looked out of the kitchen window to witness him standing over flames shooting up from the grill amidst a billow of smoke. It didn't look good for the food he had placed on the rack prior to his visitor's arrival. After smothering the fire, he placed the top back on the grill and headed inside while Sara scurried to reposition herself on the couch. Clanging a pot on the stove, the first words out of his mouth, were a little harsher than his first exclamation, all to her delight.

"Baby, I'm so sorry about dinner. All I have been able to salvage is a tossed salad. Where would you like to go tonight?" asked the defeated cook.

"Nowhere. Just the fact that you put forth the effort for me is greatly appreciated."

"You're just being nice. Let me at least order something to go with the salad," he sighed. After several suggestions and looking over a variety of take-out menus, they agreed to some barbecue grilled chicken wings from a local carry out. Although this wasn't exactly what he planned, they dined sufficiently, picnic style, on a blanket in the living room. After some entertaining small talk, he laid his head on her lap, stretched out on the floor, then put the spotlight on her.

"Now, Sara, it's my turn to hear all about you. And the same rule applies. You can tell me as little or as much as you want, just be honest," Jonathan said as he closed his eyes and with a slight smile, waited for her monologue.

Sara spent a few minutes telling him about her modest upbringing in a blue-collar family from a blue-collar town although she knew he was more interested in her adult years. But this was the ice breaker, as she massaged his scalp and twirled his twisted hair with her fingers. She fast forwarded to meeting Krista in college and moving to the Chicago area after graduation when she met Chana. "I was ready to take the corporate world by storm, dreaming of becoming an executive all the while being married to Mr. Wonderful with two adorable children. Well, I never met this imaginary husband and after working for two different Fortune 500 companies for almost twenty years I was laid off and here I am today a quality control inspector. But a good one I might add. I also suffered financially taking a big reduction in pay. Chana's business sense helped me budget and live comfortably based on my new income. I've adjusted and my life is still as rewarding as it was back in the high income pay days." She paused to sip some ice water and let him absorb her history so far. This didn't seem to faze him and it still wasn't what he wanted to hear so he opened the door into her private life.

"Why has it been so hard for you to meet your Mr. Wonderful?"

"When I was younger, I made a lot of mistakes when it came to men. I watched some of my good friends and family members go in and out of marriages and I thought I'd shield myself from those aches and pains by staying single. So for a period of about three years, I was out there, playing, partying and having fun. Not taking anyone or anything serious. I thought I was really living the good life. That lasted until I had a false pregnancy at twenty-seven, honestly not knowing which of these two guys could have been the father. One of them

213

dashed immediately. The other one stayed around long enough to find out there was no baby. After that awakening, we agreed to go our separate ways. Now I had grown tired of the emptiness I felt from the hit and run type relationships and retreated from that hollow lifestyle. Unfortunately, at age thirty I met a married man who said all the right things I wanted to hear and did all the right things I wanted him to do. For two years, I held on to a false hope that one day he would be mine, when in fact, I was just the other woman. When I finally walked away, it took almost as long for my heart to get over my love for him. Or at least that's what I thought it was." She sipped more water then, continued. "I had visited Rosebrook many times because Chana was a member when I met him. He often extended invitations to become a part of this contemporary ministry. Their emphasis on Bible study and prayer grabbed my interest and reminded me of my family's church. There I made a commitment to God that I would live a single, celibate life until my wedding day, if that's in the grand plan for me. For the past ten years, I've been happy, satisfied and sex-free." At this point, she stopped to fumble with her glass of ice water and see what kind of reaction she'd get. He appeared to be really engaged in what she was saying and didn't flinch a muscle.

"You make it sound so easy, like you've never even been tempted to be intimately pleased by a man since then," Jonathan spoke up.

"Ooooh, trust me, this is by far not an easy walk. Yes, I've had to overcome the lure of human nature for some momentary

214

gratification. So much of our society glorifies sex and tries to make it seem like abstinence is a thing of the past. The Christian community is constantly under attack on this issue, with our young people and adults as well. I have stayed grounded through my involvement at Rosebrook, with my CLEAR sisters, and daily devotionals. By faith, I stay focused on my commitment and the promises of His blessings." Once again, she used her glass of water to give him a chance to digest these words.

"I admire your ability to resist men coming on to you as I'm sure some guys have. If I had my way, we would have made love a long time ago. You know I have strong feelings for you? Not to brag, but most women I have met gave it up rather easily, including the sisters who were shouting and singing the loudest at church on Sunday morning and shouting and singing a different tune with me Sunday night," he remarked .

So this is what he's doing on some of those out of town business trips. Sara don't start tripping now! "Jonathan, there are people who go to church and people who do church. And there are those who don't block blessings and strive to keep them coming. The price we pay for being faithful is that we move in a different direction from the secular world. There have been men I've met at Rosebrook over the years that tried to get me in their bed. One man even commented that he can't believe I gave up sex. I vividly recall the look on his face when he practically shouted, 'For what?' He scored with several women then moved on someplace else. Maybe he's even gone to another denomination to see if the sex is different among Baptist,

215

Methodist, or Catholic women; who knows. Regardless, I'm trying to earn all the 'good 'n faithful servants' points I can get," she added with a smile. "And I'm very proud of it!"

"I can believe that," he said, amused while taking her right hand and laying a soft kiss on her fingertips. "Whatever happened to your married ex-lover?" That question caught her a little off guard, but she would be honest and say little.

"I have crossed paths with him from time to time, but there are no more feelings between the two of us. We've both moved on with our lives." And that was the truth.

"Do you ever see yourself getting married?" *Another unexpected question from the man I thought may have been God sent. Now I think I know the answer to that.*

"I don't know what tomorrow holds, nor will I attempt to guess or try to make things happen. I'm just going to keep living life to its fullest, one day at a time," Sara confidently replied.

"I see. It sounds to me like you aren't ruling out any possibilities. Maybe you've already met him and just don't know yet. Timing; maybe the time has not come for Mr. Wonderful to be revealed," was his final remark.

As if on cue, the doorbell rang for a second time that evening. Sara sighed a small breath of relief, although the things he said made her raise an eyebrow. *Leave it alone, Sara!*

Whoever was at the door, Jonathan did not let them enter the apartment. Instead, he excused himself and stepped outside with this visitor. It was now past eleven o'clock so she was preparing to bring this night to an end when her host returned, apologizing for the interruption. "Sara, I'd never do anything that you didn't want to do so don't take this to be anything but honorable. You are welcome to stay here in one of the spare bedrooms if you don't want to travel home tonight or any night you come into the city," he said with sincerity as he embraced her with a gentle hug. However, she knew better than to put herself in a position where the flesh could easily overpower the sense of knowing right from wrong.

"Thank you for the offer, and I know you would be nothing but a gentleman, but, I'll be fine driving home," she said, giving him a quick peck on his lips. "And by the way, you make a great tossed salad," she teased.

"Thank you for your honesty tonight and being a much welcomed guest. Now, after today, I no longer consider you a visitor and you're welcome anytime. I'd love for you to meet Mrs. Robinson, and my other sister can't wait to meet you either. Call me as soon as you get home so I can sleep in peace," he replied, walking her to the car.

The midnight hour had already struck when Sara returned home. As requested, she called Jonathan to signal her safe arrival. The sublime evening was not over for her yet. She sat on the couch for what could have been minutes or maybe hours, smiling and replaying segments of the conversation they had earlier. She certainly would not rule out any possibilities as long as he was still in the picture. Jonathan could be her planned husband, yet to be revealed. Timing is everything, isn't it?

Chapter 14

Thursday, June 14th

Sara was seemingly enjoying her day at work that Thursday. That's usually how she was when the quality control audits were at standard or above. She was making small talk with her fellow employees while congratulating them on a job well done.

"Sara, was that announcement a gift from heaven or what?" asked another happy coworker.

"You can say that again. I'm planning to take full advantage of it. I'm not sure what I'll do but I know it won't have anything to do with work," she replied.

They were referring to the announcement that had come across the manufacturing floor after lunch. Due to the slowdown in business over the past few weeks, production for tomorrow was cancelled and they had the day off. Cheers and hand claps rose from the employees as they seemed to welcome a three-day weekend, even at a last minute notice. Within half an hour, the work area was cleaned and they were dismissed for the day.

Driving home, Sara was trying to decide what she'd do with her free day. Although they would not be paid for the time off, she learned to adjust her expenses to meet the shorter paychecks. She had never been a frivolous spender even back in the corporate management days when her annual salary with bonuses and benefits easily topped one hundred grand. But now that she was doing good to earn a third as much with overtime, she now enjoyed more of the free and simpler offerings. She was happily considering her options for tomorrow. Prior to arriving home she stopped at a costume jewelry store and bought the twins a pair of earrings and matching necklace for their birthday celebration on Saturday. The gem was a replica of a pearl, their birthstone.

Still mulling over how tomorrow would be spent, she stepped inside her safe haven with a joyous pep in every movement. After grabbing a Diet Pepsi to drink with the soft pretzel purchased at the strip mall, the blinking light on the telephone caught her attention.

Hey, baby. It's me. Just wanted to let you know that Johnny and I decided to drive to New York and spend the weekend with Jasmine. We haven't seen her in over a year and I miss my baby girl. Johnny misses her too, although he won't admit it. Anyway, we're leaving early in the morning and I need to take care of a few things before I go. I'll miss you this weekend, but you have my permission to spend time with Trent if you want some company. I'll call as soon as I return.

Sara knew that was his way of making a joke, giving her permission to spend time with anyone, let alone her young neighbor. Her first instinct was to go through her PDA and find a male friend to share dinner and a movie with. However, not being one to engage in petty behavior, she just crossed Jonathan off the list of potential people and activities for Friday. The truth was her address book didn't contain one single man that she had any interest in spending time with, except Jonathan. *click, dial tone   silence...click, dial tone*

Telemarketing calls perhaps. There was a call she wanted to make so she hit the speed dial to Krista's house. Unfortunately, she had to settle for leaving a voicemail message. Knowing Krista didn't travel far from her cell phone that was her next attempt and they connected.

"What are my three favorite ladies doing this afternoon?" Sara asked.

"We're doing some shopping for the sleepover this weekend. I know I can't talk you into joining us at the mall and helping out, can I?"

"Of course not. You know me and malls; and with professionals like the three of you, I wouldn't survive long. Besides, I just came from a store picking up the girls' presents. What's on your schedule for tomorrow?"

"The girls are spending the day with Chana, Olivia, and their nephews. I'm taking my mother to see her doctor. She was fortunate they had a cancellation, but you never know how long that could take. I told you she hasn't been herself lately, always tired and just not feeling well. So I'm determined to find out what's wrong with Nola White. What's on your plate other than work?"

"Actually, we were given the day off so I was looking for someone to have fun with."

"Excuse me, but what about that handsome man who has rocked your world?" Krista inquired.

"He's going to visit his daughter in New York this weekend."

"That's why you should keep an updated little black book for times like this," she said with a giggle. Krista had an active black book back in her single days.

"Thank you, but no thank you for the advice," Sara said, taking her comment lightly. "If you need me before Saturday afternoon I'm just a call away."

With that phone call, Sara crossed five other people off her list for tomorrow. So instead of focusing on Friday, she knew she needed to take this opportunity to make the most of the rest of today. She donned her walking gear and headed to the paths of the nearby forest preserve. Here she found her sanctuary to clear her head and fill her lungs with some fresh air.

Two hours of calorie-burning walking rendered her guilt free while ordering a fried fish and shrimp dinner complete with French fries and slaw from a local fast food carry out. As an added treat, she couldn't resist the butter cookies in the glass counter that smelled and looked so inviting. *Live it up a little!,* she convinced herself.

While surfing the internet in the early evening, the ringing of the phone broke her concentration from a women's health and fitness website. Caller ID revealed this was an unexpected and unlikely caller.

"Hey, Sara. What's going on in your world?" asked a delightful Nia.

"Not much, Miss Nia. It's nice to hear your voice. You sound rather spirited today."

"I'm just trying to sound like you do most of the time, as if you live in Utopia."

"That's a nice compliment. But why are you trying? You can sound like you're a no-worries-be happy type person all the time. What's eating at you?"

"I don't know. I guess I'm just a little bored with work, tired of these worthless men I've been meeting, and doing the same ol' stuff in general," she replied with an indignation that signaled trouble in her world.

"Nia, you are definitely too young and have got too much going on to be bored with life. One thing I wish you would quit doing is spending so much valuable time focusing on men. You know you don't need a man to have meaning and purpose in your life."

"That's easy for you to say, Sara. You've got a good looking man to do things and go places with. You've got a good reason not to be bored and enjoying a good life."

"Nia, how long have you known me?"

"About three years," she answered.

"And when have you known me to complain about being bored with anything?"

"Okay, as usual, you made your point!" Nia said, laughing a little.

"By the way, Jonathan is out of town. What would it take for me to talk you into taking a day off and hanging out with me tomorrow?"

"It's a done deal. What are we going to do?" Nia asked with an uplifted voice.

"Leave it up to me. Just be ready in the morning for a fun filled ladies' day."

"Awesome, Sara. I trust you. Remember I like my men tall, handsome and rich," she playfully said, then clicked off.

Sara returned to the computer, hit a couple of local websites, spent an hour reading and jotting down a few notes, then smiled once again about the three day weekend she was looking forward to.

Friday, June 15th

Although she was awake at her usual early morning hour, Sara treated herself to lying in bed and watching her favorite cable political talk show. It also gave her a chance to see what the weather forecast was for the day she had planned. *Perfect!* Clear, sunny, temperatures in the mid-eighties, low humidity and no rain in sight. This was just what she needed to help lift Nia out of her state of boredom.

Sara could identify with Nia when she was in her twenties. As a college educated woman, she was trained to believe the world was hers to control. Being part of the first generation of post high school graduates in many African American families, all she heard growing up was if she finished college she would never have to worry about needing or wanting anything. She pictured in her mind that would mean a college educated husband and professional employment until the golden retirement age of sixty-two. They would have sent their two children to the college of their choice and spent work-free days traveling the world. *Right? Wrong!* Reality hit soon after the comfortable college days ended and the up and down roller coaster ride of life began. Sara accepted herself as a child of God, despite not having the family of her earlier dreams. Her contributions to Rosebrook as well as the community at large brought her much pleasure. Today, she wanted to aid Nia in finding her own Utopia.

Nia was in a much better mood than last night when Sara arrived. She did not badger Sara about their itinerary or if they were meeting up later with Mister tall, handsome, and rich. Instead, the ladies carried on small talk making their way through the last of the morning rush hour traffic, then existed the toll road at Oak Brook. Nia's eyes lit up like that of a child as she thought their first stop was the mall.

"Sara, I thought you were not much of a mall shopper?" she asked.

"You're right, I'm not, and we're not heading to the mall. However, our first stop is breakfast."

"Good. I'm hungry enough to eat for the both of us," Nia laughed. After they enjoyed a breakfast buffet at a local diner it was time for their adventure to begin. Nia still didn't ask any questions while Sara drove down York Road until she pulled into the parking lot of the Graue Mill and Museum.

"Sara, what is this place and why are we here?" The way Nia asked that question tickled Sara a little and she didn't try to hide it. Nia sounded like a school kid on a field trip.

"I take it you've never been here before?" Sara already knew the answer was no. She had mentioned this place once before in a CLEAR meeting.

"Not only have I not been here, but I don't think I've ever heard of this place."

"Well, Nia, one cure for the blues is to do something new and different, which is what we are about to embark on. Come on, we're going to live and learn a little about African American and Chicago history."

"I'll admit, this isn't my first pick for fun and games, but I'm open to something new."

Sara paid the small admission fee and opted for the self-guided tour. At first, Nia didn't approach the museum with much enthusiasm since it is mainly about a water mill and how it was used in the nineteenth century. As they looked at pictures and read the captions, she gave Sara a look as if to say, *I know I didn't miss a day of work for this.* But her attitude and the expression on her face changed when they came to the exhibit Sara was most interested in. The basement of the mill was used as a safe house for one of the stops along the Underground Railroad. The mill was one of several safe houses located in the western and northern suburbs of Chicago. The mill's owner, Fred Graue, was one of many white folks who secretly helped finance the freedom of many slaves in the United States.

As Sara and Nia slowly stepped down the creaky wooden stairs, stopping to view pictures and read the captions, they both began to get a feel of what their ancestors had to endure to gain their freedom. Something that was hard to imagine. Today, the basement was well lit and polished for visitors. The ladies seemed to cautiously descend the stairs even knowing that their coming down here was of their own fruition. They knew that soon they would be climbing the stairs to leave. However, the slaves had no choice but to hide in what was a cramped, dark, and damp cellar, waiting for the way to be safe before moving northwards. They studied the exhibit with a quiet and revered sense of pride.

Back upstairs, a volunteer demonstrated how corn meal was made by the giant water wheel, still operable today. A man who looked to be in his forties was quite inquisitive about the museum, engaging the workers and guests in questions and answers. Nia respectfully captivated his interest with more historical facts about slave days and the importance of places like these. He, along with others, were quite impressed and thanked her for the history lesson. One of the volunteers told her to make sure she came back in the fall for an Underground Railroad reenactment. Nia assured the woman she would put it on her list of things she must do.

Perusing the gift shop, Nia walked out after purchasing an apron, some candy, and a small bag of freshly ground corn meal.

"What are you going to do with those kitchen items?" Sara asked, amused. Like herself, Nia couldn't find her way around a kitchen without detailed instructions.

"I was so impressed, I had to buy something. I'll more than likely give this corn meal to a real cook. I can go for some candy any time. You know it's a weakness of mine."

Back at the car, Nia surprised Sara with a hug and thanks for an enriching experience. "I've heard about this safe house and others in DuPage county and have been meaning to visit them. Thanks for making that day finally happen." Sara emphasized how Nia and the male visitor became absorbed in conversation. The gist of this comment was to get her to see that she can meet all kinds of interesting people, in her case men, by getting out of her familiar zone and participating in the world, even right in her own back yard .Nia followed Sara's line of thought with a smile and remarked, "Sara, once again, you're absolutely right."

Their next stop brought them back on Chicago's far south side. They pulled up to the side of a brick row house where Nia failed to see the sign in the yard. "Who lives here?" she innocently inquired.

Sara chortled and, with a wink, replied, "You'll see."

Actually, this was Sara's first visit and a new experience also. As they approached the rear steps to the entrance they saw the sign welcoming them to the **A. Philip Randolph Pullman Porter Museum.**

"Sara, how did you know I've been meaning to come here for the longest? Have you been reading my mind?"

"I have to admit, I've had those good intentions also, just never put forth the effort or time. In our CLEAR meetings, I've heard you talk about places of significance to Black folks, not just in the Chicago area. We have mentioned these local museums before and you never indicated you attended these in particular. I'm quite impressed with your appreciation for African American history, so I thought this would be a good way to complement your day of fun and games."

"Sara, you're the best. What can I do to repay you?"

"Just relax, let Mister tall, handsome and rich find you, and invite me to the wedding," Sara said.

Nia paid the small fee and they began the tour with the documentary video on the history about the formation of the Brotherhood of the Sleeping Car Porters. This was said to be the first Black labor union in the country. Nia already knew a little about its history and organizer, A. Philip Randolph. As they strolled through the three-floor building, reading text that accompanied many photographs and news clippings, she added other bits of information about Randolph and railroad porters. Their self-guided tour ended with a ninety minute impromptu discussion with the museum's founder and director, Dr. Lyn Hughes. Again, Nia was in her element as they conversed about the past, present, and future of this historic area. Sara delighted as the listener, learning much about the woman she was enlightening, and some factual historical information. They probably could have been there for hours, but Dr. Hughes had to turn her attention to other patrons who entered the museum.

It took some doing, but Sara finally got Nia out the door, but not before they purchased a few items including a book, a coffee mug, and book markers from the small souvenir stand on the second floor. Much to her pleasure, Sara was educated and informed on a lot of history today. Nia did not contain her excitement of being able to share her passion of Black history. Sara had a feeling Nia would take another day off of work in a heartbeat, for this kind of adventure.

It was now late in the afternoon but they were not about to end their educational excursion.

"Where to next, boss?" Nia exclaimed.

"Let's head up to Bronzeville and stroll around the neighborhood. You just might stumble upon that tall, handsome, and rich man of your dreams."

"Are you sure you're not trying to run into your boyfriend? Jonathan lives there, doesn't he?"

"Yes, he does, and I told you he's out of town this weekend."

"That's even better. Let's go past Jonathan's house and see if he's secretly hiding another love interest. You've only been to his house once and that was something he planned. Maybe he stashed her away for the day. I know my cousin would have staked out his house many nights by now."

For a quick passing moment, Sara thought why not? But, in another flash she knew that would definitely be a deduction of 'good 'n faithful servant' points. "Nia, be good. I would not want Jonathan or anyone else doing that to me and neither would you. I suggested this area because of our day of discovery in African American and Chicago history. Besides, this was the place to be back in the early days and it's being renovated and revitalized to be that place again for Black folks. Not only that, it's close to your house in case I have to leave you here for misbehaving."

"Alright, Sara, you win. I should hang out with you more often. You have a positive outlook about everything. I know so many women who would keep a tight rope around a man like Jonathan."

"I'm the good woman he needs to try to keep holding on to, not vice versa," Sara boasted.

"I heard that! You go, girl," Nia said with a high five.

Sara drove out of the parking lot and turned onto Interstate-94 heading back towards downtown Chicago. As she drove, Nia got busy on her cell phone, talking to her sister, then Gloria, about their entertaining educational day.

Without much coaxing, she persuaded Gloria to meet them at the Negro League Café. Always ready for a social function Gloria could have arrived before the two of them, even with their head start.

"So, where exactly does Jonathan live?" Nia inquired, strolling around some of the newly constructed single family and townhomes.

"Do you actually think I'm going to tell you?" Sara replied, trying to sound as serious as she could without blushing.

"Sara, I'll find out. You know that. Then I can spy on him and give you the real deal about this man who just seems too perfect."

"Nia, you never heard me mention the word perfect in reference to him or any man for that matter. I'm not living some fairy tale. This is the real deal. I'm very aware that Jonathan has a past, like we all do, and there may be some things about him that just won't change. The bottom line is, he is who he is!"

"What do you mean by that? Before she could answer, Gloria's SUV pulled up next to them. *Thank goodness.* They were a block away from the restaurant. "I'm famished! Sara wore me out with our African American Chicago-style tour." She typically had a hearty appetite but didn't pack on pounds. The CLEAR ladies always commented on how jealous they were of Nia's eating habits.

"Gloria, if talking was an exercise, she burned enough calories for the both of us today. That's why she is so hungry. But, I'll admit, I enjoyed every minute of her mouth and she deserves to eat whatever her heart desires."

"Sara, you should have invited Zach so he could pick up the tab again," joked Gloria.

"Maybe Nia will meet her tall, handsome and rich man in here who'll take care of us this time," Sara replied with her own sense of humor "But just in case, the AMEX card is within reach."

Upon entering the establishment, which pays tribute to the men of the Negro Baseball League, Nia started speaking to patrons she recognized including one of the bartenders and wait staffers. She approached a table of five with greetings like she had not seen them in quite some time. Gloria and Sara followed the host to their table. They decided not to wait for Nia before ordering anything because it seemed she could be a while.

"I'll admit, this is one of my favorite places. I don't come here as often as I did when it first opened, but I'm good for a visit at least two to three times a month," Nia said when she finally made her way to the table. "Everything on the menu is good, and I mean everything. I've eaten each item at least twice," she proudly boasted. By now, someone came to take their order and Nia began recalling the day for Gloria.

While they were munching on chicken wings and crab cakes, Nia's sister, Naomi, and her cousin, Rachel, entered and joined the table. Naomi seemed to have the opposite personality of her younger sister. Rachel was just as animated and talkative but slightly louder than Nia. Naomi kept trying to get Rachel to lower her voice, but that just seemed to inspire her to raise it a decibel or two.

"You have to excuse these two," Gloria said to our waiter. "They don't get out much."

"We're used to them. They are two of our favorite customers," he said.

The two cousins were left for their own discussion while Gloria and Sara got to know a little more about Naomi. The appetizers kept coming. More acquaintances were greeted by the favorite patrons, including a gentleman who pulled up a chair, joining their table. Nia introduced the fifty-some-thing-year-old man as Sonny, the Bronzeville private eye. She said he knew everyone, saw everything, and had the inside scoop on what has or will happen. Sonny appeared to gloat being surrounded by the women. He showed his appreciation buying a round of drinks.

"So, Nia, is this Mister tall, handsome and rich?" Sara whispered.

"No, not Sonny. He's a good guy, but too old and not rich enough. But, I'll take a free drink any time," she answered.

By eight o'clock, Gloria and Sara departed, leaving the three to relish in a mini family reunion. From the hearty laughter that continued to bellow from the table, it was a sure sign that Nia's spirits were lifted and flying high.

Before ending the day Sara had rejoiced again and again about the delightful day. She was thankful for the experience and for good friends to share such events with. She prayed with assurance that Nia would find, just as she had, all the things her heart desired, through Jesus Christ. So that night, Sara went to sleep, absorbed in a feeling that all was well.

Chapter 15

Saturday, June 16th

Spending a Saturday night with ten screaming, giggling, and talkative pre-teen girls can take a lot of energy out of anyone, especially Sara. She often spent this time mellowing in a bubble bath and reading a good book. Celebrating Autumn and April's tenth birthday was worth missing out on a couple of hours sleep while and hearing Disney Channel songs blaring in her ears. Nevertheless, for her goddaughters, she'd do it again in a heartbeat! Chana and Olivia were there earlier in the evening and feasted on the twins favorite, spaghetti and meatballs, with everyone. By pajama time, it was officially girls' night only. Krista and Sara found time to talk amidst the pillow fights, second servings of cake, and the girls' version of American Idol auditions.

"The news from the doctor visit yesterday with my mom wasn't the best," Krista began when the house started to quiet a little. "I told you she had a congenital heart defect as a baby, but it was corrected. She's been on blood pressure medicine for many years and now the doctor says she has an abnormal heart rhythm. I wish she'd exercise more and give up some of the red meat, but that's an argument I've been losing for at least the past twenty years. So, I'll just do what I can do, which includes not letting the twins get on her nerves when they visit. But you know grandmothers, she loves it when all of her grandkids come around. And yes, count my sister's five wild ones."

233

"Oh, Kris, before you know it, you'll be a doting granny," Sara said.

"Whitney or Kendall better not have any kids for at least another ten to fifteen years. By then, I'll be ready to be a babysitter maybe once or twice a year. Heck, I'll just have gotten rid of the twins. Me and husband number four will need some time to ourselves so he can spoil me to no end."

"What happened to husband number three?"

"With my track record, I'll probably be married again in about two years and he'll be gone three or four years later," Krista flippantly replied.

"You don't give yourself enough credit. I give hubby number three at least a dozen years before you either loved him to death or worked him too hard to be able to afford you."

"Work, no, Sara, the next man will have enough money to afford me and only work a few hours a week so he can devote his time to me," she said as both of them laughed out loud.

Although Sara found this funny, she was not sure Krista was really believing this would be her new life soon. This was Krista's ideal lifestyle, a bit on the fantasy side, but this had always been her dream since they met. Not wanting to come off as if she was lecturing Krista, she simply responded, "Pray on it." Actually, Sara was pleasantly surprised that Bradley's name was not mentioned much in their conversation. She deduced that her good friend was letting on and moving on. *Great!*

Sunday, June 17th

The partygoers' invitation stated that attendance at Rosebrook Community Church was part of the festivities. Although it was not a condition of attending the sleepover, all of the girls, with their parents' consent, agreed to the Sunday visit. Krista started waking up the girls at eight o'clock to assure they'd get dressed and fed before the start of worship service. Mission accomplished!

Rev. Stevens acknowledged their presence while the congregation applauded their feat. That gesture may have lend itself to them sitting quietly and alert during the service. Usually, the twins would attend the youth church but today Krista had wanted everyone in the main sanctuary. Sara thought it was because they had plenty of help keeping a watchful eye on the girls.

Rev. Stevens read from 1 Peter 4:7-9 and entitled his message, Loving More Today than Yesterday. Not to frighten anyone, he reminded the congregation that as the end of the world was drawing nearer, they needed to keep praying and loving each other. Paraphrasing Scriptures, he stressed that deep, genuine love outweighs a multitude of sins, those committed by and levied against all of them. He challenged the members to share what they have with those in need. And, as if addressing Krista and Sara directly, he drove home how love will help conquer an unforgiving heart.

The pastor's deliverance was well received as Krista, the twins, and six others accepted the invitation to join Christ. Now it was Sara's turn to shed tears of joy as did Olivia. Seven of the new candidates said they were ready for baptism on the next Sunday.

At the conclusion of service, most people were engaged with the familiar hugs and kisses,

Sara being no exception. Making her way to Palmer's Place to wait for the Cunningham's to come out of their membership welcome meeting, Sara came to an abrupt stop. She was approached by an unlikely visitor who grabbed her hand. "Hello, Ms. Deyton. It's good to see you again," said the smiling, well-dressed man.

"Zach, this is quite a surprise. What brings you to Rosebrook?" was her nervous response.

"I've heard so much about this church from you and others that I decided to see for myself what all the talk is about."

"Well, I hope you enjoyed your visit and felt blessed by today's message."

"Very much so, especially having you in my presence."

"Zach, what's with all the pleasantries and formalities? You seem to be in this area quite a bit of late. Are you moving here?" Sara asked cautiously.

"Well that depends if there's someone here to make it worth my time and trouble, if you know what I mean?" he said winking.

"Good luck in finding that someone," Sara said and started moving towards Chana, who was standing nearby with Jed.

"I know I have. I just have to convince her," Zach said while trying to physically detain her. "Where's Jonathan? I'm surprised he's not on your arm today."

"Jonathan doesn't come to church to be on my arm. He's a man of God who comes to worship and fellowship," she said, trying to believe her words. "He's not here, as you can see."

"Would you like to have dinner with me today?" he asked.

"Thank you, but I have other plans," Sara said. This was a fact since she was going to help Krista clean up from last night.

"That's too bad. I was looking forward to spending some time with you so that we can talk without interruptions."

"I don't know what conversation we could hold for very long, especially that couldn't include Jonathan. Anyway, it can't be today. Now if you'll excuse me, there's someone I need to see. Have a good day, Zach," she said. Before he said another word, she quickly moved away.

"Who is that?" asked Chana.

Sara briefly filled him in on this visitor and how he managed to find his way to Rosebrook. Chana could sense she was not comfortable with Zach's presence so he and Jed approached him as they would any visitor. Sara turned her attention to the girls who were snacking on cookies and punch. She didn't know what all was said in their five minute encounter, but she was glad to see Zach leave.

"Well, anyone can see that Jonathan has some competition," Jed said. "That man wants to get his hooks in you, Sara. All I can say is may the best man win."

"There is no contest going on. Zach doesn't count as far as I'm concerned and Jonathan doesn't have to compete for anything," Sara snapped back. Although she knew Jed was only teasing her, Zach had just got next to her in a negative way.

"Chill out, Sara, Don't let that guy ruffle your feathers. I don't think he'll bother you again. We made it quite clear to him that he needs to find some- one else to get to know better, that you're off limits," Chana said. He changed the subject and inquired about Jonathan. "Speaking of Jonathan, where is that man of yours?"

"He and his son went to New York to visit his daughter."

"Wait until I have a talk with him. He'll never go out of town again without you, especially if he wants to find that you're still available when he returns," Jed kept teasing. This time, Sara shared in on the laugh. At this moment, she was hoping Jonathan would return from New York early enough for her to see him today. But, that was only wishful thinking.

Back at Krista's house, the twins were in their room, playing with their new gifts as the two ladies relaxed in the family room. It was a quiet afternoon again as the remnants of the party were put away and the steady Summer rainfall complemented its serenity. It would have been very easy for Sara to cuddle in the recliner and take a nap if it was not for Krista bombarding her with questions about Zach, Jonathan, her job, a man at church who caught her eye, and anything else that popped into her head.

This reminded Sara of their college days when they sometimes stayed up all night, laughing and talking about the parties they attended, some of the interesting people in their classes, and their plans after graduation. Sara's mission had been to solve the world's problems while she had dreams of becoming the first Black First Lady of the United States. They thought they had all the answers back then. Today, they laugh at how little about life they really knew .The fact that Krista was laughing and talking about life was enough to make Sara stay up all night again. Thank goodness it was not necessary.

They both must have dosed off from the drone of the rain and their voices. They didn't wake up until the girls came into the room to announce they were hungry. Understandably, it was now five o'clock and they were all ready to eat something else. The leftover spaghetti and meatballs decided the dinner menu and satisfied everyone. Autumn and April retreated to their room again. This gave Krista and Sara another chance to clean up the kitchen and talk in private.

"Are you a little worried about this Zach guy knowing where you live? I'm sure he knows that if he knows where you go to church," Krista said.

"I'll admit, it's not a comfortable feeling, but there's nothing I can do about it now. Thanks in part to the internet. I'll just try to be more aware of my surroundings at all times. And you know all I have to do is inform my neighbors and they'll look out for me. No doubt about that," Sara said consoling her own fears.

"Hey, maybe you might need to call upon your old friend, Marcus Richardson. Sara, I'll bet he'll come running if you just mention his name. You know men, all of them are no good. He'll probably think you want him, the way it used to be."

"First of all, nothing will get to the point where I'll need Marcus in his professional capacity. Secondly, if I ever did need him, he'll know exactly what for because I'll be very specific, leaving nothing to his imagination. And third, he does have a woman in his life and they have a son. And....," Sara said with a little hesitation, "I do have Jonathan."

"You don't sound as excited about him now. Are you having any doubts?"

Sara knew she had to answer Krista satisfactorily or she would just keep pressing. So she proceeded carefully. "Maybe I was very excited from the start, and in my mind wanted him to fit my image of a perfect relation- ship. But, now that I can see a little more clearly, he may not be heaven sent after all. He has had a problem with being totally committed in the past and that's something I know I can't change about him. There are signs that point to the fact he may still be that way today. So, with that said, I don't know where we'll be in one, three, six months or a year from now. Today, we are good friends and I'm just enjoying that."

"Where do you want to be with him in six months or a year?" she asked, just not ready to end this topic yet.

This caught Sara a little off guard because she was the only person to ask such a poignant question about Jonathan. She laughed a little as she thought about her answer. She also knew she couldn't fool Krista. Better yet, she had to be honest with herself. "I want both of us to be more mature in our spiritual growth. That will determine where we'll be in our personal lives," Sara finally replied. And that was the truth!

"Since you didn't quite answer my question, let me put it another way? Do you see yourself being Mrs. Jonathan Tate?"

"If all conditions were right, yes, I'd marry him." That answer apparently satisfied Krista's curiosity and gave her a victorious laugh. Sara was grateful when Krista's phone rang.

"Hey, Chana. Thanks again to you and Olivia for helping make the girls birthday so special," said Krista. "Yes, she's here. Would you like to speak to her?" Handing Sara the phone, she teased and said, "He's checking up on you for Jonathan." Sara hit her with one of her sofa pillows and took the cordless.

"Good evening. This is Ms. Deyton. May I help you?" she kidded.

"So there you are. I've called your home and cell phone a couple of times before I thought this is where you might be. Anyway, I was just concerned about this Zach character coming out of nowhere. You be careful going home tonight," he said.

"Thanks for thinking about me. I'm going to call Jed just before I get home and ask him to be on the look-out for me. You know he'll keep his eyes on the entire neighborhood for Zach or anyone else."

"That's a good idea. Don't be out too late."

"Yes, daddy," Sara replied.

"We're very lucky to have him for a friend, aren't we?" Krista remarked.

"Yes, we are. And he's right. I need to get home while there's still some daylight," she said. Sara gathered all of her belongings from the weekend and headed towards the door.

"I hate that you have to go I've really enjoyed your company these past two days," Krista solemnly said. She gave Sara a long, passionate hug.

"You know I'm always here for you, anytime you need or just want me around," Sara said cheerfully.

"Sara, I wish I was as positive and easy going as you are. Give me a little of what you've got, please?"

"Krista, it's called faith. You already have it. Just keep trusting and believing in the Lord. Everything, no matter what it is, will be worked out for your best!"

"I know that's what all of you keep telling me. But there are times when I feel so empty, like I have absolutely nothing to have faith in."

"Believe me, I know how you feel. A long time ago, when I was beginning my new faith walk, Rev. Stevens told me to always remember this thought. When you feel like you are running on empty and are down to nothing, that's when God's greatness will show you that He has been doing something all along. That something will be the plans He has laid out for you from day one! And I've found those words to be so true. Hang tough Krista and talk to God. He already knows what you're going through and He'll help you get past these issues and challenges. Before you know it, you'll have forgotten all about your troubles because they'll seem so insignificant. We've all been there."

"You make it sound so easy," she said, echoing Jonathan's words.

"It gets easier over time. You're going to always have something happening in your life, but as you learn to turn things over to God and let Him work it out, you'll get past it sooner. And, you'll have your friends who'll be there right by your side. That's why it looks so easy."

"Okay, Sara, if you say so," she replied.

"I know so! Now, kiss the girls goodnight for me and I'll talk to you tomorrow," Sara said.

"Call me when you get home. Smooches." She stayed at the door, watching Sara get in the car and drive away.

It wasn't until Sara turned onto her street that she remembered to call Jed. However, as she got closer to her house and saw two male figures standing in front, she realized her best friend had taken care of things for her. There was Jed and Bill, another man from the neighborhood seemingly amused in casual conversation. She pulled into the garage and joined them for a few minutes. Her assumption was correct. Chana had called Jed and the neighborhood watch was in motion. Sara described Zach and the car he was driving the night they had dinner. Neither of them recalled seeing him in the neighborhood. Knowing her dear neighbor Jed, she was bracing herself for his comments and he did not disappoint.

"Oh, poor Jonathan. I guess while the cat is away, the mouse will play."

"Nobody is doing any playing, especially when it comes to Zach. Besides, I don't have to wait for Jonathan to go out of town if I want to see another male friend," she said. Her attempt at sounding serious was not working.

"Yeah, right!" both men said.

"Seriously, thanks for being on the lookout for me. I appreciate it."

"Sara, you know I'll do anything for you anytime," said Jed.

"I know and I won't hesitate to call if I have to," Sara said.

"I'm going to tell Jonathan he'd better hire a bodyguard for you next time he's not around."

Sara just waved them off and went into the house while they lingered on, laughing and talking. She was glad to be home where she always did feel safe. However, she immediately turned on lights in several rooms as soon as she made sure the door was locked. All was well. She quickly called Krista to let her know she arrived safely and thanked Chana for being her constant protector. Then she listened to messages.

Hello, sweetheart. I just wanted to let you know it'll be Monday before we get back to Chicago. Although we had a great weekend, I missed seeing you and hope you missed me too. I'll talk to you tomorrow. Have a good night.

Hearing Jonathan's voice brought a smile to her face. But the next voice she heard quickly erased it.

Click, dial tone

Delete.

Hi, Sara. I was hoping I could change your mind about dinner, but I guess I can't. Well, at least not tonight. There's always tomorrow. Call me if you have a change in heart or appetite.

Delete.

Click, dial tone

Delete.

Zach! Doesn't he know how to take no for an answer? His persistence was not flattering. She refused to let him ruin her good mood. Sara took several deep breaths and replayed the first message, twice.

Chapter 16

The week had been quieter and less eventful than the previous one; a welcome and much needed change. Monday and Tuesday had been rain-soaked and dreary. However, after that, the heat was on again. Jonathan and Sara had dinner on Tuesday at her house. While it was nothing fancy that required much preparation, her homemade lasagna, Caesar salad, and garlic bread was a hit. He shared the New York visit with his daughter and the good time they had. The pride he had for his children was clearly displayed on his face and in his voice. It was another side of him she was seeing for a second time, only in more detail. Sara found his enthusiasm quite impressive and oddly relaxing.

He invited her to a White Sox baseball game on Friday, which she happily accepted, especially since it was a fireworks night. Once again, she was able to spend time with him, taking each moment for what it was and not wrestling with any visions. The calm, relaxed Sara just went with the flow and it was all good. *Very good! Too good!*

Krista and Sara talked every day. She even convinced Sara to go shopping with her and the girls on Saturday after the fitness program. Sara still was unsuccessful in getting Krista involved in the youth activities, but April made sure she and Autumn were in attendance and on time. The anticipation of their baptism on Sunday led them to beg their mother for a new outfit. Persistence paid off and Krista conceded. So, the four of them spent the better part of that afternoon at an outlet mall, picking out colorful dresses, matching shoes and play clothes for the cookout to follow at the Hemings'. Sara couldn't pass on a few bargain buys several stores offered, although she didn't have a need for anything. She knew Gloria would be proud of her doing some impulse shopping. All of their hands were toting bags and boxes when they finally made their way back to the minivan and cruised home.

Sara's contribution for Sunday's cookout would be a seven layer salad and a pound cake, another easy recipe passed on to her by her mother. So that evening, after recuperating from the shopping excursion, she prepared the pound cake batter. No sooner had she put the round cake pan in the oven, the phone rang. It wasn't until then that she realized she had at least one message waiting.

Before lifting the cordless, the caller ID displayed 'Unknown Number Unknown Name'. Thinking that it was Zach on the other end, she let the call go to voicemail. Several minutes later she listened to the messages.

Click

Hi, Blake. It's Tamecka. I'm still waiting to hear from you.

Sorry, Tamecka, you'll be waiting a little longer; wrong number.

Hey, sweetheart. I was hoping to reach you but I guess you're out enjoying your day. Deacon has some family emergency and wants me to go out of town with him. I'll try my best to get back in time for the baptism. If not, I'll definitely come over to the cookout. I'm sure I'll make it back by then. I miss you already!

Sara was disappointed, but she refused to let that phone call upset her cheerful disposition. Was it her imagination or was Jonathan deliberately avoiding talking to her, thus using her voicemail to announce his plans to be any place she was not? His business trips, the weekend in New York, and now coming to Deacon's rescue, were communicated to her via the Bell invention. These were more signs, clear signs, warning signs, to keep her emotions in check. His actions were a reminder that she was attracted to a commitment phobic. That's how she saw him and why she would continue to guard her heart; for now!

Sunday, June 24th

Sunday was picturesque! Beautiful sunshine, clear blue skies, and various colorful flowers were everywhere. This made the baptism of Krista, Autumn, April and twelve other adults and children so special. Rosebrook's visitors' list included Winston, Whitney, Kendall and Mrs. Nola White. They were here to witness the start of a new life for their loved ones. Kendall and Chana were equipped with cameras for lasting memories. Mrs. White was ecstatic to be surrounded by her favorite son-in-law and grandchildren. Although Winston and Krista had been divorced for many years, Mrs. White still considered him to be part of the family. Mainly because he has custody of his kids and was doing a commendable job of raising them. She always bragged about Winston and all of the children's academic and social success. It was also no secret to anyone that Krista's mother never developed a close relationship with Bradley. It was several years into their marriage that she quit referring to him simply as Krista's husband. Mrs. White had confided in Sara more than once that her prayer was for Krista and

Winston to find their way back to each other. However, they both knew the probability of that happening was next to impossible.

At the end of service, Sara was approached again by Zach, who, by now, totally annoyed her. This time, Jed was there to move in to the space Zach attempted to create for them. He asked her to dinner and again she had a good reason to turn him down, although the fact that she didn't want to go out with him was good enough. His tenacious behavior towards her could have been considered flattering if it was someone else. But her cautious, now eerie, feeling about him from the beginning had not wavered. If anything it was gaining more intensity. Again, he inquired about Jonathan, but before she could reply, Jed mentioned Jonathan would be at his house later in the afternoon. Zach could sense his presence was not welcome at the cookout. So he started towards the exit, stopping to greet several ladies, one of whom he appeared to be acquainted with. Hopefully, one of them would be his dinner companion today and every day after that as far as Sara was concerned. She smiled victoriously and joined Krista's family for pictures.

Mrs. White didn't feel up to the cookout so Krista took her home and said she would join everyone later. The twins came with Sara so they could spend most of their time with the three T's. The Barrett family had other plans for the rest of their day and graciously opted out of the afternoon cookout. Jed was always prepared for a large number of people when he lit up the grill and today would be no different.

By four o'clock that afternoon the yard was full of friends and relatives, including Rev. J.C. and his now steady companion, Taylor. Plates were piled high with ribs, chicken, burgers, corn-on-the-cob, several different kinds of salads, and other hot foods. Music, laughter, and voices of all ages filled the air that surrounded this joyous and festive occasion. Sara still had not heard from Jonathan, but that fact did not occupy any of her thoughts. Instead, it was Krista's no show that was beginning to concern her.

"What am I going to do with the two of you? I wouldn't be surprised if she was at home having her own private pity party. I'll just have to drag her out of that house, the same thing I'd do to you," Chana said in between bites of food. And she knew he would do just that if necessary. So after he completed a second plate, he and Olivia left to escort Krista to the festivities. Meanwhile, Sara got on the makeshift dance floor with the kids, attempting to learn the latest dance.

As the old saying goes, 'time flies when you are having fun.' Most of the guest had left and all the kids were actually starting to wear down. By ten o'clock, Sara got the girls back to her house and ready for bed. They were so busy playing with all the other children, they never realized their mother hadn't shown up. Uncle Chana had told the girls he'd be right back, and did not return. Sara hid her worry from them because she knew Chana had everything, whatever was going on, under control. She really just wanted to hear from them and know for sure. What a relief she felt when the phone rang.

"Hi, Sara. I'm surprised you answered the phone. Isn't Jonathan keeping you busy tonight?" inquired Nia. This was not the voice she was hoping to hear but, glad nevertheless.

"Jonathan is not the only thing going on in my life. As a matter of fact, I just left a party surrounded by men and he wasn't one of them."

"You go, girl. That's what I'm talking about. Keep your PDA up to date and active. You never know when it will come in handy. And speaking of men, I went out Friday night with a man I met at the Negro League Café. You and Gloria left too early and missed the brothers who showed up after the White Sox game. He turned out to be a good catch, has some potential," Nia boasted.

"It's my turn; you go, girl. Please, don't rush into anything and expect too much too soon," Sara replied. She was happy for Nia's new interest.

"I won't and I won't tell Jonathan about your hot dates today if you don't!" she giggled and clicked off.

Sara fell back on the couch, losing the battle to keep her eyes open as tiredness was beginning to overcome her. The next thing she remembered hearing was the clock chime for the midnight hour. A short time later, the ringing phone jolted her to sit straight up and reach for it, not bothering to check caller ID. Chana told her he was pulling into the driveway and would be the one at the door in less than a minute. She jumped up to let them in hoping to see three of her favorite friends. And three people did approach her door, Chana, Olivia and Rev. J.C. They entered slowly.

"Are the girls already asleep?" he asked.

"Yes, they've been in bed for a couple of hours. Where's Krista?"

Without saying a word Chana gave Sara a tight and comforting embrace. Next, he quietly cried in her ear, "Krista is dead."

Chapter 17

Hours after her crying had been repressed and those three words, *Krista is dead,* had been absorbed as reality, Sara was desperately seeking Jonathan. Earlier, she had felt their relationship would eventually drift away, but that didn't matter now. She needed to feel his consoling arms holding her close and his voice telling her everything would be all right. As the darkness began to fade into the dawning of a new day, she had left three messages on his voicemail. Her best friend had left this earth much sooner than she was prepared to accept. *Where is Jonathan?* He was hours past his stated arrival. Poor Sara! All she could think was *Lord, now what?*

Up all night and still in shock, Sara was able to muster up enough strength to be with Chana and Olivia as they delivered the heartbreaking news to Autumn and April. The news of Krista's death spread rapidly throughout Sara's neighborhood and the condolences started flowing her way. Trent displayed an impressive level of maturity as he supported the grieving girls. He knew firsthand the pain of losing parents; his father to prison and his mother to drugs. He and his siblings were examples of how their young lives would go on behind the loving care of responsible adults, who stepped in to clean up a disastrous situation.

Prior to gathering at Mrs. White's house, Chana gave Sara the details of the past twenty-four hours. After Krista had taken her mother home from church, she went back to her own house, apparently more depressed than any of them had known. She wrote a note, climbed into bed, and swallowed antidepressants and scotch. None of her family or friends knew she had been under a doctor's care and had a prescription for Prozac. When she didn't answer the door Chana used the key he had made for himself when they changed the locks after Bradley left. He was too late. She was already dead. After calling emergency, he contacted Winston, who arrived within minutes, with Kendall. They made the official identification then delivered the bad news to Krista's mother. Rev. J.C. stayed with Chana until the medical examiner removed her body. Their final difficult task was at Sara's house.

Friends and family were filing in and out of Mrs. White's house. The grieving matriarch stayed in bed the entire day. Kendall's bravery was astounding as he handled the well-wishers while looking after his grandmother. Winston was home, trying to comfort a devastated Whitney. The early outpour of prayers and love helped soothe all of their wounded hearts. Chana had been on his phone much of the day. Taylor and Gloria were just two of the many people who stopped by briefly, offering their services for whatever was needed. No one talked about how Krista died, but everyone spoke highly of how she lived!

Sara's CLEAR sisters' presence made her oblivious of the time. They even managed to get a few laughs from her. As the lack of sleep began to catch up with most of them, everybody started to make their way back home. When Chana pulled up to Sara's house and she recognized the black Navigator in the driveway, the tears that she thought were behind her resurfaced. She leaped from Chana's car and into Jonathan's open arms and collapsed.

Sitting on the couch with her still in his arms, Jonathan explained why he didn't get her messages until early that evening. Sara didn't focus on what he said because he was there now and would be until the next morning. That was all that mattered. He let her do most of the talking and all of the crying. She read from several different devotionals about God's constant love for everyone and His presence in the time of need. These reminders brought with it the peace she would need to get through the week. Between tears of sadness and joy, they both took quick naps, which for her probably amounted to two hours of sleep. Closing in on six o'clock a.m. with the sun's brilliant rays peeking through her windows, she called off work for another day.

Jonathan refused to leave her alone, maybe feeling a bit guilty for abandoning her the previous days. He listened as Sara reminisced about the years she shared with Krista through old photo albums and enough stories for a novel. He kept Sara close by his side as he stressed more than once how sorry he was for not being around on Sunday like he promised. Sara refused to give it any thought. When she closed her eyes again, he stepped outside to catch a breath of fresh air. Jonathan spoke to an inquiring Jed about Sara's disposition. As good of neighbors as they were, Jed and Rhoda came over with some homemade cream of chicken and rice soup. Not only was this a favorite of Sara's, but Jed said it contained the nutrients she needed to make it through this day and all the ones that would follow.

Finally, as the evening's orange sun began to set, she convinced Jonathan he should leave and get some rest. She also wanted to return some of the calls that had been left on her voicemail. He resisted at first, admitting his guilt for his absence, but she insisted that she needed some time to herself. With the quietness afforded by a calm summer's night, few stars visible to her weary eyes, Sara bid him a good night and watched tearfully as he drove away.

Kendall, who had his father's good looks and demeanor, took care of most of the funeral arrangements. Sara spent most of her time with the twins as Krista's siblings and other relatives consoled her mother. Mrs. White had just one request that the service be kept short, simple, and sweet, the way Krista would have wanted it. They were all aware that Krista never liked long funeral services or the traditional dirges. She even joked once about wanting hers to be the express version with a luncheon afterwards to remember. She promised to haunt anyone who didn't comply with her wishes. So they agreed and planned to honor her request as a fond celebration of her life.

Sara had gone back to work on Wednesday and Thursday, which helped ease her sadness. She concentrated on the present and future, not the past. With the inflow of people from out of town, including Sara's family, and the careful attention given to Autumn and April, she didn't give it much thought that Chana was out of town from Wednesday afternoon until early Thursday evening. He didn't tell her why and Sara didn't raise any questions. She just wanted

Friday's express funeral for her best friend to be perfect.

Friday, June 29th

Beautiful floral and balloon arrangements lined the front of the sanctuary and surrounded Krista's white casket. The pews were filled with many people, some of whom were familiar faces of days gone by. All of Bradley's immediate family was there in his absence. Keeping with the spirit of celebration, everyone who got up to speak commented that they were on a timer and had to be quick, including Rev. Stevens, who officiated, and Rev. J.C. who gave the eulogy. Kendall, who showed remarkable composure, spoke for his sisters, told the mourners he tried to have the funeral before noon on Tuesday, but was told not to be that quick. Overall, there was more laughter and frowns that were turned upside down, than tears from aching hearts.

At the cemetery, her sorority sisters sang their hymn and released forty-three silver balloons, one for each year of her life. When the services had concluded, Sara scanned the cemetery, hoping to get a glimpse of Bradley. She thought that just maybe he was trying to go unnoticed. Even though she didn't know for a fact, Sara had a feeling he was well aware of what had happened and would come back to face all of those he disappointed. However, that would not be the case. He was nowhere in sight.

The last item on the short-order service menu was the gathering of mourners in Palmer's Place. Sara was not in a mood to eat, so she mingled, greeting those who came to pay their respects. Her first encounter was with none other than Marcus Richardson.

"Sara J, I was shocked to hear about your best friend," he said after he gave her a hug and kiss on the cheek. "If it wasn't for her, we probably would not have met, at least not that night," he continued. He gave her a wink still holding her a little too close for comfort.

"Yes, Marcus, I doubt that I would know anything more about you except that you're Adelaine Richardson's baby boy,"

"Aren't you glad it didn't turn out that way?" he asked.

"How's Brittany and Marc?" she asked. Sara was trying to change the subject while wriggling free of his embrace.

"You mean Brianna, don't you?" he replied with a letdown in his voice.

"I'm sorry, I got your wife's name wrong, again," she said mannishly.

"She's not my wife," he sternly said.

"Sorry again," she said. Moving away from him and over to the table where her CLEAR sisters were sitting, she saw that Nia was back in her usual flirtatious mode.

"Sara, who is that fine brother over there in that killer blue suit?" she asked, staring at one of Kendall's cousins.

"I don't know his name, but I could find out for you?"

"No need. I'll check him out myself," and off she went in his direction. "You can't take that girl anywhere and expect her to act right, can you?" said Gloria. Once again, she had all of them laughing.

"Let her have fun. We know she's harmless," Sara said.

"Speaking of harmless," Gloria continued, "that hug Marcus gave you didn't look all that innocent to me. He seemed like he wanted to console you until the next funeral. It's too bad all of those good looks are squashed by his reputation."

"Gloria, don't start no mess. We all know how he is and he means nothing to me. Now you need to behave yourself as well." They were all still laughing when Jonathan approached.

"Baby, I've got to go and take care of some business. How long is your family going to be here?" he asked. She thought it was funny he would bring them up because he avoided being with her family as much as he could. She didn't know why since she never made him out to be anyone of great significance in her life.

"They might be here until Sunday," she said. Sara just wanted to see him squirm a little. Actually they were leaving that day, but he didn't need to know that.

"O.K., I'll see them later. If you need me, just give me a call." With a gentle hug and kiss on the cheek, he waved to her family and made his exit. Marcus must have been watching them. No sooner was Jonathan out of sight than he was right in front of Sara, again.

"Where's your man going in such a hurry? I was looking forward to meeting my competition," he said.

"Oh really, and what are you competing for?"
"You!"

"Marcus, you're still full of it. I know Brandy would have something to say about that now wouldn't she?"

"Brianna. Why are you so concerned about her? That's my problem to deal with and she

258

doesn't have anything to do with us," he said conceitedly.

"Us? There is no us. That was then, Marcus, and this is now, a whole new day and time. Thank you again for coming, now good bye!" Sara turned and walked away, somewhat miffed by his nonchalant attitude about the state of his relationship, but more about his lack of respect for hers. *Darn that Jonathan for having to take care of some business at this time!*

Sara's brother, Kid, was standing up and stretching when she got back to her family. Eddie and her mom were chatting and laughing with each other.

"Who is that good looking man who seems to be interested in you?" Eddie asked, referring to Marcus.

"Just an old friend of ours."

"Is that all, just an old friend? I wouldn't mind making him a new friend of mine. What's his status?" Eddie quizzed.

"Unavailable and probably has a long waiting list," was her final answer on the subject of Marcus.

"Tell these two old ladies we have to get a move on it," Kid said.

"Oh, he's the only one in a hurry. That desperate girlfriend of his has him on a short, tight leash," remarked Eddie.

"Please, I'd stay longer, but there are too many women here who have been giving me the eye all day. I wouldn't want to break anyone's heart," Kid stated. The three women laughed at his inflated ego.

"That Jonathan seems to be a nice young man. He kept paying a lot of attention to you. Is he someone special that we should know about?

I still don't understand why you and Charles never got together. I know he would have made a fine husband. His new wife looks so happy, she's glowing. When am I going to see that kind of glow on your face?" asked her mother.

Sara couldn't believe her mother still hadn't accepted her twenty-year friendship with Chana as being just that. They had had that conversation before, more than a few times. Sara didn't want to get her mom's hopes up for the son-in-law she claimed to be sadly missing. So she down played the answer to the questions about Jonathan.

"He is quite a considerate man. What you need to know is that he is the good friend you saw in him today. Nothing more and nothing less," she said with crossed fingers. That seemed to satisfy her family's curiosity. *Thank goodness!* They prepared to make the four hour drive home. They were at ease with all the people they saw and met today, knowing Sara had enough support for the days ahead of missing her friend.

Palmer's Place was almost empty by three o'clock. Sara sat quietly, reflecting on the beauty of the day and how Krista got her wish. Tears were starting to swell when she switched her thoughts; to Jonathan, who seemed uncomfortable in the presence of her family; to Nia and her constant flirtatious behavior; to her sister and brother, going at each other just like they did as children; and to Marcus being his usual womanizing self. All of these incidents reminded her that she was still among the land of the living. Her frown quickly turned upside down and she couldn't help but laugh out loud.

As early evening's gorgeous sunset lit up the western sky Sara settled into her home and relished the solitude. That lasted for about fifteen minutes when the phone rang. Her first thought was to just let it ring, but she knew some people would be worried about her state of mind. So, she conceded to the caller.

"Hey, baby. What are you and your family doing?" asked Jonathan.

"Nothing. They left this afternoon."

"Would you like me to keep you company again tonight? I'm all yours." he said, sounding relieved.

"No, thank you, Jonathan. The only thing I need is a good night's sleep. I appreciate your offer, but I'd like to spend this evening alone."

"I understand, but you know I'm just a phone call away."

"I know. I'll call you tomorrow. Have a good night," she said and hung up. His last comment gave her a chuckle as she recalled how she couldn't reach him the night she really did need him. *That's O.K., he came through eventually.*

There were unheard messages on her voicemail from earlier in the day so she took a few minutes to listen to them.

Hello, Sara. I heard about your friend. I started to come to the funeral today, but some of your church members don't seem to want me around you. The dinner invitation still stands. If you need me, just call. I'll be there in a flash.

Zach! Delete

Hello, baby. I just wanted to let you know we made it home safely. Call me if you want to talk. Love you!

Mom

Sara, all of that man's fine looks are wasted on the fact that he's gay! What's up with these brothers? What's the real deal on Marcus? He can arrest me anytime. I'd love to play cop and criminal with him. Talk to you later!

Nia! Sara just shook her head and giggled at those comments. *Click, dial tone*

For one final laugh, she replayed Nia's message and, for a brief moment, thought about Marcus, but not with a fondness. She shook off his image since she did not have any interest in him at all. Instead, she wondered how Nia knew Kendall's cousin was gay. Maybe she didn't get the results she was after and used homosexuality as a defense for her disappointment. After a brief wellness call from Gloria and Chana she turned the ringer off and pushed the phone to the side.

Before retiring, Sara picked up her Bible and turned to the last chapter of Job. The footnote in her Bible stated that people may ask, "If God is in control, how could He let this happen?" This very question had filled her head for the past week. The passage continued, saying that people must often choose between doubt and trust because people limit their scope to a brief time frame. Lastly, it asked the question, "Will you trust God with your unanswered questions?" She briefly pondered her answer, knowing that it was always, *Yes*. Sara then fell into a peaceful sleep.

Chapter 18

Weeks passed and they were all trying to get back to a place of normalcy. Sara was spending time with Mrs. White, whose health was in a state of decline, although she insisted on having custody of the girls. April seemed to accept losing her parents with a little more ease than Autumn. Kendall and Whitney were settling their mother's estate with the help of Attorney Gordon. In time, all four of Krista's children, with the love and support of her extended family, would adjust to life without her.

The youth fitness program at Rosebrook had come to an end. Sara was absent for the final weeks of activities due to her fragile state of mind. With the persistence of Trent, she would not miss the recognition banquet that awarded all the participants for their efforts. After the celebration of trophies and ribbons was over, Chana gave Trent a cell phone in honor of his demonstrated leadership in the way he looked out for his siblings and the twins. Chana had told Trent if he ever needed to talk man to man, they could do it through the privacy of his own phone. That small gesture led to an exuberant amount of pride and responsibility that matured Trent well beyond his thirteen years. Their newfound bonding resulted in the three T's referring to him as Uncle Chana instead of Mr. Charles. Uncle Chana's chest swelled with pride, graciously accepting the tenacious trio as family members.

Undeniably, Sara's ongoing grieving contributed to the declining relationship with Jonathan. They had not seen much of each other, which didn't seem to weigh too heavy on her mind. Phone calls were less frequent, but cordial. He had made another trip or two out of town and had not attended church with her since the funeral. Sara did not raise any questions and he volunteered no information. She only knew that things were not the way they used to be. These were surely the signs she had been seeking to put this phase of her life in perspective. Their friendship had definitely become nothing more; hopefully nothing less, so she thought.

This particular Saturday morning had the appearance of rain at any time with its over-cast gray clouds. The weather report called for late afternoon showers, creating a humid and muggy evening. Sara didn't want to waste the entire day indoors since Summer was rapidly drawing to an end. Walking, her therapeutic cure-all medicine, was her remedy for this ho-hum kind of day. Sara dressed in workout attire and set out for the forest preserve. Imagine her surprise when she opened the front door to find Jonathan standing there, about to knock.

"I see it worked," he said, clothed in sweat pants, tee shirt, and athletic shoes.

"What worked?"

"I wanted to surprise you and join you for one of your nature walks. From the look on your face, it worked. You are clad in your walking gear?"

"Yes, I was going for a walk and I'd love to have some company." She grabbed another bottle of water and off they went into the woods with miles of asphalt paths ahead.

Their pace started out a swift stride, but the more they got into conversation, that stride became more casual. With nowhere to be and nothing to do, they walked along and talked about a little of everything but nothing particular. Since she had determined that Jonathan was just meant to be a friend, there was no need in trying to get answers to what was causing them to drift apart. There was no need to know what his out of town trips were about. Sadly, she had accepted the fact that his church going had been on her account, not his personal relationship with the Lord. They filled the time with idle dialogue that was comfortable for both of them.

According to her pedometer, they had advanced four miles when the clouds were darkening and moving in rapidly from the northwest. Turning around, they stepped it up a notch in case the rain would not wait for them to be sheltered. And it did not. Three blocks from the house, the rain drops fell bigger and faster. At the sound of thunder and flash of lightning Sara's scream caused a laughing Jonathan to grab her hand as they ran the final distance to her home.

"I don't know about you, but I've worked up a huge appetite," he said while toweling himself off.

"Yes, I could eat a really big meal myself. Give me about twenty minutes to shower and slip into some dry clothes, then we can head to your house for the same. I've got the taste for some good southern fried chicken from one of Chicago's south side favorites. How does that sound to you?"

"Great, especially since I'm hungry enough to eat the entire bird! Hurry up before I dissolve," he teased.

Sara told him to make himself at home, that old hospitable cliché, and moved to quickly rejoin him, clean and dry. The warm water and shower gel was a refreshing compliment to the earlier physical and mental regimen. Although she told Jonathan she'd be ready in twenty minutes, she could have used all that time being pampered under the massaging and soothing showerhead. Lost in thought, she had no idea how long she had been in the shower. It wasn't until she felt a breeze created by the shower curtains that snapped her back to the present. She knew the window was not open so the blowing curtains had to be the result of the bathroom door being opened. When she peeked around the curtains, she saw the door closing.

"Jonathan!" she called out, but got no response.

She just shrugged it off as his way of saying hurry up. While the shower was providing the same kind of relaxation as the walk, Sara found herself using the water to wash away the tears she was starting to shed. Krista, gone; Jonathan, going; Marcus, arrogant as ever, wishing he'd stay away; and Zach, why he found her at all. Suddenly, the previous months started playing out in her head with sadness. She cried, hopefully for the last time, then prayed with thanksgiving for the blessings each had contributed to her life. She was regaining her composure when once again, the bathroom door opened.

"Okay Jonathan, I get the message!" she hollered out. But, the door didn't close. Instead, his footsteps came closer inside the bathroom. She peaked around the shower curtain and got a glimpse of him in the vanity mirror. He was naked from the waist up that she could see. Maybe he'd removed his wet tee shirt while waiting on her. When she called his name again, he backed away and shut the door. *That was strange.*

Dashing from the bathroom to her bedroom, Sara yelled, "Okay, Jonathan, I'm hurrying as fast as I can." Still there was no answer. *Perhaps he settled into a little nap while waiting.* By now she was moving a bit faster remembering he was sitting in the living room in wet clothes.

Dressed in a pair of denim shorts and tank top, she bolted into the living room after briefly blow drying her hair. Oddly, the room was empty. *Maybe he stepped out to his car now that it had stopped raining.* Following that thought, she looked out on the driveway to find his Navigator was gone. *Hmmmmm, that's even stranger!*

Maybe he got tired of waiting and dashed out to get something at the store? Or maybe he has another surprise for me? Or maybe he got a call on his cell phone and had to take care of some business at the last minute? These were just a few of the thoughts that ran through her mind before she called his cell phone to inquire of his whereabouts. The fact that the call went straight to his voice mail did nothing to clear up the mystery.

An hour, two hours, three hours later she got more of the same, voice mail. Perplexed, she tried to pass the time by working a Sudoku puzzle. Unable to solve yet another puzzle, she threw the book across the room, grabbed her keys, and left to eat the chicken she still had a taste for. But, with this uncharacteristic move by Jonathan, she ended up at Gloria's house first.

"He did what?" was her reaction to Sara's recollection of the earlier events.

Convinced that an emergency phone call took him away with no time to explain yet, the ladies went to a local buffet specializing in southern cooking where they splurged on chicken, pork chops, fish and too many side dishes to mention. The good food and Gloria's great company eased her worries a little, for now.

Once Sara returned home later that evening to find no messages on either phone, her mind started racing again with maybes. Her strength was waning and finally tears fell freely down her face. Falling across the bed she'd find herself still dressed when she awoke Sunday morning.

Sunday, July 29th

At the conclusion of the church service, Sara tried to mask her disappointment to meet and greet the members and visitors as usual. Most of her prayers today had included the request to finally hear from Jonathan and that he and his children were not in any harm or danger. That's what she attempted to convey since no one at Rosebrook knew anything about yesterday, but several people asked about him. She hid her anguish from everyone except her best friend. Chana knew her too well, as she must have been wearing her worries on her forehead.

"What's wrong with you, Sara? You look like you're troubled by something. Is everything alright?" he sincerely asked.

"Yes, Chana, I'm fine. You know I still have a few bad times every now and then, but for the most part, I'm okay," she said with fingers crossed.

"You'd tell me if something or someone was bothering you, wouldn't you?" he demanded.

"Yes, you know I would without any hesitation. Now stop worrying about me," she said. With a soft peck on his cheek, she quickly got away before he questioned her again.

On her short drive home, she repeated over and over, Psalm 3:3: But you, O Lord, are a shield around me, my glory, and the one who lifts my head high. This helped her stay positive and excited when she saw the message indicator blinking on the phone.

Hi, Sara. It's Gloria. Have you heard from Jonathan yet? Call me as soon as you get the chance.

Silence, then Click.

Click, dial tone.

Sara phoned Gloria back and received a dinner invitation, one she gladly accepted as the diversion she badly needed.

The two of them spent hours talking and laughing about the things in the past that gave them so much joy and pain. This held Sara's attention for a while, but eventually, she couldn't stop thinking about the bizarre behavior of Jonathan Tate, the man who had been wonderful and compassionate from the time they met, yet, mysterious and complex when it came to his past personal involvement with women. She had already left two messages yesterday and one from this morning. When she got his voice mail again for the hundredth time, she just hung up immediately. Seeing the pain on her face Gloria grabbed her keys and Sara's hand. Not saying a word, Gloria headed straight to Jonathan's house.

As Sara expected, he did not answer the door after they knocked and rang the bell. Gloria's patience grew thinner than Sara's as she kicked the door and used her fist to pound on it. Out of frustration, she began to yell, "Jonathan, open up this door. We know you're in there, punk."

This outburst got the attention of his upstairs tenant and a passing police car. Sara was a little amused at Gloria's violent antics.

"Gloria, let's go. We're starting to disturb the peace," she said.

"Is everything alright?" asked the police officer, stopping in front of the house.

"Yes, sir, we're leaving," Sara said, leading Gloria off of his porch and back to the car.

"He's not home," said someone who yelled from the upstairs window.

"Thanks," Sara replied in an apologetic manner. "Gloria, it's not a problem. We know who's got everything under control," she said. Actually, Sara was trying to convince herself more than Gloria.

"What a punk! I'll kick his butt the next time I see him," Gloria angrily said. "I finally remembered why his name was so familiar to me. He used to date my cousin's daughter, Candace. She was so much in love with that man. I vaguely remember seeing him once at a family picnic several years ago. After that, I don't recall him being with her whenever we had other gatherings. But you couldn't tell Candace anything. Her mother tried to warn her from the beginning, if she really wanted to get married, don't move him in to her house. She wanted to convince Candace this man didn't love her unconditionally. He only loved the convenience of having a good home and bed partner. Candace was devastated when they broke up. I heard she gave him an ultimatum, marriage or get out. We know which road he took."

"What a small world. I met Candace at the birthday party on that after noon cruise. She made an effort to warn me not to expect a husband out of him. Now you see why I held fast to my vow of celibacy. I refuse to have any more hit and run affairs. That's not what I want, not ever again. That's why I stand on my faith, my beliefs, and stand my ground!" Sara said with determination.

After that revelation, they rode home mostly in silence except Gloria venting her anger by taking it out on passing cars. Sara was having a hard time believing this was happening to her. For the past eight months he was so attentive and caring. He had proclaimed her as his woman and she regarded him as her man. They had laughed, talked, cried, and prayed together. His kisses use to melt her heart and his arms brought her a sense of comfort and security. Now in the past twenty-four hours all of that was in question. One thing she was well aware of during their brief courtship; Jonathan not once uttered the words "I love you". She was grateful he never told that lie.

Before retiring that night Sara prayed and read Psalm 51:10: *Create in me a clean heart, O God. Renew a right spirit within me.* With no more tears and no more wondering, she was soon peacefully out for the night.

Wednesday, August 1st

Three days had passed and all was quiet in her world. Going through a mini rut, Sara went to work, came home and shut out the world, except Gloria. She was concerned that Sara was handling this too calm, for her comfort. The truth had come to light that Jonathan Tate was not her Heaven sent man. Knowing this, her tears had dried up and life would go on, just as it did prior to that December enchanted evening when they first met. To help put Gloria's mind at ease, Wednesday evening, Sara was planning to attend Bible study. She was relieved that Sara was not becoming a recluse.

Pulling into the driveway returning from work Sara noticed an object at her front door. Examining it upon approach, she saw a beautiful bouquet of colorful roses in a gorgeous crystal vase. Jed headed her way and wasted no time bombarding her with questions.

"So, what's the occasion? Jonathan quickly dropped them off and kept going. He must have really done something to tick you off. Is this some kind of makeup gift or is something else going on? I have to give him credit, he didn't spare a dime for whatever reason." Jed was right. The flowers and vase were absolutely beautiful. He included a card which she reserved to read in private. Sara picked up the vase, but still remained silent, not answering his inquisitive mind. "Is everything alright, Sara? I haven't seen much of Jonathan around here lately. Have you given him his walking papers already?" Jed said humorously.

"We've decided we need some time apart," she said, breaking the silence emotionlessly.

"That's too bad. I liked that young man. Is there anything I can do?" he sincerely asked.

"No, thanks, Jed. I don't need anything."

He accepted her statement and left her to read the card and admire the gift, if only for a moment. The card displayed a single rose on the front and a brief handwritten note inside.

My beautiful Sara, please forgive me. I have some personal issues that I must work out. It's not you, it's me. I can understand if you move on and meet someone who honestly deserves you. Unfortunately, at this time, I'm not the one. Please pray for me.

Love, Jonathan

After reading the card twice, it only allowed her to have more questions and not enough answers. The more she marveled at the lovely arrangement, she knew it would hinder her ability to move on. So she took the card to the kitchen sink and lit a match to it. As she watched it turn into ashes she silently prayed for the help he needed to resolve his personal issues. In a sense this was her personal Burn the B.S. "Goodbye, Jonathan", she whispered.

Before Bible study, she asked Rev. Stevens if she could leave the flowers in the lobby for everyone to enjoy. He delightfully agreed and asked what was the reason and who was the benefactor. With a smile, she gave the credit where it belonged but said no more. Rev. Stevens had the wisdom to know something was not right, but he also didn't push the issue. He extended his ear if she required any counseling. Sara thanked him for the offer but declined any help at this time.

Saturday, August 4ᵗʰ

Saturday's CLEAR meeting was suspiciously quiet other than the discussion of this month's selection by Gloria. First, there was Nia who brought a guest named Chelsea. She introduced her as someone interested in being a part of CLEAR. They were encouraged and delighted since their membership had been reduced by two in less than a year. Chelsea's presence coincided with a subdued Nia, something they were not used to observing. Not that anyone complained, but their nonverbal expressions told the story.

Then there was Gloria, who still showed signs of anxiety about what Sara had experienced the past week. She applauded her for getting rid of the flowers since she viewed this gesture as his way of *punking out*. For some unknown reason, Taylor was absent today, a rarity.

At the conclusion of the book review, Sara spoke up first and informed the ladies that she and Jonathan had agreed to end their relationship and to pray for a resolution to some personal issues he was having. Her statement spurred Nia to break her unusual calm and sent her into a tantrum.

"Men! What's his problem? Does he expect you to wait around for him to get over his troubles? What about you? You did just lose your best friend as the result of some man's personal issues. I can't take this anymore. I've had enough!" she cried.

"Nia, please, calm down. I agree with our decision. I had a life before I met him and my life will go on without him. No, I'm not putting my life on hold for him, not that he asked me to either. Remember, God is with me, you, and every other woman in the universe at all times!"

"Amen, to that! Having God in your life is the only sure thing any of us can ever count on. Sara, I'm sorry to hear about you and Jonathan. You've been through a lot in the past few weeks. If you ever need to talk, you can call me anytime of the day or night," said Erin with a warm hug.

"Sara, you are a much better person than me and I admire your strength and faith. The Lord has a lot of 'good 'n faithful servant' points for you. I'll admit, I would have hit it at least once before he got away," Gloria said humorously.

"Gloria, coming from you that means a lot!" Sara replied.

Holding hands, Erin led them in prayer, asking to heal Nia's anger towards men and to find her true companion in Christ's love. Gloria's name was mentioned to not fall back into her habit of using men to satisfy her physical desires. She also shed tears for Jonathan's personal issues, but she was the only one who did. Sara's had dried up (for good)!

Chapter 19

Now that school was back in session, Sara spent as much time as she could with the twins. Whenever they were at her house, the three T's had an open invitation and they took advantage of every opportunity. It was a win-win situation since they all entertained each other and her only role was that of referee and provider of food and snacks.

One Friday evening, Chana came to see Sara. They hadn't spent much time together in the recent weeks. He was genuinely concerned since two significant people were no longer a part of her life.

"Sara, if I had known Jonathan was this kind of a jerk, I would have never introduced you to him. I have no idea what his personal issues are and I'm sure he had them long before he met you. Of course, I hope it's nothing serious, but I can't trust him anymore. As a matter of fact, I'd be more comfortable if you never got close to him again."

"Chana, don't blame yourself for anything. I don't regret meeting him and I appreciated the time we had. But, it's over and that's that. I didn't see it coming, especially the way he disappeared without a word. Yes, it hurt for a brief moment, but really, I'm over him. My plate is now full with kids, work, CLEAR, Rosebrook and occasionally Toastmasters. Rev. Stevens has hinted again that he would like for me to take a more active role with the singles ministry. So, my dear, there's no time for me to dwell on the past, which is where Jonathan belongs and will stay."

276

He accepted her case even though he was not thoroughly convinced. Her actions would just have to prove this to be true. To change the subject, she made some popcorn and started talking about work, Olivia's family, and her plans for a much needed vacation. As they indulged in the crunchy snack and small talk, it occurred to her that this was the most fun she had had on a Friday night in many weeks. In some ways, it reminded her of the good old days when the two of them had no relationships except their platonic one. He was the only male she could count on to be a true friend. That evening they even engaged in a pillow fight that ended with Sara claiming victory.

Saturday, September 15th

With the crisp Autumn days now in full bloom, this particular Saturday morning was calling for fair weather outdoorsmen to take advantage of the cool temperatures and colorful foliage. This was also a good time to stay in bed and do nothing. Compromising, she released the bed at ten o'clock, donned walking attire, and put her feet to the pavement. Nature's sounds filled her ears in addition to footsteps she could hear at a close distance. Looking behind, she saw Trent about twenty feet away.

"Where are you going?" Sara asked.

"I'm out for some exercise. Don't worry, I'm not following you. I know how you like to go for walks by yourself," Trent replied.

"Well, then, have a good workout," she said Actually, Sara knew he'd be behind her the entire time and she didn't mind the company. Besides, the forest preserve was large enough to accommodate two more weekend athletes.

The walking path had a number of runners, walkers, and bikers taking advantage of the kind of day that would be too few before the cold and snow would leave most of them housebound. As they crossed paths, they exchanged greetings and high fives, encouraging each other to shed those unwanted pounds or get the heart pumping stronger and longer. Trent kept a close, safe distance, while the music on his headphones had his head bobbing and fingers snapping. At one point, Sara tried to add a little jog to her routine, but shortly went back a walk mode. Jogging was just not for her, even as easy as the seasoned joggers made it look. At the end of a two-hour mind and body cleansing power walk, she slowed down for her not quite workout partner to be by her side.

"That felt good, didn't it?" she asked.

"Yeah, and it made me work up a big appetite," he responded.

"Yeah, I could eat something too."

"So, Miss Sara Smile, what are you going to fix for lunch?" he asked with a big hungry grin.

"I was about to ask you the same question."

As they approached her house, Trent noticed a new blue car slowing down next to them. The surprise came when this shiny Buick LaCrosse parked on her driveway and out stepped Zach Lewis.

"Sara, it's good to see you again. I was beginning to worry about you since all of my messages went unreturned. How are you?"

"Fine, Zach, and yourself?"

"Great, especially since I'm standing in front of you and see no reason for you to decline my lunch invitation."

278

"Actually, I was just about to cook lunch for me and my workout partner, Trent."

"Well, am I invited? Do you mind if I join you, young man?"

"Nope, it's okeydokey with me," replied Trent.

This was not how Sara wanted to spend her Saturday afternoon but it appeared she had no choice. "Come in and get ready for some lip-smacking wings and fries," Sara said with no enthusiasm. This time, she had no intention to jump in the shower and freshen up. Maybe her sweaty odor would send Zach running a lot sooner than later. Hesitantly, she made her way to the kitchen to prepare lunch for her invited guest and intruder. A sigh of relief came upon her when the telephone rang. Dashing to respond to the caller and inform them of her unexpected visitor, she received another surprise as Zach prohibited her from picking up the cordless.

"Let voicemail handle it. I want to spend some uninterrupted time with you."

"That might be Jonathan or Miss Lizzie, Trent's grandmother, or even another one of my neighbors. I really should get this so nobody will be wondering what's going on. Besides, we're not alone," she said eyeing Trent.

"The kid will be leaving after we eat, if not sooner. Now leave the phone alone," Zach insisted.

"Okay, Zach Lewis. Take it easy, I won't answer the phone," she said trying to bring a sense of calmness back into the room.

"I have to go to the bathroom," declared Trent as he stood to head in that direction.

"No, sit down," demanded Zach.

"What's wrong with you Zach? This is my house and you'll have to leave if you can't act like the visitor that you are. Go ahead to the bathroom Trent," Sara said sternly. But then fear ran down her spine as the phone rang again and Zach brandished a gun, taking over control of her house.

"I said no one move or answer this phone. Let someone other than me have to speak to your voicemail. Sara, I haven't seen Jonathan around here in a while so I don't think he'll be disturbing us. I wasn't planning on the kid being here, but for right now, I'll put up with him until I decide what to do."

"Zach, what is this all about? Why are you doing this?" she cried.

"I have wanted you for myself for quite some time, even back in high school when you paid no attention to me. After our ten year reunion I've kept up with where you lived and what's been going on. I even know about that cop you were involved with several years ago. I should have moved in on you after that ended but my circumstances didn't allow it. Now I have another chance to convince you that I'm the man for you. Not one of those jerks you dated know how to treat a good woman, even if you gave them instructions on a golden platter," Zach stated.

"Then why don't you let Trent go and we can talk, just the two of us? That is how you want it?"

"Not just yet. I don't think this kid knows how serious I am. He might run out of here and immediately call the police."

"No, I won't," replied Trent.

"Shut up, kid, and let me think," he said.

Sara couldn't believe what was happening. A man she barely knew was holding her hostage in her own home, her safe haven. Once again, Trent was an innocent victim, falling prey to an irresponsible and irrational adult. *Lord, now what?* Of course, in her heart she knew that God had this situation under control and she would listen to Him for instructions in this situation. She sat on the couch next to Trent, put her arm around his shoulder, and gave him an apologetic look, while Zach stood over them with gun in hand, planning his next move.

"Don't worry, Miss Sara Smile, I won't let anything happen to you," whispered Trent. He actually gave her something to smile about. Before long, the doorbell rang, which came as no surprise.

"Zach, I'm going to have to answer it or someone might think something's wrong in here. Remember, your car is parked in front."

"Okay, but quickly get rid of whoever it is and don't try anything," he said, holding the gun on Trent.

With a deep breath, Sara opened the door to find Tyree and Tamala standing there with smiling faces.

"Hi Miss Sara Smile, Grandma told us to tell Trent to come home since you got company over here," said Tyree.

"Well, Tyree, tell your grandmother that it's okay because Trent is keeping Zach and me company. You two go back home and your brother will be there a little later."

They didn't have a problem buying that explanation and off they went, back across the street. In the meantime, Trent continued to sit on the couch, rubbing his legs from his ankles to his thighs and stretching them out.

"At least let me make lunch since that's what we started to do in the first place," Sara reasoned.

"No, I don't want any greasy chicken and fries. When you're with me, you will only eat the best. Caviar, lobster, filet mignon, whatever your heart desires. Maybe chicken and hamburgers is all Jonathan could afford, but with me, there's no limit to the finest things life has to offer. How does that sound, baby?" Zach asked.

"That's just great, Zach," Sara said. She even detected a smirk on Trent's face. He kept stretching and rubbing his legs. Zach finally turned his attention to Trent.

"What are you doing, kid?"

"After exercising this morning, I didn't get a chance to stretch out and cool down. My coach taught us this was an important part of the total workout. Do you mind if I sit on the floor and stretch? It also helps since you won't let me go to the bathroom," Trent replied.

"Go ahead and stretch," huffed Zach. So Trent got down on the floor and began stretching, including holding his ankles and bending forward as far as he could. Zach sat next to Sara and continued babbling about what he could do for her if she would just let him. Since he was in control, she allowed him to let his imagination run as wild as he wanted it to. In her heart and mind, she was saying no way! Another twenty minutes had passed and the phone rang again. Still she was not permitted to answer it, so it was again no surprise that the doorbell rang less than five minutes later.

"Same thing applies. Get rid of them," said Zach. But when she opened the door she knew this would not be an easy task.

"Good afternoon, officers. What can I do for you?" she asked the two uniformed police officers standing before her.

"Good afternoon, ma'am. We received a 9-1-1 call signal from this location and no one answered the phone when the station called your house. Is everything alright?" asked the dark-haired policeman.

"Yes, sir, we're fine. I don't know how you received a 9-1-1 call from here. No one has used the phone since we've been in the house."

"It came from a cell phone. Is it alright if we come in and take a look around for ourselves?"

Just then, Zach appeared at the door with her and spoke up. "Hello, officers. Is there a problem?"

"Well, there doesn't appear to be, but we need to take a brief look for ourselves if you don't mind?"

"No! Please come in," she said and gladly opened the door, not knowing what was going to happen next.

"May I get your name please?" the same officer asked. She gave him her name and before anyone else could say a word, Zach spoke up. "I'm David Washington."

"Is that your rental car out there?" the officer continued.

"Yes."

"Who are you, young man?" he asked Trent, who was getting off the floor with a look of relief.

"I'm Trent Miller. I live across the street with my grandmother Elizabeth Payne. I have to go

283

to the bathroom," he said running from the room.

"See, officers, we're just fine. I don't know why you got a distress call from here. Sara was going to fix us some lunch, but I'm going to take her out instead."

"Is that right, Miss Sara?" asked the officer.

"Yes, sir. There's no problem here."

"Well, thank you for your time and have a good day," replied the officer. The two left without further conversation.

Zach turned to her, looking puzzled. "Cell phone signal? Where did that come from and where's the boy? Trent, get your butt back out here," Zach yelled. "Trent, I said get out here now!"

Failing to get a response, he went to get Trent out of the bathroom. To his dismay, the room was empty and the window was open. Swearing, he relocked the window and closed the blinds.

Meanwhile, Trent flagged down the officers and told them what was really going on inside. In less than three minutes sirens could be heard coming to a screeching halt in front of her house and flashing blue and red lights could be seen, although Zach had closed all the window treatments.

"What, now, Zach, or shall I call you David?"

"Shut up and let me think!" he shouted. A few minutes later he quieted down and continued, "Oh, Sara, my love, I didn't mean to holler at you. I'll never disrespect you like that again. Please say you forgive me."

Surprised by his change in demeanor, she knew she needed to play right into his mood swing to keep him subdued.

"Zach, I know you will never hurt me because you love me. Stay calm and this will all be over soon."

It was apparent that Zach was in need of professional mental help, especially since he had it in his mind that she wanted a life with him. What seemed liked hours had passed as the house was now surrounded by law enforcement officials. Zach refused to talk on the phone and pulled the cord from the wall jack. The negotiator had to use a speaker to communicate. Since they were barricaded inside, Zach had to show the officials that Sara was not harmed. She briefly came to the front door with a gun pointed at her head to emphasize his seriousness.

"Sweetie," she said, "You don't want everyone in the neighborhood to know about our plans, do you? Why don't you use the telephone so the only people who will know what's going on is you, me, and the negotiator."

"Is that what you want, baby?"

"Yes."

"I'll do anything for you, Sara. When we leave here, you just name it and it's yours," he replied, grinning broadly.

Finally, Zach was convinced to plug the land line phone back into the wall. As soon as he did, the phone rang and he immediately answered it. The only thing he demanded was that he be able to freely leave and take her with him so they could start a life together. Of course, she knew that wasn't going to happen, so the wait continued. Sara was prepared to wait as long as it took to get this deranged man out of her house. She silently prayed no harm would come to either of them.

As the afternoon turned into evening the phone rang again. This time, Zach handed it to her after he had a brief exchange of words with whoever was on the other end. A familiar and welcome voice was on the line.

"Sara J, this is Marcus. Nothing's going to happen to you, not as long as I'm out here; and I'm not going anywhere."

"Thanks, I'm relieved to know you're here," she said before Zach grabbed the phone and clicked off.

"Who was that?" he asked.

"I thought you knew all about me since you've been following me around."

"Did I miss another one of your men? What kind of game are you running?"

"I'm not a game player. That was Lieutenant Marcus Richardson. Remember him? He's still a cop and good friend."

"So you mean he's my competition again? Well, Richardson can forget about you. You're all mine now, the next Mrs. Zach Lewis."

"Whatever you say, Zach," she conceded to his disturbed mind.

"I thought you wanted a good man to take care of you? I'm offering that to you. Marcus and Jonathan both blew their chance. I'm your man now and forever. I love you, Sara. Tell me that you love me too."

Zach started pacing the floor with sweat pouring down his face and neck. His hands started shaking, causing her to keep her eyes on the gun he still held.

"I love you, Zach," she said, playing his mind game.

"Say it again and again," he demanded with a wild excited look.

"I love you, Zach. I love you, Zach." she repeated out of fear.

He became so wildly excited that the gun accidentally discharged into the floor, causing both of them to jump from the startling sound. Immediately, the phone rang again. As Zach stared at the hole in the floor she answered the phone, assuring the officers nobody was harmed by the unintentional shooting. Quickly, he snapped back to the current situation and ordered her to hang up the phone. Sara obeyed.

After another fifteen minutes of silence, the phone again was the needed distraction. Zach quickly grabbed it and said, "Is this Lieutenant Richardson? ...Well, put him on now." Turning his attention to her, he stated, "I've got some news for this two bit cop... Richardson, I know you and Sara were friends. That was then and it's a new day. That's all you'll ever have because she has consented to be my wife. I'd say congratulations are in order, don't you?" With a big grin on his face, he handed the phone to her after Marcus must have pacified him.

"Listen, Sara J, Trent told us your rear bedroom window has a broken lock. Did you get it repaired?"

"No, sir," she carefully said.

"Good. Keep him talking. We're coming in. I'm ready to get you out of this mess."

"Yes, that's right. I'm going to be his wife in the near future. Thank you."

Handing the phone back to Zach, he was pleased that she said what he wanted to hear. That was just the start. She kept saying whatever made Zach happy and holding his attention.

"I could tell Marcus was a bit upset by our news, but he'll have to get over it quickly. Maybe we should invite him to the wedding so he can witness firsthand how happy we are. As a matter of fact, Zach, we should have a big wedding and invite everybody so they can all be jealous of our love. What do you say about that, honey?"

Zach was taking this all in as reality. He relaxed his hold on the gun as he fantasized about them through her concoction. "Whatever you want, Sara. Just name it. We'll have the biggest wedding anyone can imagine. We need to start planning it today. Of course it will take place at Rosebrook so all of those church folks can see that I was the best man for you after all. Let's make sure Gloria and Jonathan are there. Maybe those two are really meant for each other. It'll be great! Just wait and see."

By now, Zach's voice was full of excitement, rising above the normal conversational level. Sara could have won an Oscar for her performance because she was definitely winning him over. Although it seemed like forever, within minutes, four S.W.A.T. officers and Marcus jumped into the living room and this seven-hour nightmare came to an end.

Exhausted and somewhat shaken, Sara was able to release her emotions in Marcus' arms while Zach Lewis was escorted out of her home and life in handcuffs. As soon as the door closed, it opened again immediately by an excited Trent, leaping into the living room. Saying nothing at first, he and Sara just embraced as she was never happier to see him. Entering the house behind Trent was the negotiator.

"You should be extremely proud of this young man. He helped us with information about Zach and he remembered the broken lock on that bedroom window. But before that, tell her how you called 9-1-1, son."

"While I was stretching, I reached under my pants legs and dialed my cell phone which was in my socks. Uncle Chana told me this was a good place to hide my phone and have it on vibrate instead of ringing all the time. That's really cool, don't you think so, Miss Sara Smile?" asked Trent.

"Yes, it is, and I'm so proud of how well you handled this situation. You are my hero!"

"There's a mob outside who wants to see you, Miss Deyton, but first I need to ask you a few questions, then we'll be on our way," said the negotiator.

"Uncle Chana, Rev. J.C., and everybody is outside. They've been here all day long," said Trent.

Sara asked Trent to get Chana and to let everyone else know that she's going to be just fine. After a tight hug from a worried Chana, she asked him to send everyone home so that she could get some much needed rest. He reluctantly obliged and she turned her attention to the officer with Marcus by her side.

"Zach Lewis has been on our watch list for some time now. He's a little smarter than most criminals, but in the end, they all end up losers. He's been tied to drug trafficking from Florida to Kentucky. He's got several paternity suits filed against him and his first wife learned he's a bigamist. Apparently, they never divorced, he moved out of state and married two more women, whom he has since left and was working on making you number four," said the officer.

"That would have never happened," she said. "Not in this lifetime."

After a few more questions and a reassurance that she was not harmed, the officer left, leaving Marcus at her request. She was finally able to make an attempt to relax. Marcus went through the house and checked all the doors and windows, even the broken one.

"I'll make sure to fix this one first thing tomorrow," he said. "What you need now is a nice hot shower or bath to help you relax. You do that and I'll keep all the well-wishers away." He made that remark in response to the doorbell ringing.

So she did as she was told and let him take care of everything else. After a lengthy lavender bubble bath, she climbed into her bed where she felt safe. Still numb over the events of the day, it helped that Marcus had refused to leave and said he'd stay with her as long as needed. Sara couldn't cry, couldn't eat, and at first, she couldn't sleep. Marcus just let her sit still in his arms while he kept assuring her the ordeal was over and Zach would be put away for a long time. The last thing Sara remembered that night was Marcus saying he would be watching over her. And he did. When she woke up at seven o'clock in the morning, he was sitting on the couch in the living room where he had been all night.

Chapter 20

Saturday, October 6th

The passing weeks helped Sara's life return to that which she was accustomed to. Work was a forty hour per week, five day routine; they were preparing for the annual Fall festival at Rosebrook; Sara spoke again at a Toastmasters meeting; and then there was CLEAR. These Christian women were still enthusiastic about reading, but their beliefs were about to be challenged.

This month's discussion was held at Sara's house. Instead of a book discussion, they held another Burn the B.S. ceremony. This time, she was the one jotting down several concerns that required three sheets of paper. Sara was being specific about what she was releasing into the hands of the Lord. With the fire ablaze, they took turns destroying the papers, sending the ashes to drift away so the blessings could flow down. Although her blessing stoppers seemed many, they paled in comparison to her thankfulness for the abundant gifts she continued to receive. The testimonies of the group were in agreement as well.

Taylor informed them that she had been in contact with her sister. She didn't go into much detail except that Teena and Adrian were alive and well. Gloria reported that Cecily and Mario were adjusting well to life in Dallas. Her house in Calumet Park had sold, she was working through a temporary agency, and Mario was enrolled in a high school with a reputation for academic success. Serena was in California last month and had spent a day with Danielle, who was comfortable being back home and working in downtown Oakland. Erin was delighted to inform them that her daughter decided to go to law school and perhaps join Pierre's practice. Her son had completed his first year of medical school. Then Nia made her announcement that none of them saw coming.

"Ladies, Chelsea would love to join our group. I'm sure you'll find her to be intelligent, witty, and an avid reader like all of us. She has been an inspiration and has helped me find my way in this sinful and upside down world. Since we are living in the final days on earth, I'm happy that I've found someone to live with peacefully and lovingly. You see, Chelsea is more than just a friend. She's my soulmate, and lover. I've never been this happy and excited about anyone in my life."

Silence fell across the room. Coffee cups almost fell back on the table. Water bottles were lifted to lubricate suddenly dry throats or occupy the mouths that were left wide open. From their nonverbal reaction, it was safe to say that Nia had dropped a bomb on them.

Eventually, Erin, poised and proper, spoke up in a diplomatic way. "Nia, this came as a surprise to me, maybe others in the group as well. As in the past with all new members we need to discuss Chelsea's membership because everyone will have to agree to accept her into CLEAR."

"I concur," said Serena.

"Listen, ladies, I know some of you may be uneasy with my relationship with Nia and I didn't mean to put anyone on the spot. I'll leave now so that you can have the good time you generally have at these meetings," stated Chelsea.

"No, please don't leave like this, Chelsea. This is not the CLEAR way of doing things. We don't want you to walk away with a negative feeling," said Erin.

"I agree Chelsea. CLEAR doesn't operate like that and neither do I when it comes to visitors in my home. Please stay," Sara insisted.

Chelsea did and they continued burning blessing stoppers, more papers being tossed in the fire as the mood took an unexpected turn.

Taylor dismissed the meeting with prayer. Chelsea and Nia were the first ones out the door. This gave the rest of the ladies an opportunity to digest Nia's words and react. "I'm not a believer where I feel homosexuals are committing a capital crime and should be put to death, but I strongly feel it is a sin. Granted, all of us are sinners and I pray we repent daily. However, I do not condone the practice of homosexuality and I would personally have a problem with Chelsea and Nia being a part of our Christian group," stated Serena.

"I agree with Serena. To take my view one step further, if we are trying to be leaders among other women, especially young ladies like the Roses, we have to stand firm on the characteristics of a Godly woman. God wants us to be lovers of men, not women, and He wants us to seek Him and His will for our lives. I honestly believe God wants all women to wait on the husband he has in store for us and not turn to another woman for that type of relationship," said Taylor.

"Hold on, ladies. Are we being a little too hard on Nia? Is she any more sinful than me being with a man and I'm not married?

Sometimes I think we put too much emphasis on male/female relationships instead of just relationships. If she's truly happy with Chelsea; what's the problem? I'd rather see her in a loving and non-abusive relationship than what Cecily and I put up with," commented Gloria.

"No, Gloria, we're not saying Nia is any more or less of a sinner than any one of us. The difference is I'm believing in the Lord for the man He has planned for me. If there is no man in my future, I won't go back into the world and seek out an alternative. And, like Taylor, I'd have a hard time trying to encourage young ladies to wait if I show acceptance to Nia's lifestyle choice. Besides, I really think Nia doesn't know what she wants in her personal life. Just a few weeks ago, she was still actively seeking Mister tall, handsome, and rich," Sara said.

Erin spoke up. "I love Nia like a little sister and I pray she'll reconsider her personal choice in intimate companions. I never liked her outwardly flirtatious behavior, but I can honestly say, I never heard her talk about any sexual exploits. I think we just kind of assumed some things about her. But since she admitted her involvement with Chelsea, that's something I can't ignore. I hope I'm not judging anyone. It's not homosexuals I don't like, it's their practice. Also, I have no desire to understand the lifestyle."

"So in other words, you don't hate the players, just the game," Gloria said lightheartedly.

"I think we should give Nia some time to see if she changes her mind. We know she is more liberal about her social life than most of us. It wouldn't surprise me if she has a new Mister tall, handsome, and rich by Christmas. As funny as that sounds, it's not beyond Nia. I'm willing to wait, but if she continues to be in a love relationship with Chelsea, then perhaps we should suggest they find a reading group more in concert with their beliefs," said Serena.

They agreed and changed the conversation while munching on the rest of the snacks Sara had prepared. As much as she tried not to talk about the events of her life recently she was questioned anyway. Sara kept her answers very short and simple, indicating she wanted to let go of the past. The only real information she gave out was that Zach was in jail in Florida where he'd be for a very long time. And she assured Gloria that there was nothing going on with Marcus. Besides, Sara wanted to hear more news about Cecily and Danielle. Little did she know she'd soon be getting the facts up front and personal, just like old times.

With the house to herself again, she decided to do nothing for the rest of the day. She flopped on the couch and flipped through the television channels. She thought this would be her entertainment tonight until the phone rang.

"What's a good looking single woman doing sitting at home on a Saturday evening? You haven't forgotten how to line dance, have you?" joked the friendly voice of Chana.

"Let's just say I've semi-retired my stepping shoes for the time being. What are you doing at home on this beautiful Fall night?"

"I'm resting after a full day of noisy kids. The twins are spending the weekend with as well as Olivia's nephews. We played in the leaves at Starved Rock State Park and cooked hotdogs and marshmallows on an open fire. The kids had a blast and now I'm worn out. You should have joined in on the fun."

"The CLEAR meeting was at my house today. It was an interesting one, quite different from any of the previous gatherings. But I'll definitely take you up on the offer the next time you invade one of my favorite places in Illinois. How's Olivia?"

"Lovely and loving every minute of the time we spend with these kids. She's helping the girls get ready for bed as we speak. They're looking forward to seeing you and the Millers at church in the morning. One reason for this call is that I wanted to let you know I've been in contact with Bradley. To be honest with you, this is the third time I've had a conversation with him," Chana said, getting straight to the point.

"That...that," Sara couldn't find anything good to say so she didn't continue.

"Sara, watch your mouth and just listen. He's very aware of Krista and the situation with the girls. Right now, he has his own troubles, which could land him in jail for a long time. Teena and her son live a short and comfortable distance from where he is staying, but, they are, for all practical purposes, with him. I'm sure you probably knew that anyway. He's making an effort to do what is best for the girls, which includes staying away and not having contact with them. They know nothing about my dealings with their dad and I want it to stay that way."

"Does he think that little money he left Krista will make it right for Autumn and April?" she asked obviously still upset.

"No, Sara, it's not about the money. Honestly, I believe Bradley is sincerely devastated by the way everything has turned out, especially Krista. He broke down and cried, stating that he never would have left if he had any notion she was that vulnerable. He would have faced jail instead of walking out on the family. But, that's a moot point now. His legal troubles are on him. My concern is for the girls. There's not much else to say now, but I'll keep you informed later about what is being done. I know I can trust you to keep this conversation between us, right, Ms. Deyton?" Chana said seriously. She could tell because he called her by her last name. That was rare.

"Yes, Uncle Chana. I know you're all about taking care of business, especially when it concerns any of your women. That's what we love about you," she fondly replied.

"Good. Now the other reason for the call is to check in on you. With all the recent ups and downs in your life, I want to make sure that you're taking care of yourself. Don't be afraid to seek professional help if you need to."

"You sound like Marcus. Thank you for your concern but I'm handling things well. I've gotten a lot of support from my CLEAR sisters and of course our Rosebrook family. Rev. Stevens and Portia have been there for me whenever I needed them. You know as well as I do that prayer is powerful. But, Chana, I'm still having a hard time understanding why. Krista was my best friend. How could she take her own life and I couldn't do anything about it? Did I miss something? Was I too busy with my own issues that I wasn't available in her time of need? Where and how did I fail?"

"Listen, sweetheart, you didn't do anything wrong and you didn't fail Krista at all. She absolutely adored you to the very end. I have deliberately not shared with you the note she left behind, but one of these days, I will. Please know that there was nothing more you or any of us could do. She masked her hurt and depression from all of us who knew her well. I want you to keep smiling; there are many people who love you because of the way you affect their lives. Now let me see you smile this very minute!" he lovingly demanded.

She did and he knew it. That call gave her a little inspiration as only Chana could. But soon after his call, the next one really gave her a breakthrough.

"If I'm disturbing you that's just too bad", teased Danielle, a former CLEAR sister. "Sara, what else is going on with you except all the negative things I've heard lately? Come on, girl, tell me something good."

Sara was so glad to hear Danielle's voice and welcomed it with a lot of enthusiasm. That kicked off a three hour conversation detailing events of the past few months. Two weeks later, Sara was in sunny Oakland where the fun and laughter escalated.

Chapter 21

Wednesday, October 24th

Stepping out of the Metropolitan Oakland International Airport and getting a whiff of the waters of the San Francisco Bay, Sara anticipated frolicking about Fisherman's Wharf, shopping and savoring the ever-pleasing taste of sourdough bread, great seafood and of course a world famous Irish coffee. Indeed, that would come during her weeklong visit, amongst other memorable events.

"You look absolutely fantastic. I love the new look!" she proclaimed. Danielle embraced Sara when they met at the passenger pick up area. She was sporting a short, natural coiffure in a mixture of gray and brown, complementing her attractive face and stylish eye glasses.

"No more hours in the salon for relaxers and permanent colors for me. Every two or three weeks, I visit my nephew's barbershop where I'm in and out in usually less than an hour. The money I've been saving on my head has been going straight to my hips! Girl, I've put on ten pounds since I've been here and loving every ounce of it," Danielle stated as they both got a good laugh at her modeling move. "And speaking of good looking, you've got it going on yourself. Has this Jonathan guy I heard so much about lost his mind or what?"

"Who?" Sara flippantly responded.

Passing the Oakland Coliseum, gazing up into the hills and the world famous bay reminded Sara that she was indeed taking a much needed retreat at her girlfriend's west coast dwelling. Northern California's natural beauty beckoned many to get away and fall in love again with God's creation. That was the only thing on her agenda.

Danielle had informed her that they would be stopping by Maxwell's Lounge, a popular place for socializing. Her niece was celebrating the opening of her own advertising agency. She referred to tonight as her 'get down before getting down' to serious business. Arriving at the already crowded club, Danielle was being greeted by family and friends as they weaved their way towards the woman of the hour.

"Are you sure this party isn't for you, or is this place one of your regular stomping grounds?" teased Sara.

"Not hardly. My stomping days anywhere except home are long gone," she stated.

But they both knew Danielle wasn't very serious. As they approached her niece, who was finger popping and moving to the beat of the music, she led them directly to the dance floor where the electric slide was in full progress. When fifteen minutes had passed and the dance floor revelers had doubled, Sara and Danielle departed to quench their thirst and rest their feet.

"Lovely chicks of a feather flock together, I see," remarked a nice looking man. He made his way to the table managing to finagle a seat.

"Wyatt, you always have a line or two for any woman you see. I'm glad you made it. This is my good friend, Sara, that I was telling you about."

After kissing the back of her hand, Wyatt looked Sara in the eyes and said, "I only speak the truth. Definitely, the pleasure is all mine, Ms. Sara. Ms. Danielle had me almost as excited as she was about your arrival." He said this all the while smoothly and flirtatiously planting a kiss on her left hand. "Just checking," he remarked. And he added an all too familiar wink!

Wyatt Earp Hendrickson was an accountant at the firm where Danielle worked as a part time administrative assistant. During the next hour, he revealed that he was thirty-five, divorced, not ready to settle down again anytime soon, had been with the company for eight years, had a CPA and was a year away from getting his MBA. His parents were big fans of western movies and television shows, thus naming him after the heroic gunman. His younger brother was named Jesse James and sister was named Josie Jane. Throughout the getting-to-know-you colloquy mainly between Wyatt and Sara; Danielle intentionally removed herself. He was approached by several ladies who wanted to make their presence known or try to coax him to the dance floor. He acknowledged most of them by rising to his feet and giving them a kiss on their cheek, but declined the dance. Sara assured him she was not trying to monopolize his evening and encouraged him to heed the desires of those in need of a dance partner. Wyatt claimed he was not much of a dancer and that he was enjoying their conversation. So they engaged for about another hour.

Drawing closer to the eleven o'clock hour, Sara's internal clock was beginning to slow down, yearning to lie down. Besides, it was Wednesday and tomorrow was a workday for most, including her hostess and most recent acquaintance. When Danielle put her dancing feet to rest again, Wyatt walked them to the car and they bid each other a goodnight.

Thursday, October 25th

Rising around seven the next morning after a well-rested night, Sara spent some quiet time gazing out the living room window of Danielle's Emeryville apartment, overlooking the east bay hills. During this solitude, her body, soul, and mind began to assuage the anguish of the past few months. An exigent manifestation from her spiritual being whispered to her heart that today was the first of new days to enjoy and live like no others. So Sara would do just that!

By now, Danielle was up and a bit startled to find Sara raring to make the most of her weeklong visit.

"I call myself being quiet and letting you sleep in, but you've beat me to the draw," she said in her burgundy silk gown and matching kimono.

"I can sleep when I get back home. I'm in California with every intention to see and do as much as I can in a few short days."

"So Miss Hot Stuff, what's on your agenda? Or shall I say who's on it? You and Wyatt were enthralled in some serious conversation last night," she teased.

"Yes, I enjoyed talking to him, but we didn't exchange phone numbers or anything and that's fine with me. Besides, I came out here to spend time with you, not some man who'll be here today and gone tomorrow."

"Wyatt seems to be a nice man. His personal life isn't the talk of the office so that lets me know he's at least discreet with whatever he's doing socially. Not only that, but he doesn't

302

appear to be a 'player'," she said while making quotation signs with her fingers and emphasizing the last word.

"Whatever! You know me, I'm still a tourist at heart and can't wait to go back to Pier 39 and Jack London Square. Not to mention getting a look at the bay from Coit Tower and of course hiking up and down Lombard Street for some exercise."

"Well you better not go to the Pier or Jack London Square without me, but you can have that crooked street and tourist tower all you want. As I told you, I have to work the next two days, but we'll have all next week to the point where you might get tired of looking at me," she said. Danielle was talking and laughing while in the kitchen, brewing a pot of coffee.

"Shopping is your bailiwick, not mine. I wouldn't know what to do or where to go. I need you to help me pick out some nice things whether it's for my body or my home. I haven't changed when it comes to navigating through stores, hoping to emerge with a bargain buy or two. It's never been my forte."

"I've got you covered," she said in between sips, heading back to her bedroom to get dressed. An hour later, they were both walking out the door to begin the day's activities; Danielle's work, Sara's play.

"Now, check in with me later so that I'll know where you are. Did I remember to give you my work number? Of course, you can reach me on my cell too. Call me if you need anything at all. I'll be back no later than four o'clock," she finally took a breath from her motherly bantering.

"Yes, ma'am, I'll call you at noon to give you my whereabouts. Yes, ma'am, I have your work, cell, home, and mother's phone numbers. I promise to call you if I need anything, unless I run across some good looking public servant in a police uniform. And I'll try to be back before you get home. Now, Mother, can I go? Please, please, please?" Sara whined. The two women hugged and then she skipped off in the direction of her mode of transportation.

Although Sara could not see her face, she could feel the smile while she rode BART into San Francisco like a first time visitor. This trip was supposed to be one of relaxation and rejuvenation. Having only been in the area for less than a day, she already felt like it was mission accomplished! Exiting at the Powell Street station; taking a brief walk to the Powell-Hyde cable car; hearing the operator yell out Lombard Street; she was one of several eager pedestrians about to traverse one of the world's most famous blocks. Looking down at the curves, flowers and superb mansions that align the street she stretched a little and took off; down one side, up the other. *Not bad,* she thought to herself. Down again and back up again, a little bit slower this time. She stopped for a rest break and to enjoy the scenery. Then, down one side again, and slowly making her way back to the top. Midway through the block, her cell phone broke her *lento* stride, a welcomed sound to her ears.

"Yes, Mother," she answered out of breath. "Is it noon already?"

"Mother, I'm sorry to disappoint you. But, I can call back if you were expecting another call?" responded Wyatt. She recognized his voice right off.

"No, I thought you were Danielle checking up on me. Good morning Wyatt," Sara said laughing.

"I begged her for your phone number and told her I'd come to your rescue if you were in any kind of trouble. So tell me, do I need to mount my horse and defend you from any evils out there in San Francisco? Sounds like you were running or something."

"I'm happy to report that all is well and I'm just getting a little exercise in addition to some sightseeing. How are you this afternoon?" she asked grinning from ear to ear.

"Just another day at the J-O-B. I see you didn't waste any time gracing the Bay area with your presence. I'm impressed and jealous that others get to see you before I do again. So, make a brother happy and have dinner with me tonight?"

"Thank you for the flattery. I needed that. But, I haven't spent any time with my good friend yet. I'd appreciate it if I could take you up on your offer later in the week."

"I'll be heading out of town on business in a couple of days and don't want to miss out on the opportunity to spend a little time with you myself."

Even though Sara was thinking to herself, *He's so full of it,* she was taking in the wheedling nonetheless. "I promise. It's a date!"

A few more minutes of lighthearted conversing and they ended the call. Sara continued to sit and gather her thoughts and go over his invitation again when the phone rang for a second time. This time, she answered like she normally would only to have Danielle pleasantly scolding her.

"What do you mean you can't go out with Wyatt tonight? Have you lost your mind? I'd be disappointed if you stayed home with me instead of going out with him. When was the last time you met a good looking, available, professionally employed man who doesn't have a million and one issues? And Lord only knows when another one will come along again. If you don't tell this man yes, I'll go out with him and leave you at home!"

After that amusing tirade, Sara calmly conceded, "Yes, Mother, I'll have dinner with Wyatt. Can I stay out past my ten o'clock curfew?"

"Only until ten-thirty. Here's Wyatt," she said.

"So, I'll see you tonight at six," he said with the upper hand and clicked off with all celerity, allowing no response.

Motionless, her windedness from conquering the hill was now an ebullient exhalation in anticipation of this evening. So much so that she mustered up the energy to finish the climb up the street then descended for the last time. Now she was off to Coit Tower, to relish in some fond memories and visualize possible new ones.

Later, when they were back at the apartment, Danielle and Sara carried on like a couple of teenagers, dressing for her dinner date.

"Look a little sexy, show some cleavage, tease him a little," Danielle said. She handed Sara a gold color, spaghetti strap, silk camisole. "Your outfit is fine if you were going to a church convention." This was in reference to Sara's selection of a burgundy pants suit and rose color silk T-shirt. Admittedly, the camisole did spice up the ensemble. Of course, Sara brought enough earrings to choose among three pair.

"You deserve to enjoy a good time with a good man. Who knows? Maybe he's the one."

"Stop right there," Sara said, raising her hand palm out a short distance in front of her face. "Danielle, the last thing I need right now is another man who could be the one. Been there recently and don't want that again. Let me just have dinner with your coworker and be done with it."

"Whatever you say," she replied, continuing her teasing. She walked away humming the tune to Here Comes the Bride. Sara facetiously threw a pillow at her and waited for the doorbell to ring.

"So how was your first day back on the west coast?" asked Wyatt as they were driving to their dinner destination. He arrived promptly at six o'clock with two single red roses, one for each of them. He was stylishly dressed in navy blue pants and a sports jacket with a silk, royal blue, button down shirt. Wyatt had the corporate look with a close, short cut hair, clean shaven, and gold wire rimmed glasses. Yes, he was very easy on any woman's eyes. Sara took a silent, deep breath and listened to her spirit tell her to loosen up and enjoy the evening.

She tried to appear as if today was just another ambulatory day with the side note being that it was in San Francisco, not Chicago. However, the modulation in her voice told a different story and she was sure he sensed her excitement. While crossing the Golden Gate Bridge, her shrilling gasp could no longer hide her true feelings. Wyatt just laughed a little and said, "Go ahead and enjoy the ride. You deserve every minute of it." And so she did.

The restaurant he had chosen in Sausalito boasted an intimate ambiance and a superb seafood cuisine, as she would soon discover. Picturesque views of the Bay and city skyline caressed the splendor of the evening. While they ate a seafood sampler appetizer, the ice breaker conversation was simply about a little bit of everything but nothing too serious. She shared about her involvement with Rosebrook, sisterly bond with CLEAR, and her job. Sara carefully chose her topics to keep her personal data as much away from his knowledge as possible. Wyatt, however, spilled more facts about his job and what the future held. Surprisingly, he added details about his marriage and other past involvements, as he kept referring to them. Actually, it was a little too much information than she really wanted to know. Even while savoring their dinners of sole almandine and pan seared Mahi, Wyatt continued on and on about his exes. Sara had to give Wyatt credit that his popularity with women seemed to be effortless on his part. So she kept on enjoying the evening's ride, even if it included knowing a bit about Tiffany, Jessica, Rachel, and Ebony. In fact, it seemed he was being open and honest, a character trait she highly appreciated in a man. Therefore, she did a good job of pretending to be very interested in what he was saying. Then he put the ball in her court attempting to delve into her personal life.

"Enough about me. How has a beautiful woman like you escaped marriage? I can't believe you haven't even come close to tying the knot."

Apparently, Danielle had never mentioned anything too personal about Sara and neither would she. "I won't deny that I thought I was in love a few years ago, but it turned out to be a lopsided affair. Lately, the men I've met don't understand that they can't compete with my relationship to Christ. I'm not trying to sound like I'm some kind of saint, but I don't live as worldly as I did back when I was in my twenties and early thirties. So if I'm to be married, he'll have to be Heaven sent. I've learned my lessons on trying to make things happen myself."

"Sara, I know what you mean. My parents raised us in church and they were very strict with my sister, making sure she at least made it through high school as a virgin. I was very proud of her when she told me her husband was the only man she had ever had sex with. Unfortunately they're divorced now, but she still lives by her Christian values."

"Good for her. What about you?" Sara asked, catching him off guard. But she quickly let him off the hook. "You don't have to answer that. Your intimate life is none of my business."

Wyatt just chuckled and finished pouring the bottle of white wine. "Let's just say I have my limits," he remarked.

The sound of a vacuum cleaner interrupted their laugher and brought to their awareness that they were the last patrons and it was time to get out. To show his appreciation and good natured humor, the manager gave Wyatt his business card with an offer of a ten percent discount on his next visit. Wyatt commented that in the future, he'd come a little earlier.

Outside, they kept on talking as Wyatt pointed out some of his favorite places throughout the bay. Not wanting the night to end, Sara was trying to ignore the chill of the light wind that swept across the bay. She was even wearing the heavy sweater that Danielle insisted she bring.

"Is it getting too cold out here for you? I thought you'd be used to this type of night breeze coming from the Windy City?" He started rubbing her arms, generating some warmth.

"I'm fine, just need to acclimate my body to being out here as opposed to in there. And you're right, living in Chicago has prepared me for any kind of climate. So, I can handle it," she said, trying not to shiver too much. Wyatt just laughed and gave her a big hug. Even as the employees' cars were pulling away from the parking lot their date lingered on past the stroke of midnight.

Shortly after the last car left, leaving the two of them under a brilliant moonlight, Wyatt turned to her and sat her upon the hood of his car. Their talkativeness had begun to wane due to the lateness of the night, or earliness of the morning. In the midst of silence, he planted a soft kiss on both her cheeks, then on the lips. The softness grew more passionate and the internal battle heated up between Sara's heart and head. Her head was winning, allowing her to bask in the moment and enjoy the attention. At first she withheld returning his affection as the inner battle intensified. Her head was telling her to completely let go and release all of the built up stress as a result of the past tumultuous months. Yes, she wanted this, she needed this and she was convinced she deserved to feel this good sensation. It did not matter that she knew very little about this man. It was just enough to win over her head if for nothing more than the here and now. Especially after he whispered in her ear, "Don't fight it. Let go and trust me." Foolishly, she acquiesced. With her guard down and human nature taking over he drew her closer into a strong embrace. Sara began caressing the back of his neck and stroking his smooth face. All the while, their tongues played patty cake as his lips covered hers. And seemingly, because this felt so good, it had to be right. At least that was the affirmation coming from her head because she wanted it to be right.

Wyatt sensed her body becoming almost jelly-like and maybe his head was telling him the same, that she was his for the taking. So he commenced to take this physical meandering to the next level. He positioned his body in between her legs, pulling her so close that she could feel him. Their hearts were both beating rapidly, perhaps for different reasons. As she felt his hands slide up her thighs and start to fumble with her clothes, suddenly her heart began to overpower the battle.

Guilt crept into what had felt good. Knowing she had gone too far already, she knew she had to end what the world at large would have approved. However, The Lord she served would disapprove. Her hard earned 'good 'n faithful servant' points would be diminished due to self-indulgent immediate gratification. Abruptly, she backed off the kissing and gently but firmly pushed him away.

"Wyatt, I can't do this. I'm sorry for letting my emotions get the best of me, but we can't take this any farther. Please forgive me, but we have to stop now."

"Sara, I know you have this thing about obeying God, but right now He can't make you feel like I can." Wyatt was panting while pushing himself into her so that she could feel his hardness rubbing against her upper thighs and in between.

"I know. He can make me feel better. Please, Wyatt. I'm sorry, but this isn't what I'm about, not anymore."

Much to his chagrin, he proved he was indeed a gentleman and abided by her plea to cease. They both spent a few minutes collecting themselves before he started the trip back to Oakland. Showing his manhood in a different fashion, one that Sara greatly appreciated, Wyatt kissed her on her left cheek and said apologetically, "I'm sorry for taking you for granted, that sex would be a part of this date as it is with so many women I encounter. And believe me, I'm not always the aggressor."

"You didn't take me for granted because both of us got a little carried away. In the past, I was one of those aggressive women. Today, I'm more like your sister."

"And I respect you for that. Now sit back and enjoy the ride," he said bringing a smile to her face. So she did.

Listening to the smooth sounds of a classic jazz favorite sent both of them into a head swaying, finger snapping mode. It was the late Grover Washington's, *Mr. Magic*. Towards the end of the song Wyatt broke the silence with more personal facts. "Mr. Magic was my nickname in college. A couple of ladies still call me that today."

A moniker she was sure he bestowed upon himself. This time it was her turn to be amused.

"What's so funny?" he asked.

"Nothing, Mr. Magic."

Because Sara was absorbing the autumn atmosphere, she didn't see him take his cell phone out of this jacket pocket and turn it on. It started to ring after they crossed the bridge.

"Hello....I told you I had something to do tonight before I go out of town....It's a little late, don't you think?....I'll have to call you later, baby." Sara said nothing because it was none of her business, although she did briefly think, *So I was something to do tonight.* Quickly dismissing what she overheard, he felt he needed to offer some sort of explanation for an early morning call. "That was Ebony, a good friend of mine."

Her only reaction was, "Oh". By the time they reached the Bay Bridge, the phone sounded again.

"Hello.... Hey, lady I tried to reach you last night...... No, not right now.... Maybe. I'll give you a call back.....Okay, baby." Silence again. "Excuse me, Sara, I'll be out of town most of next week so I need to get a few things done before I go. That was Jessica. We go way back."

"Wyatt, don't let me stop you from doing whatever you need to do. I'm just enjoying the ride," she reminded him of his command. By the time they arrived at Danielle's, the phone rang once again. This time, he put the caller on hold while he walked her to the door and waited to be buzzed in.

"Let me see you to the door like I promised Danielle I would," he said.

"That won't be necessary. Besides, you shouldn't keep your caller waiting too long. Thanks for a lovely, memorable evening ."

"Well, have it your way. The pleasure was all mine." With that said, he kissed her on the forehead and left. The cell phone was to his ear before he got back in the car. Maybe he would make some lady feel good tonight after all. It just wouldn't be her. And that was the last of Wyatt for the rest of her vacation.

Danielle tried to give her the third degree, but she claimed to be too tired and went straight to bed. Sara feigned sleep the next morning until Danielle left for work. But when Danielle came home that afternoon she resumed her interrogation until Sara gave in and told her some things, but not all, definitely leaving out the parking lot scene.

"Wyatt was in meetings most of the day. He must have had a good time because he took a few minutes to tell me how nice he thinks you are and that it was one of the best dates he's had in a while. So, did you two make plans for another date before you leave?"

"No, he's going out of town and I didn't come out here to spend time with Wyatt, remember? The rest of my vacation is about me and you, unless of course you have a date, then I'll stay here and catch up on some reading."

"No, honey, and I'm not looking for one. I was married for almost thirty years and raised two wonderful children. If Nylan were alive, I'd still be married to him. But," she hesitated as if to fight back tears, "let's just say I'm engaged in some much needed me time."

"Ms. Grant, I'm with you on that," Sara said with a high five.

"Sara, all kidding aside, I admire your strength in the wake of all that you've endured recently. Serena told me about your girlfriend, then your breakup with a man they all seemed to be crazy about. And finally, to be held at gunpoint in your own house. I'd probably be a basket case by now."

"Danielle, you know as well as I do about the amazing power of prayer. My church, family, and friends all lifted me up in their prayers and that has gotten me through these difficult times. Some of the days were painful, but I never felt any of these events were the end of my life. Deep down, I knew there was always tomorrow. And that tomorrow is today, here with you and I'm as happy as can be."

"I'm sure Wyatt had something to do with that big smile on your face, too," she insisted.

"Yes, I won't lie. Last night was very nice. However, the rest of the time it's all about you, girlfriend," she said giving Danielle a hug.

And that's how it was for the next five days. Their random agenda included a fish fry at her mother's house, an afternoon hanging out at Jack London Square, a tour of the newly developing lofts in the Central Station neighborhood (where Danielle had already purchased one), and of course two ferry rides to Pier 39.

Strolling around downtown and the loft complex, Danielle explained to Sara her move from a suburban lifestyle for many years to the heart of urban life.

"The suburbs are a great place for family, especially raising kids. But mine are on their own and I don't plan on raising grand babies, if the Lord is willing. There is a famous quote by Jack London that says, 'The proper function of man is to live, not exist.' I existed for two years after Nylan died, now it's time for me to start living again. Down here, I'm five minutes from work by bus, can walk if I want on a good day. My mother's house is fifteen minutes from here. And best of all, I can shop and eat until my heart is content! Life can't get any better than this!"

Sara responded, "Here's to single woman holding their own by standing strong on their faith, their commitments, and standing their ground." To that, they saluted each other with a playful fist bump.

Chapter 22

Monday, December 31st

Winter again! Already! Where did the year go? Sara was contemplating the year ahead as she lay across her bed, getting some rest before going to Rosebrook for the New Year's Eve service. She declined Gloria's offer as well as some co-workers for dinner and board games to ring in another year. Tonight, she wanted this time for reflections of the past and revelations for the future. She looked at the three feet of snow that had already blanketed the area. Meteorologists were predicting a harsh Winter ahead with possible record low temperatures and snow- fall. This aided her decision to stay close to home tonight. Sara had stayed home the entire holiday season. She had accepted a promotion at work to quality manager when the current manager announced her family was moving to Arizona. She used some time during the annual shutdown to familiarize herself with her new duties and staff. Several openings, created from retirements and voluntary separations, would need to be filled in the coming weeks. Sara made her first goal to work smarter, not longer and harder.

When the time drew nearer for her to bundle up to leave for church, one offer she did not decline was to ride the few blocks with Jed and Rhoda. Sara seldom turned down the opportunity to be a passenger and leave the driving to someone else. She and Rhoda chatted as Jed maneuvered the SUV through the crunching snow and slick spots on the pavement. Judging by the number of cars that were in the church parking lot, many people had decided to say good-bye to the old and welcome the upcoming year in prayer and thanksgiving. They recognized some of the vehicles as the faithful who were usually in attendance at Rosebrook functions. Others were less obvious, but just as pleasing to the sight. Once inside, the inspirational crowd warmed their spirit, forgetting about the bone-chilling wind and thigh high snow.

One by one, people came to the front of the sanctuary, offering testimonies of what the past year was like and the hope for a better tomorrow. There were so many people who wanted to say something, that, Rev. Stevens had to cut the testimonials off so that they would be in prayer at the midnight hour. He purposely allowed one family to address the congregation because he said they had made the request in advance. He also felt it was a special announcement that they would appreciate hearing, adding a little suspense to the service. Sara was a little perplexed when Chana, Olivia, and the twins came to the front.

"I'm going to keep this brief and to the point. My wife and I are proud to announce the expansion of our family to include our newly adopted daughters, Autumn and April. Please keep us in yours prayers, especially me, as I get use to this fatherhood thing," Chana said.

The entire church rose to their feet applauding, and laughing. There were also those who had delightful tears in their eyes. Initially, Sara's reaction was to mildly scold Chana for not telling her, but that was short lived. Four of her favorite people were a family, which was all that mattered.

At the ringing of midnight, there was plenty of loud praising to the only One worthy to be praised. Rev. Stevens shouted to everyone to claim this year to be a very good year, starting now. He repeated it over and over, a very good year, a very good year! At twelve-thirty the church was dismissed to begin another year, a very good year!

Rosebrook's traditional spaghetti dinner was being held in Palmer Place to allow for fellowshipping and to give the outside revelers a chance to wind down. Sara made a quick dash towards the Nash family, as did others. Before she got to them she was elated to see the Barrett clan, Winston, Whitney, and Kendall. With outstretched arms they embraced in a group hug.

"We came to support their little sisters and give the Nash family our blessing," Winston said. "You'll also be proud to hear that Kendall is graduating early and has been accepted at Harvard law school. Whitney is returning to college next week and will be spending the summer in France." Whitney had been mourning Krista, her mother's death, by sitting out a semester. Now she was prepared to keep living her own life. Kendall had stayed focused, as usual, in pursuit of his dreams, and it had paid off.

"Now let's hear about you, Dad," Sara turned to Winston.

"I'm just getting older every day," he jokingly replied.

Actually, Winston was still a very handsome man, but a bit too solemn as suggested by several women who had attempted to date him. He would still be a very good husband to a woman one day. He just had to decide to open his heart again. As for he and Sara, their relationship had always been and would probably remain like that of siblings.

"Hi, everybody," sang the twins as they joined in with hugs and kisses for all of them. "Aunt Sara Smile, did you know Uncle Chana was going to adopt us?" asked Autumn.

"No, sweetie, this was a big, wonderful surprise. I'm so happy for all of you." At that moment, Chana and Olivia approached . Sara took one look at him and her eyes began to water again.

Her dear friend gave her a hug and whispered, "I'll tell you all about it later."

She graciously responded with all sincerity, "No need, this is all that counts."

The twins met up with the three T's and ran towards the food. The Barrett's left and said they'd see everyone later that day at the Nash residence for dinner. More well-wishers were greeting Olivia and Chana as Sara started to ease towards Palmer Place. Stopping her in her tracks was an all too familiar voice.

"Happy New Year, Sara J. Can a brother get a hug and kiss for old and new times?" said Marcus.

Now this was a reason to rejoice as his presence caught her off guard. Sara hadn't seen Marcus since his mother's funeral in mid-November. Adelaine Richardson had shocked the church family when she suffered a massive stroke and died suddenly. Maybe her dying had a positive spiritual influence on her only son and he was ready to return to church, like it was when he was growing up.

"Happy New Year, Marcus," she responded and happily obliged. "This is quite a treat seeing you here. But where are Marc and his mother?" The truth was she noticed Brianna was not sitting with Marcus at the funeral. She had raised an eyebrow but kept her mouth shut. She should have done the same thing tonight but, oops, too late.

"My son is staying with his mother tonight. I'll pick him up in the morning. As if you didn't know, Brianna and I are no longer together. She lives in the house and I've moved into my mother's place. We share custody of Marc."

"I'm sorry to hear that you've ended another relationship. Maybe you'll get the next one right," Sara said, all joking aside.

"I'll bet you're sorry. Maybe the next one will be the one I should have kept ten years ago," he said winking again. "I'm going to rehab the house from top to bottom after I get rid of all the stuff she kept over the past fifty years. I could sure use a good woman's touch. What do you say, baby?"

Now why did he have to say that! We're not going there again. "I'm sure your sisters will be glad to give you a hand. Besides, they may want some of that stuff," she replied with a wink of her own.

"Touche', Sara J."

Then she took his hand and got a little serious. "Marcus, you know I'm here for whatever you need, just as you were for me. It'll be fun helping you fix up your house. I got some help when I redecorated earlier so I'll share some of the Feng Shui tips and advice I received."

"Whatever that is. We can start tonight, talking about what has to be done. How about joining me for a cup of coffee? There are plenty of places open, including my own kitchen," he remarked.

Cautiously Sara thanked him for the offer but declined. She knew better than to have a late date with Marcus, even if it was an innocent cup of coffee. He had recently dropped one woman and may be in search of another. To make matters worse, Marcus was still very attractive and quite charming. This time, she knew who his victim wasn't going to be. Besides, Sara was tired and looking forward to climbing into bed. Without fail, Chana rescued her from any further conversation with the man he still held at a distance.

"Sara, are you going to have those chicken wings ready on time? I have a taste for them already," Chana said.

"Of course! All three flavors, each with a special ingredient of my own."

"What, Sara J is going to cook? Is that some sort of New Year's resolution?" teased Marcus as Chana laughed at the remarks.

"I know my way around a kitchen." She paused a little while Chana gave her a look that caused her to qualify the statement. "Alright, at least a little bit but what I do know usually turns out very good."

"Marcus, you're welcome to join us and taste her wings for yourself." Chana's invitation was another surprise this evening.

"Thanks," said Marcus extending a hand to Chana. "I just might do that. Congratulations on the adoption. Fatherhood is something I know a lot about. There aren't any concrete rules. You just have to love them and teach them not to turn out like you."

Miracles never cease. This was probably the first time in many years that the two of them shared something in common worth talking about and shaking hands. Sara didn't think they connected like this since that dreadful day at her house. *But then, look whose house they're standing in!* Marcus gave her another kiss on the forehead, then exited the church. She was so touched that she would call him to make sure he had the address to Chana's house in case he decided to join them for this special New Year's Day celebration.

Chana used the time they had to themselves to brief her on the adoption. Sara really didn't care about the details. She was sincerely ecstatic about the newly formed Nash family. He told her, along with Olivia, that she had her work cut out for her as Auntie Sara Smile, a role she already relished.

Digesting that news Sara literally bumped into Miss Lizzie, who was holding the hand of her sleepy granddaughter. She could sympathize with little Tamala because it was now almost one o'clock and she wanted her warm bed also.

"Happy New Year, Sara; this just may be the good year for our children," she said. Tamala sat in a chair nearby and started to doze off. "My daughter called earlier today. She's been out of rehab and drug free for a month. She's been interviewing for a new job and has started fixing up their house. She wants the kids back, but I told her to give herself time to start getting her life in order. These kids have been through enough and I don't want them to be disappointed again by their mother. If she keeps clean and holds down a job, then I'll probably let them go back after school is out. But she has to prove herself first. Lord knows I need the break and they really need their mother, but if I don't feel it's safe for them to return, they'll stay right here with me. We will not mention anything to them until they finish this school year. These kids don't need any more distractions."

"Miss Lizzie, this is great news. We'll keep Rayanna lifted up in prayer that she stays on the road to recovery. As much as we've all come to love the kids, we know their place is with their parents. Hopefully, prayers will release their father sooner than later and he can rejoin his family too."

"That's been my prayer since the first day he was locked up. I still have hope for both of them and you too."

"Me? What's your hope for me?" Sara exclaimed.

"That you will find a good man for keeps," she said smiling.

Sara had to laugh at Miss Lizzie's comment. "Miss Lizzie, I'm just fine as a single woman. Let's keep our focus on the Miller family. Now get your granddaughter and I'll see you later today at the Nash home." After her last relationship fizzled out, Miss Lizzie told her that she just knew he was meant to be her husband and blamed herself for not fervently praying her intuition. Sara begged her to dismiss that thought. A wolf in sheep's clothing can mislead anyone, as they had recently witnessed. Miss Lizzie gathered the kids and the Nash family also left Palmer Place together.

The church was emptying fast as Jed's laughter could be heard across the room. Sara was hoping they would not be the last to leave when she heard her name called one more time, hopefully the last.

"I know you don't think you can get out of here without speaking to me," said Taylor. She and Rev. J.C. were walking her way, smiling as usual. This was the first time Sara had seen her tonight.

"I didn't know you were here. Happy New Year, you two, and best wishes for the upcoming twelve months, a very good year."

"And the same to you," Taylor responded. Then she threw up her left hand and flashed a beautiful marquis-cut, diamond engagement ring. For one of the few rare moments in Sara's life, she was speechless. Thank goodness Rev. J.C. spoke up.

"We were going to announce it tonight, but decided to save it for another day and let the Nash family have the spotlight. They deserved it more than us. We've only told a select group of people so far, but I'm sure as soon as the rest of CLEAR finds out, the world will know," he said poking fun at their sisterhood.

"My sincere congratulations on your upcoming marriage. It has been anointed from Heaven above. Be prepared for all of your little ones to be spoiled by Aunt Sara. I promise I won't be the one to spread the word to CLEAR," she said. She tried to sound as convincing as possible, but her broad smile said otherwise.

"Erin already knows, which means Serena probably does too. If you don't call Gloria later today, then I will," revealed Taylor. She had a brilliant glow about her. Rev. J.C. hugged Taylor before they made a dash to their car.

Approaching the table where the Hemings' were sitting, Rhoda took one look at Sara and knew exactly how she felt. "Please help me get Jed out of here. I'm so ready to go to sleep. You know he can talk until the sun comes up." So the two ladies put on their coats and helped Jed into his. He caught on to the hint and escorted them safely home.

Tuesday, January 1st

Once Sara turned the key and entered her house, she was no longer sleepy. Having digested all that had transpired at church actually woke her up. Instead of falling into the bed, she reached for the mail that laid on the coffee table and the box that had been left at the front door. In the small stack of envelopes were two bills, three credit card offers, two offers to refinance her mortgage and three more Christmas cards. One card was from Uncle Dillon which included a VISA gift card. He penned a little note saying the gift card should be used for her wedding dress. *That's Uncle Dillon. He'll never give up his hope to see his niece become someone's wife and he doesn't really care who it is, just that the event will happen.* Sara and her uncle had had this conversation more than once. She hadn't persuaded him to set his heart on something else. Anyway, Sara had several ideas where that gift card could be used and a bridal shop was not one of them.

The next card was addressed from Oakland so she just knew this was from Danielle. Wrong!

Handwritten under the printed words inside 'Best Wishes for a Prosperous New Year' read,

'Hope to see you again soon. Enjoy the Ride! Wyatt.'

When she stopped reading those simple words over and over she eventually put the card down. Recalling their dinner date, in her mind, she found herself hoping that would not be their one and only. Now that she had his address, she would return correspondence after she figured out what to say and how best to say it. The last card was from Nia including a typewritten note to CLEAR:

'Hey, ladies, Chelsea and I are sorry if we put you on the spot. One of the things I learned from all of you is to make life happen for myself. So we have started our own group, Ladies Loving Life, (L to the third power is how I like to describe us). We not only read and discuss, but get out and do a variety of activities, such as skiing, where we've just returned from. So far, three other like-minded women have joined our venture. Maybe you'd like to join forces with us one day for some really big fun! Peace & Love.'

Sara truly loved Nia's adventuresome spirit and her zeal for life. She was looking forward to the times when they would get together again, for whatever. Lastly, she opened the box from her sister. Would she continue her trend of giving her something in white: either a sweater, sweatshirt, jacket, robe, or pajamas? And the winner was (opening the box) a soft, white, fleece jacket trimmed in red and gold. It was very pretty and would get plenty of use in the weeks and months ahead.

Tossing the box aside, presuming it to be empty, what seemed like a large-sized booklet fell out. Sara laughed out loud at the calendar of Chicago's finest firefighters and police officers gracing the twelve months. Flipping through the pages she could tell it was going to be a very good year! Now that Sara was very alert and feeling good, she picked up the phone to chat with Gloria.

"Hey, sleepy head. Wake up. I've got some good news," Sara blurted out when she answered the phone.

"And Happy New Year to you too, Sara. What's so hot you had to wake me from my dream with Denzel?"

"Taylor and Rev. J.C. are engaged!"

"You act like you're surprised. They seem to be meant for each other. I'll have to congratulate her later today. I know that's not all that's got you bubbling over with excitement. What else is going on in your world?"

"Guess who was in church tonight by himself? Marcus Richardson. Can you believe it? Also, Wyatt sent me a Christmas card and stated he hopes to see me again soon. Maybe. Who knows what tomorrow holds? But enough about them. Did you get a card and note from Nia?"

"Yes, I did. Isn't that Nia something? Good for her, Chelsea and the rest of L to the third power. I understand why you're so happy this early in the morning. Earlier, I heard from all of my kids. I've got some news of my own. I'll share it with you later today when I'm wide awake. For now, I'll get back to Denzel and you get some sleep, too. Good night!"

Sara was about to take her friends advice but picked up the phone to call Danielle. After several minutes of hearty laughter, they vowed to talk more often in the weeks ahead. Climbing into bed, sleepy and exhausted, Sara filled her mind with the possibilities of tomorrow. She imagined more fun with the twins and the three T's. She was already looking forward to Taylor's wedding even though there were no details at this time. Marcus and Wyatt briefly sailed across her mind, but had no lingering affect. Sara finally fell asleep just knowing the next three hundred and sixty-five days were going to be a very good year. In her dream, she stared into a beautiful sunlit blue sky and dutifully asked, "Lord, now what?"

THE END

Look for Sara and others returning soon in

This Year's Clouds

by Judith L. Dammons

About the Author

Judith Dammons has enjoyed reading most of her life. She had a successful career in manufacturing management and for several years as a real estate appraiser. Now, she is doing something she really enjoys, reading and writing. She has written and published several short stories, as well as content writing for web pages and blogs. This is her first attempt at a novel of contemporary fiction, her favorite literature genre.

She'd like to hear from you. She's on Facebook or you can email her at jldammons@gmail.com.

Thanks for your support, not only to me but those who are facing a food crisis. A portion of the sales will go to feeding people across the U.S and Africa.

Made in the USA
Charleston, SC
15 January 2013